The Locust Hunter

The Locust Hunter

Po Wah Lam

Published by BlackAmber Books Limited
3 Queen Square, London WC1N 3AU
www.blackamber.com

First published 2004

1 3 5 7 9 10 8 6 4 2

Copyright © Po Wah Lam 2004
www.locusthunter.com

A CIP record for this book is available from the British Library.

Illustrations by Po Wah Lam

Typeset in 12.5/13.5 pt Garamond Three by
RefineCatch Limited, Bungay, Suffolk

Printed by WS Bookwell, Finland

ISBN 1–901969–19–3

Para mi tio Hui de Ying King,
maestro Jon Cook, guru Norman
Griffith, y mi hermano

1

Three Hundred Million Years' Catch

THE PLACE COULDN'T have been just anywhere or any-time. It was 'somewhere'. That much was clear. Some-where and the right time, where if you wanted to forget who you were and what you were, all you needed was a quick wrist. A trick of the wrist.

Each evening this was how we left the village and the real world behind. We knew *they* were out in their thousands. The hills were swimming in the beguiling music of grasshoppers, which has to be the world's most hypnotic sound; with their amazing dual ability to either jump evasively or fly from predators, grass-hoppers are one of the most perfect organisms ever cre-ated. Of course, people have made out that the game's attraction was strictly money, since we traded them in later for petty cash to buy ice cream and drinks and so forth. That was our reward for catching them, snatch-ing them out of the green and blue.

Looking back now I don't think it was always about money, although a 7UP did refresh the spirit and helped us forget about our homework. As a child when troubled or overcome by grief, unlike adults who could take to the bottle, out here in Hong Kong's back of beyond, this was our great escape. But that is not the real reason why I've been sitting in this classroom, crying for hours like a baby. There is something else I can never forget. Some*one* I can never forget. Lord Baltimore . . .

3

'Can you "catch"?'
'Yes.'
'Anything?'
'Yes.'
'I bet there is one thing you can't catch.'
'Name it.'
'. . . three hundred million years.'

Those were the days when I thought I was 'smart' because I was earning more money than a grown-up. When Lord Baltimore, a tortoise who had been with us for more than two hundred years, was alive and living among us like leaves in the forest. Lord Baltimore was no ordinary tortoise. She was sacred, as essential to the village as an engine is to a motorcar. She had been a part of the village and us from the beginning so naturally that in a naïve way I'd always expected her to be with us to the very end. We looked out for her and she in turn looked out for us. There was something in those great deep brown eyes that communicated wisdom and inspired confidence. You see, I was once the fast catcher, hunter, obtainer of entomology. I was that all right, and probably a little bit more. To people like Locust-man, who travelled the rural regions collecting insects for the Bird Market at the Street of Singers, Kowloon, I was quite an important person to know. I provided the commodity, while he was the buyer, the touring stock-broker of the insect market. Always trying to catch me out on price and current info, because he reckoned he knew better, and at times perhaps he did.

'*All of you. Treasure this,*' he once said. '*It's not going to last for ever . . .*'

If your football coach suddenly came up to you and

said: 'There's going to be no more football tomorrow. Ever,' how would you feel about that? Would you take it as fact and start packing? Or would you play on? Well, here in old Honkers that's exactly what happened. We played on, to the bitter end. This is a story of how our national sport faded away like the last sunset along with Lord Baltimore and the village. And it didn't just happen that way, 'somebody' was responsible. The game was jokingly simple. We hunted. We caught insects. The prize was money. I'd take 40 per cent of what I'd earned and the rest I would pawn out on the evening table for Grandma as *my* contribution towards food and the cost of daily living. And six or seven dollars a week was enough to keep us in grand style. In other words I made a living from catching grasshoppers. And what a fine way it was to make a living.

How can I explain it? Once you heard them, your mind was lost. Tuned into another time and place more primal, more predatory. Out here it was all part of the evening process. Their whispers like chimes in the air, a call, a summon to game. There were no particular restrictions to age, race, sex or class other than it had to be evening, round about six o'clock, when shadows moved faster than people. Within an hour it would all be over, for darkness, in this part of geography, descends like a guillotine. As I said, the only trick was lightning reaction, a conjuror's quick wrist. Listen, locate, home in. Then you pounce. Smash down the way thunder smashes down.

It was supposed to be a simple after-school game with which to earn a few cents, but in the end we were taking home three or four times the wages of a common farmer. Our delectable stock of live lizards and locusts and grasshoppers was destined to satisfy the appetite of caged birds, which in the psyche of Hong Kong society are the most prized of all luxuries. Almost every evening we would receive payment without fail. A figure of dusk known as the 'Mang Lo' or 'Locustman' would call into our village and be seen handing out fiscal rewards in return for harmless bags of live insects. Those two enormous baskets he kept at the back end of his bicycle, protruding like panniers, contained 'catches' of all shapes and sizes of what must be a billion raptures, a trapped universe. It was surreal, meeting him just before night fell, where the dark iron billboard overlooked the mauve road, watching him appear in the distance like something holy. Perhaps I was too young and inexperienced then to understand such apparitions, to realise he was more than a gatherer of insects. The way he must leave each evening, the way all things must end.

We children wanted nothing to end. We desired above all to carry on dancing through the grass for ever, to meet again, and again the same time the next day. That was what we worked for, to keep all of this alive – our village, the wisdom, the perfection, our friendships among the harmony of nature.

But he was right. The Locustman was right. Such beauty could not have lasted.

Now, as I sit in the classroom's abandoned silence, with my bandaged right thumb 'they' so mercilessly crushed, I struggle to write what you are now reading. Next to a very sentimental flower named *Michelia*, my words are trying hard not to sound too traumatised by the suddenness of it all. Questions torment me. How was it possible they all vanished before my very eyes – my

friends and sweetheart and most of all, Lord Baltimore?
How did I get this four-week-old scar across my
forehead? How did the village population dwindle
down to a waterless well? It had something to do with
the supernatural. Animism. A curse. I was sure of it. Or
was it coincidence or the natural progress of time?

All things have a beginning, and so did our village of
Tortoise Spring. According to ancestral records, in the
year 1789 a man seeking new lands came upon a giant
tortoise. Believing it to be divine, he followed and it
led him to a stream where the decision was made that
here a village should arise, which it did thanks to this
holy tortoise. In my childhood there was the great Lord
Baltimore, a second-generation descendant of this original divine tortoise.

In size she was impressive. About 80 centimetres and
weighing in the region of 121 pounds. You will have to
pardon me if I make her sound like a real person. I
swear, if you had met her, saw her come up to you, look
you up and down like a wise sage, taking you in, there's
no way you could remain aloof. My fondest memory
was of how she'd let me sit and lean against her tex-
tured shell that we waxed and kept as well polished as if
she was a car. In those days she could be found by the
village pond, along with all the other turtles and ducks,
but as the years passed and she grew older, her preference was solitude. From then on she was known as 'The
Cow Herder's Friend'. The journey from the pond to
her new home took her three days, a journey which a
human could do in thirty minutes. Till eventually she
reached the brook south-west within the circle of trees,
the place she saw as solitude. Her contact with humans
from then on was minimal, except for myself and a few

others. Still feeding her. Still believing tortoises were immortal and still uncertain whether she was a *she* or a *he*. Yet Three-Eye, who always preferred a comic stuck close to his face and knew pretty much how society worked, said there was no doubt she was a *she* due to the markings on her back typical of female tortoise-shells.

In our local Ancestral Hall, which is the heart of any community, where anything and everything that mattered took place, a room of names, you will still find the legend of our village inscribed by the first ancestor.

But on the fourteenth night of February 1973, year of the Ox, the Locustman was right. It all came to a blunt end.

THE WOUND

Maybe he was tipped off. He was in the 'business', after all. It was supposed to be a night just like any other night. High moon. Dew in the air. But all the same the great Lord Baltimore, part-god and part-mortal, vanished.

We, the children, guarded her day and night. Some of us took turns skipping school just to be there, crouching by the watered rocks and the fall of blood-red leaves. Watching, waiting. Our hands held either a stone or a sling or a spear, ready to strike out the second something appeared, be it a cow or a wolf, or even a man. We trusted nothing.

But in the end, what came was something out of this world. Something we had heard about but for which we had no solid preparation.

The 'Supernatural'.

Maybe it was all my own fault. I just loved animals far too much. And in Hong Kong, this was not a wise thing to do. It was not something to be proud of, but nor was it something to be ashamed about. Even somebody like Big Voice the Ghost, almost in his fourteenth year, almost a man, gleaming with energy and my best friend, found it hard to answer that question people tended to ask: 'Could you eat your own pet dog?' In other words, are you a man or a wimp?

'Of course!' he stamped, chest up high, almighty. 'Why not?'

Why not indeed?

Yet this was the same boy who couldn't sleep for a whole night after he slit a chicken's throat during the New Year and ended up chasing the half-decapitated body for a full 100 yards before it ran smack into a low wall and came to a halt, the head hanging from the bloodied neck like a pendulum. And when he finally caught it, one eye actually winked back at him! So how could he sleep, ever, if he had to kill his own pet dog?

I went through some sleepless nights myself, in which I dreamed I could hear the pitiful screams of Lord Baltimore, pleading for mercy, yet knowing well such mammals can emit no vocal cries of pain. Our beloved Lord Baltimore, who was worth several thousand HK dollars if sold to the right bidder, the right restaurant, was thrown into the back of a Triumph TR6, her legs and head in total retraction. We learned later that she was driven towards the city of Kowloon and sold that very night. The entire slaughter took twenty-five minutes and two men. The incision was made at the belly. It was pure, premeditated murder. No doubt about it.

9

And then what followed immediately after – the next day, was and still is the one thing I cannot explain. As if in horror and condemnation of this terrible crime, the roof of the old Ancestral Hall cracked, and came crashing down on top of the Sacred Candle and its Ancestral Tablets, pretty much destroying 300 years of written history. Of course, this may have been due to the building's poor structure and age, and anyone with a rational mind wouldn't be wrong for assuming that. But whether this is to be believed or not doesn't matter. What did matter was that to almost everyone who lived in Tortoise Spring at the time, this was seen as nothing less than a bad omen. Goodness, luck, and prosperity had obviously gone from the place, and if you had an ounce of sense you would pack up and move on, move out. So that was what they did, except for those too old to move like Grandma or too young like myself.

By the summer of 1973 the school was closed and all seven windows and two exits silenced. The forest and leaves were starting to creep in and enclose as they do when man is no longer present. The entire village of Tortoise Spring was virtually devoid of movement. Lord Baltimore was gone and within a few weeks so was everybody else.

But you must remember that only five months ago it all looked and sounded so very different. You could hear the verses of books being sung drifting from the school and over the shimmering rice fields, and in them were the images of angels. The precise mood and order. Wind and air were calibrated. V waves from a spear of moving ducks. Only half a year ago, our hunt after grasshoppers was in full swing. The village mood one of joy as time plunged towards the big day, a day of revenge and

10

justice. The great day of 21 June 1973, on which only the best could emerge through the hallucinogenic sea of fire.

THE VILLAGE

Tortoise Spring was by far the strangest place to grow up. To the north of us, about 500 yards distant, was China, known to us as 'The Big Amber', barred off from the rest of the world, while to the west was the distant city soon to become a brighter constellation in the night. We lived peacefully and nobly in what had to be the best-looking village by the border. So good-looking, as a matter of fact, the Brits couldn't keep their eyes off it; they had a special dark green metallic watch-tower perched on top of the hill next to the border, and every morning when I got up and walked through the door this was the first thing I saw. The image of the Union Jack cocking a snook in the face of indignant China.

The village plan, like all villages, was developed according to feng shui. It consisted of a grove, an enclosed valley, and a series of terraces shaped like a horseshoe. Our house was number 73, part of a six-house terrace with smoking chimneys and neighbours who were about as perfect as you can get. Neighbours like Mao Zedong the record-playing man who, as his nickname implies, obviously worshipped *you know who* and had three framed pictures of *you know who* inside his house, positioned where you would normally find family photos. I had no personal dislike of him as a neighbour, but I *was* mildly shocked to discover that the

11

world at large thought that all Chinese people looked like Mao! A bulging, mould-ridden, balding egg of a man was our chosen representative! Until, thank the Lord, heaven sent us Bruce Lee, a lean, good-looking hero. And suddenly WHAM! As if at the wave of a magic wand, the world at last saw us differently. Ever since then, Mao's Red Army March: *'One, two, one, with a fiery badge and Red flag prepare to sing . . .'* played flat out every morning on his gramophone bang on at 7 a.m. no longer spoiled breakfast but actually made my day begin with a smile.

And who could forget the Malaysian Black Widow, who lived entirely by herself. This tired old lady whom Grandma called a 'snitch' and who was her only enemy, did once offer me a dried date from an ancient jar that I ended up chewing for hours like a goat. Or how about the eighty-nine-year-old woman with the Russian hat and nursemaid? All she ever seemed to do was sit three feet outside her front door, and no matter how many times I said Hello, she wouldn't respond, her sagged, motionless face like stone. Till one afternoon a cursed centipede crawled past her leg and I saw her move, fast. She killed it with a single, well-timed stamp of her right foot – *crunch!* – and I realised she *could* move, almost as fast as Bruce Lee himself. She was there then and always, just like Aunt Smart, who lived right at the other end at number 77 and who didn't farm and was already on a flight to Canada before it all came to a sad end. They were all there. Our almost perfect neighbours.

In 73, Tortoise Spring Terrace, at 8.30 prompt every morning, I clapped my hands twice like a good citizen, just to hear the wings-like reverberations come back to me against a wall in the distance. Washing, brushing my teeth, doing both like a good citizen, in case the Brits were watching. It would not surprise me if they were watching my every move, even my sojourn past the chickens and ducks and their droppings after hearing the electric bell ring one minute away in the distance. This could mean only one thing: class was about to begin.

The village school was nothing more than four cream walls topped by a sheet of corrugated iron and enclosed by spooky trees and gods and waters. No one could have imagined a classroom so close to The Big Amber. Our school day began about nine, broke for lunch at twelve and ended abruptly round about four. In between these hours, the silence would be awesome. *Hush, hush. Swoosh, swoosh.* That was all. Only the movement of swooping birds was audible.

'Is there *anything* you are good at?'

That was Mad Dog, our village schoolteacher's favourite question. His voice, always looming over my shoulders like peregrines before a storm. How many times did he ask me? And why bother, when he already knew the answer? I was good at precisely nothing.

'Let me tell you all why I am here,' he said. 'Why the school is here, this far out. Because there is nothing here for you. Once you reach adulthood, you will all abandon this. It's the only option. Your future is out there in the city.'

I watched his chalky finger briefly indicate west. He was a man who by profession was never wrong.

But personally speaking, all that talk was not my style. I could never pay attention to maths the same way I paid attention to insects. I was taught by them way before I was ever taught by books. Words are not physical, not mortal in the way life can be caught in the hand and be taken in and understood. It is a far more passionate language. To be outside, out there, on the great openness of the grass plateau is to be alert. Not wilting under the humid flicker of the electric fan's shadow facing the blackboard. No inspiration there. The worst time of the day for me was the comprehension lesson. To distract myself, I'd watch Mrs Mad Dog brush the playground leaves just as she always did at that time of the day. Her slow limp caused at birth. And through the south window I would watch her. My head nearing the desktop, still watching her. A comforting motion, a softer rhythm. *Sweep. Swish.* Sleep. Then *thud!* I have lost count of how many times I have received *thwacks* across the head from Mad Dog. 'Like the swatting of flies!' he kept saying. I would blearily regard him as he sloped away, a book in his hand and a keen soldiering objective to smash another snoring head.

At four o'clock, with the shadows less heavy and sunlight seeming to come out of the ground, I'd be heading home accompanied by my dog. By 5.30, my homework done and the evening meal under slow preparation, Grandma off feeding the animals and time getting short and the village rebounding endlessly in the soft echo of dogs . . . this was the time when I could become somebody else or be my true self, away from the haunted classroom where, in the eyes of Mad Dog I was nothing. Only at this long shadows time of the day could I step out of reality.

As usual we all gathered secretly behind the woods just south of the village, where hundreds of others had already begun. In our evening expeditions there were five of us. Big Voice the Ghost, sounding and looking more like Bruce Lee every day, always led the way (naturally), because he was the eldest, and because he said he *knew* 'The Way'. He was followed by Ar-Fun, the youngest, the little mute who came along, I think, because she liked to. Three-Eye was next: he was twelve, and liked to call birds 'angels' rather than 'birds'. Finally there was Amber, Amber Shyamalan, a girl five months younger than myself who was well-dressed and well-mannered – in fact, she was a well-off city princess who would never have known about the kind of life I led till she saw it with her own eyes. This was our team. Each one of us so different, yet somehow the mixture worked.

As I stood with Echo, my big trusty Akita mongrel – as I always did, arms akimbo with a grasshopper basket slung just below each hip – we exchanged our usual mantra.

'*Ready?*' 'Ready.' 'Easier than eating raw cabbage, right?'

A QUICK PRIZE LIST

Species	Size (mm)	Price (cents)
Grass Lizard	*100–300*	*7–10*
Bombay Locust	*60–80*	*7–8*
Cotton Locust	*60–80*	*5–8*
Large Brown Hopper	*40*	*1 or less*
Rice Hopper	*30*	*less*

In the humid days of 1973 a prized bottle of 7UP cost 3 cents. Each Bombay Locust was worth two 7UPs. Two bottles of icy 7UP down your throat on a burning hot day is like . . . Well, I think you get what I mean.

So this was the *game*. The soiled and blackened

15

moneybag Locustman carried the *prize*. But compared to other species caught for food i.e. dogs, cats, pangolins and the odd tortoise, the locust game was worth peanuts.

THE BIG GAME
(Unofficial List)

Species	Kilos	Price ($)
Dog (puppy)	5	37
Cats	10	10
Pangolin	5	45
Tiger	5	300
Tortoise	5	59

See the kind of money you could make? For 5 kilos of tiger meat you could get 300 dollars, or possibly more because tigers were difficult to locate: I had never seen one locally. Yet Grandma reckoned they were around until the mid-1960s so I guess they simply got hunted into extinction. Of course, a tortoise was no substitute for the King of the Jungle, but tortoise was local and easy game, a lot easier than gunning down a big cat.

That was what the Locustman was telling us all along. He could see things from a broader perspective: we couldn't. He had witnessed how the population gradually through the years had left the village one by one, but unlike before, were not coming back and didn't care. There was no future here. This sluggish life was no match for the city, just as our insect game was no match for the illegal 'Big Game'. Perhaps, if we had had the initiative to ask, he could have told us *who* was going to destroy Lord Baltimore.

Still, the point was, we didn't. And Lord Baltimore

was gone. We should have foreseen it, should have worked it out for ourselves, known who would take her.

> *The Locustman is,*   *'Tap, tap, tap.'*
> *The Bagman was,*   *'Rap, rap, rap.'*

Wherever you see Locustman, Bagman will be somewhere nearby. It's his shadow – the other, far darker side of himself. One is legal while the other is seemingly beyond the law.

Hong Kong is a bird society in much the way some countries are a cat or dog society. People here prefer birds over radio and opera (in any case radios are only used to check out the race results). The reason why we went hunting for grasshoppers was of course to feed this bird society. *Live* food, it was rumoured (not tin-food), can prolong a bird's life on earth.

Just as birds have food preferences, so do humans. They kept talking about dog meat, tortoise meat. Delicacies. Aphrodisiacs. I didn't listen, didn't believe them. As long as there was English rule in Hong Kong, human consumption of dog and cat would be forbidden. But that was only the Law. It was illegal to kill a dog – but you had to catch the perpetrator in the act of doing so. It was no crime to cage them and bag them and cart them away. Out here you could bribe anybody and their head would turn, their eye would not see. And this was Bagman, a collector, a middleman. So when he appeared, someone else must provide the goods. And this someone else must be the shadow we were after. The murderer of Lord Baltimore.

It was that simple. Or so we thought.

In every rural community in Hong Kong there is a

communal place of worship called the Ancestral Hall, a remembrance shrine governing the heart of pastoral life. Marriages, New Year, birth, exam successes and death – all such events are acknowledged here. It is part of the spiritual constitution. Ancestors and gods are evoked; protection and blessings given. In most circumstances the wealth of particular clans can be expressed through sheer architectural grandeur. The depth of interior, the process of 'journey' through three inner compounds housing intricate reliefs and carvings. The experience can offer the appreciation of space, passing through the anteroom, the open court and halls and skylight before the arrival of final worship at the room of Ancestral Tablets.

The most elaborate Hall I have ever seen anywhere belonged to a clan called Loh. They are one of the five 'great surnames'. And when somebody is that great, that rich and powerful and that well-connected, especially with the Triads, they can no longer be just human; they are considered to be immortal – 'Supernatural'.

Our real problem was that this thief, this killer we were gunning for, was a Loh. A 'Supernatural'.

I was nine going on ten the year it happened. Was supposed to have substance. Attained something. A suit and tie. A comb. A girlfriend. A streetwise swagger and maybe even marriage which, I suppose, does sound rather comic, but Hong Kong is a fast train and it is never too early to think about the future. For me, manhood was just round the corner. The big wide world. But this didn't necessarily mean I knew what was going on. I was still trying to work it out.

18

There are Myth Hunters and Treasure Hunters and even hunters who hunt hunters, but Immortality Hunters, I have to acknowledge, were truly something else. You can compare peanuts to gold and talk about what it means to you personally, but at the end of the day it's just peanuts. The Aphrodisiac Industry *is* gold. It is the truth. To dine on the flesh of a tiger or even a tortoise can, in theory, make you live a second longer, or possibly even a milli-second longer. A gullible donkey I may be, and I can believe in the fantastic – magic carpets and spiders that metamorphose into wasps – but to believe in the forever, living for ever: how can anyone be so gullible? Lord Baltimore died because of this belief in immortality. Just as the place of childhood died because of Lord Baltimore's death. A chain of events had been started, and all we could do was watch Tortoise Spring slowly die. Villagers were running about, dropping this, dropping that, that basket or that scythe, scuttering as they do when things go missing. To people like us it was no fairy-tale. Communities evolved this way, through geomancy, animism, ancestral worship. There was a love of order and continuity. Rivers and birds must flow and so forth.

It was all very easy to ambush insects since we had no feelings for them. We used to tear the legs off the bamboo weevil virtually crippling it, then play around with it for days simply watching it get nowhere. It wasn't anything to do with cruelty, but we were taught to ambush certain creatures considered unbeneficial to mankind. And mankind? Werewolf-kind? Well. I didn't know enough about revenge to ambush *them*.

'We'll get him anyway,' Big Voice vowed.

19

But how?

Of course none of us knew exactly how. The only honest answer seemed to lay in what was coming out of Big Voice's bottomless mouth. 'When someone rips out your heart and eats it right before you, you have to do something about it!'

And he was right. Once Bagman took something, legally or illegally it would become part of the Aphrodisiac Industry. I have seen the way they slaughter, in alleyways and below snack canopies, the creatures they have purchased: the snakes, lizards, spiders, barking deer and rhesus monkeys – creatures that do no one any real harm but which are supposed to be edible. But do they have to torment them, burn them with cigarettes before putting them under the guillotine?

Big Voice the Ghost was normally more interested in money and Bruce Lee than pride, but that evening, after the shock of the news of Lord Baltimore's disappearance had penetrated the village and with zero interest from local police, there was something honest and noble about his outrage.

There was only one place to go now. The west, sunset. The city.

THE PHARMACY

P.O.T, 7, Tseun Fu Street, Sheung Shui, New Territories

There was a room in the hazy distance called P.O.T., a room hiding hundreds of other smaller room-like drawers which, if opened, could transport you into a thousand or more places: *Cassia, Imperata, Solidago.* Each wooden drawer was neatly set side by side into

20

the wall and housed an incredible collection of herbs that could heal. A room we would enter when life encountered a problem.

Our nearest city, Sheung Shui was not much of a city since the tallest buildings were no more than ten storeys high, and it had a village community built around it with more hawkers per street than any other town. You wouldn't find any parked cars or trucks on the road here, just hawkers selling anything from a plastic gun to dried salted egg yolks. The average working day per person was twelve hours, in return for a pittance.

As a boy, my whole experience of the world seemed to have started in the village and ended here, within this room inside our nearest city. A pair of shoes being the magic ticket out. The only time we wore shoes was when going to school or to the city. At other times I remained comfortably barefoot. To us from the back of beyond, the city was like another planet. Standing in the backs of off-duty trucks, from the Closed Area we passed the fire depot at Tak Wuling then joined the Man Kam To Road, a famous road, its trucks still trading in and out of the enigmatic Big Amber even during the anti-English period of the Red Guards. Just before Sheung Shui there was the checkpoint by the river. Most of the time a cop in shorts would examine ID cards in an attempt to snoop out illegal immigrants, also known as *Snakes*.

Once 'in', it was pure technicolour. When we jumped off the truck we entered a dazzling zone of street tables, sweep-stake tickets, calculators and watery pools of bottled Schweppes. Here, all desires were tempted. To reach the pharmacist's room, you had to pass through all this. The river of faces, the cries of, 'Don't stand in the way of my business, boy!'

At the apothecary shop named Po On Tong, or P.O.T, belonging to the man we called Mad Uncle, one was forever surrounded by wall cupboards, pulled opened like drawers, like pockets. Inside, nothing lived. It was either dead or dehydrated; some of the species were reportedly extinct.

As usual, round about five o'clock we would pull up a stool each and sit. Then somebody would tweak my face, as grown-ups normally do to a juvenile. Probably one of Mad Uncle's wives. (One of many).

Mad Uncle himself was a very methodical, grey-bearded old man sat in a wheelchair, now and then drinking tea from a steel mug. To us he always seemed to roughly scribble, and only his assistant at the glass counter could make sense from it all. Drawers were opened and herbs weighed. 'The Lohs of Amalan,' he said, in a slow drawl, so unlike his speedy prescriptions. 'A Werewolf clan. A family genealogy going back to the invention of gun powder . . .'

At 5.30, Mad Uncle beckoned. Three-Eye was engrossed in staring at packaged antlers and I was similarly mesmerised by the mysterious *Buddha Magic Balls*'. Mad Uncle's left hand was still on a patient's wrist, listening to her pulse, when Big Voice received a scolding for saying the word *revenge*.

'Ever tried not living up to your nickname?' Mad Uncle snapped, then turned away, annoyed. He continued his analysis of pulse, then tongue, constitutions of the body, his mind seeming miles away.

But Big Voice continued, 'We know who he is now. We don't know how he did it but we know his name.

22

Man Wai Loh. He's twelve this year. The youngest son. Drives a Triumph TR6. Goes to a Christian school and can snap a dog's neck with just one hand . . .'

But even after all that, what good was it going to do? We were talking about somebody extremely rich, and powerful.

'We're not scared.' Big Voice boasted.

'No? Well, I am.' And Mad Uncle sat back, as if astounded. 'Right down to my dinosaur bone I am. You could try for a hundred years – one, zero, zero – and still you will never catch him. Why? Because people like him are as elusive as hell. Know why he *did* you? Because you can't touch him. He is Young Master of the House. Born with a designer name and has already seen America and more countries than your herd brain can think of. This kind of person can get away with any crime, can get away with anything.

'And stop jigging your legs when I am talking!'

There was a pause as he completed another prescription.

'Just will not learn, will you? You should be old enough to think for yourselves now. But you keep coming back here hoping for a solution as if there is always going to be a cure. This may be a medicine shop but never does it specify a cure for mankind in general. You know how old I am this year? I could be boxed up tomorrow and where would you be? You've got to start picking up the Art of Being Smart *fast*. Learn fast. You're not just talking about a twelve-year-old thug here, it's more like eight hundred years of history. You are dealing with Triads! They can swat you like a fly! *Splat!* Know what I am saying?'

A train went by and the whole shop seemed to shake.

This happened every five to ten minutes since the old building sat next to the railway – the last station in the last city before the great lost plateau known as The Big Amber.

'You.'

'*Yes, sir!*'

'I hear you can catch locusts.'

'Yes, sir!'

'I asked *him*, not you, Big Voice! But if you cannot, then the three of you are wasting my time which I have not much of anyway.' Mad Uncle paused, took out his tobacco pipe, then settled down to tell us the following story.

THE PRESCRIPTION

'Every ten years there is a contest chaired by the Lohs known as the Day of the Locust. Ever heard of it? No? It's a contest of wit and youth and speed of the wrist, to see how many grasshoppers young people like you can catch. It was supposed to select the best out of the best, but in its three-hundred-year history only the Lohs have won, which is not surprising since it's their own game. There was a rumour that someone other than a Loh did once win – but that was long ago. As far as the Werewolf record is concerned, they cannot be beaten. It's downright impossible.

'The game dates back to harsh times when nothing could be done against the plague of locusts and grasshoppers. The Lohs, a Hakka people from central China, were forced to migrate here three hundred years ago due to a plague of locusts. The game therefore exists as

24

a symbol of their defiance, for nobody likes to be forced off their own patch, in particular by something as inferior as insects. So just as Lord Baltimore was everything to us, this game to the Lohs is everything to them.

'You cannot get even with them. You cannot kill their Lord Baltimore the same way they killed yours because they don't have one. All they have is power. So whatever it is you do, it has to be OFFICIAL. People like the Lohs, like Chinese anywhere, uphold a proud name. The trick is: if you can beat that name in public, not by devious means but Fair and Square, you have them.

'Sources tell me this dog thief is due to uphold the family's proud name, so very likely he will be present on that day. And this is where you come in. One of you will have to win this contest. Win their Gold Medal. I don't know how good *he* is – that's your homework. The real challenge will be done Fair and Square. The only catch is: winning a prize that was never designed to be won. Can that be done?'

His eyes were wide open now, like a hungry dog, staring at us for many seconds. Then he went sagely on: 'You have no money and no guts, but the young will think of a way. You have to. You are the future. If *you* lose the contest, it will be no big deal, since we are already losers. However, if *he* loses, know what will happen? The family will come down on him like a ton of bricks. Goodbye, little Master Dog Thief. And *that* is where you will get your revenge. In justice. In the Art of Being Smart.

'Want to be hotshots? You've got four months to prove it. The contest was last held in 1963, so the next one is due in June this year. Get prepared! People will be there – hordes of them. The Day of the Locust occurs once every ten years and it is OFFICIAL. If they lose, the Lohs will lose for a decade. Lose "face" as well.'

By the time we walked back onto the street it was 6.30. Darkness had fallen, and neon signs straddled the crowded pavements. The night now belonged to knick-knack sellers and sugar cane freshly squeezed. A world made out of smell.

II
Discovering Angels

THEY EMERGED DURING the late Carboniferous period, which makes them about 300 million years old. In the Bible they are mentioned thirty-four times. They can be found on the walls of pyramids and were documented by Aristotle in 350BC. Wherever they appear, there will be devastation and famine: some cultures have even linked them to cholera. The first known recorded use of chemical controls, sodium arsenite, came in 1885. Ancient methods involved sweeping them into ditches and burying them or burning them. The 'classic' Kansas County Grasshopper Army Act of 1877 saw every able-bodied American aged between twelve to sixty-five enlisted with brooms and spades, bravely going against this menace.

But not until the late twentieth century, in colonial Hong Kong, did the first great hunt begin.

A common grasshopper is composed of the following.

1. Head. 2. Thorax. 3. Abdomen.

The thorax and abdomen are the parts that birds prefer to eat. The head, therefore, was usually thrown away. The bewildering *'tssskkk'* sound which makes up the beguiling *sea of whispers*, which talks to you and gives their position away, is caused by stridulations of two bodily parts called the 'hind femora' and 'forewing'. The two rub against each other to emit a papery sound much like that of a rattlesnake's soft whisper. And with thousands and thousands around you, all singing their song, the real world is shut out. People who keep fish will tell you it gives them a feeling of calm just by watching the fish swim. The Sea of Whispers can do the same thing: evoke calm by its song.

But my life so far, even as a hunter of insects governed by the need for a chilled drink, was more about my friends than anything else. There was no sense in gaming if you just bagged quantity. It was about who you were with and who would stay with you to the end. The general talk was of rhythm and getting into tune, but that was only the introduction. If someone wants the full methodology I'd say it's in the casual step. This is what detects the catch, not the ear. The rhythm, the sea of whispers is too distracting to be of any use. Amber used to call it the 'tap dance' because that's the only way to bring *them* out of the grass and into focus. One, two, three. Left and right, kicking through the green and blue as if with a ball yet always with control. Just enough not to scare the blur out of them before snatching them.

So yes, I can say, with a bright smile: I was living a fruitfully happy life till Lord Baltimore was taken from us and the village fell apart. I had a job I loved doing and a pretty fine social life added to it. Great buddies who always stuck up for me, who saved me from snake-bites and drowning. Not to mention a rather fine-looking girlfriend. And I say 'girlfriend' very carefully, not in the casual way grown-ups use it, meaning an intimate relationship that could end up in 'girlfriend' becoming 'wife'. Amber's full name was Ar-Wan Shyamalan, a name that was half-Chinese and half-Indian. I once heard her say her ancestors were from Pondicherry. This obviously explained those big eyes and the colourful dresses she wore, as though she was emerging through a rainbow. When you were with her, in the city or countryside, she justifiably shone.

It was, and still is, amazing to me that she enjoyed my rough-and-ready company so much, or was it more amazing that she came to see me almost every evening, at Tortoise Spring, chauffeur-driven in a Jaguar XJ12, when she could have been with Simon, her boyfriend, who I believe had a Rolls?

I am a regular working-class boy, I keep telling myself. I should not delve into matters that are beyond me. I should only think about the things that matter.

IMMEDIATE EVENINGS

There was no sensation like the one of hearing the four o'clock bell chime through a corridor of leaves. After four hours sat composed and rigid, any kind of noise was like the sound of ancient harps. Yet there was no mad scramble across the playground. The landslide of faces which followed, after the silence, was orderly, almost majestic.

There cannot be many schools like ours, I am sure. The class so well-behaved, homework always in on time, our exercise books neat and spotless. This was a school where the teacher could leave the room for ten minutes or up to an entire hour, then return to find nothing wrong. The truth is: Tortoise Spring was a place that had bred passive people for centuries. You could exchange 'passive' for 'soft' or, if you want to be more blunt, 'selfish'. I am not selfish but neither am I a hero. All I know is, I was born somewhere else and belong to no clan. Like Grandma, I too came in from the outside, except of course she was a widow and was about half a century older than me, and could wrestle any so-called tough guy onto the ground and force him to eat dry mud, no problem. And by that happy fact it gives me great satisfaction to know she is *my* grandma and nobody else's. I think she achieved her incredible strength by chewing all the time. Fruits, seeds, nuts – dried, salted, anything. In fact, she looked quite hip and cool, walking back and forth, tailed by her soldiering formation of ducks, a hoe over her right shoulder and her mouth continually working, as if she was chewing Wrigley's spearmint gum.

In class, I sat about three desks away from the blackboard and from Mad Dog's desk. I was close to the windows on my left facing dusty sunlight, the kind of greenframed windows I could blame for turning me into a part-time daydreamer. The only painful punishment – and no doubt it was deserved – was the famous 'swatting of flies', because falling asleep during class was a crime. But I can tell you now, it was not easy to stay awake. The heat, the hypnotic rush of five electric fans spinning above, plus the silence of essay-writing and the comfort of knowing you were cocooned by leaves – it was all too soporific.

Our teacher, Mad Dog, or Sir Wong, was actually more like a man of steel than a madman. He had been at the school for as long as I can remember; it was his life. As for his inappropriate nickname, known by many including himself, I can only assume it was connected to the popular myth of his World War Two days, when as a young soldier he fought gloriously, and madly, against the Nazi-Japanese. This explained the standing to attention and the orderly single files and, more evidently, his hatred for anything Japan-made. In Hong Kong right now it's hard to turn a corner and not find something from Japan – watches, pens, radios, comics and toys, you name it. I drew this Japanese cartoon robot once, the arm winging forward as a missile. Quite a normal subject, I had thought, quite harmless, but not to Mad Dog. He wasn't buying it. 'This is Japanese filth!' Needless to say I never saw that drawing again or drew anything else Japanese. He had his demons. An ex-soldier's demons, I guess.

But it's thanks to him that I am now doodling my small account in English. And whether I am doing a good job so far in making my story coherent and interesting, I'll find out soon enough. But should the score be against me, then the fault is all mine. A good teacher of English is one thing: an interested student is another. Mad Dog was a good teacher of English. In his mind he was vigorously fighting a daydreamer's ignorance much the same way he fought the Nazi-Japanese. And I, with good reason, wanted his fight to be triumphant the same way he was triumphant with Big Voice the Ghost before he successfully graduated on to Sing Ming High School situated six miles from Tortoise Spring. 'If you leave school with bad grades and can't find a decent job,' Mad Dog kept telling the class, 'you can always be a taxi driver or a tour guide because you know English.' And what bullet-proof truth! No one needs to be hit over the head to know that English would be a useful skill in a place ruled by the English. But for me, the

English language meant much more – and that I will reveal a little later on.

From our class of about thirty pupils, half did some form of locust hunting at one time or another. The big difference with me was, I did it almost every day.

In 1972 we had begun exploring the possibilities of a northern region known as Robin's Nest, a high mountain range that edged into the border with The Big Amber and almost seemed to disappear. We were looking for even greater catches, on the track of *Schistocera*. The Desert Locust.

Globally there are more than 23,000 grasshopper species. The *Orthoptera*, which include grasshoppers, locusts, katydids and crickets, generally present no threat to mankind until they gather in numbers, like the Desert Locust. Within the talk of total eradication there is only, realistically, 'control'. Historically, it remains the most feared and revered *Orthopteroid*. The Desert Locust can swarm and migrate 100 kilometres a day, and those among them lucky enough to escape aerial poisoning will again migrate and breed, *phenomenally*. You kill a dog or a tortoise, people will be outraged because we feel human emotions for such creatures, but you could kill millions of the dreaded *Orthoptera* and no one will complain. Tigers and sharks can be hunted into extinction but not these critters.

So it wasn't wrong to say we were doing the world a great favour. Each catch was a celebration.

'Look, everyone! Look how much money I've earned!'

I used to make something of it, used to think it was all that mattered. But Grandma was never too impressed. She was always too occupied in helping others. Most evenings she would be like this, tense but casual. Somebody sat across from her darkness – a dishevelled, shadow-filled creature. *A Snake.* She would give all she could, knowing well it was illegal, but as Big Voice once said, 'She is almost a saint.' Her gifts consisted of petty cash, rice, tea, and if the Snake was a man, clothes that had once belonged to her late Buddhist husband, and also a map. Then she would point in the direction of the city and say, 'The best of wishes.' Leaving herself to face the possibility of police arrest for aiding illegal immigrants.

'Won't you end up in prison, Grandma?' I'd fret.

'Shut up!'

Once, on a burned-out sunny afternoon, I walked barefoot across concrete so hot that even camels would have had to hop. For this I was nicknamed 'Yat Mo', meaning 'Sundance'. A name I can live with, but not for ever, I hope. Dancing, after all, is more a lady's thing. And sooner or later, no matter how bad my loser's luck can get, I know there has to be something better.

However, if names are anything to go by, then Man Wai Loh, translated literally as 'Millions, Brilliant' spoke to the world as loudly as a trumpet. And that wasn't even a nickname.

'Three-Eye', whose English name was Steven, didn't pack the same kind of power punch, but he was a fair contender. His was what locals would term a 'cracking good nickname' though most of the time he got called 'Four-Eyes' instead. He would, of course, make sure they got it right, since *getting it right* was to him a passion. I remember when he almost received the beating of his life from the heavy, chain-smoking butcher after he accused him of daylight robbery. This happened on a regular basis with Three-Eye. 'Mind your own business, boy. Now move on!' But he didn't 'move on'. He always stood his ground. He kept insisting it was cheaper round the corner as if it was his religious mission in life, and naturally enough, the butcher went berserk. My dear friend would not be here now, I am very sure, if Big Voice hadn't been around, all 173 cm of him. One shove was all it took to send the butcher falling back against the chopping board, astounded. 'Ay! Who do you think you are? Bruce Lee or something?'

So maybe life wasn't that bad, not in the company of a Bruce look-alike. And in any case, who would bother mashing somebody who, without his glasses, groped about like a zombie? Three-Eye was just another regular citizen, except he thought life should be fair, which it wasn't. He wore glasses from the moment he woke, even wore them in the shower. His thick lenses with their dark dozy frames always confused people as to why it was three and not four eyes. But here I can tell the world that his nickname was in reference to the Third Eye of the Buddha. Meaning he always read into things well ahead of everyone, or to put it another way: he read the papers and race results every morning and was the first person to inform me about the word 'computer'.

In old Honkers where Cantonese was the main dialect, some numbers represented luck and good things to come, like the number 3. When you say this number casually, it can also sound like the Cantonese word for 'birth'. Three-Eye's nickname was given to him by his mother after he picked a winning horse from one of Happy Valley's many race days. A true 'Bionic Woman', his mother almost single-handedly ran the 'Ho Sien Sian' rice shop with the rattly China-made bicycle parked outside. It was a good place for us to meet, just a few paces down from Mad Uncle's shop. Plus it was always an experience to be in his mother's presence, a lady Big Voice and I both agreed was probably *the* nicest working-class lady we'd ever come across. 'Why don't you have some rice cakes?' she'd say, with what would have been a perfect set of teeth on show, were it not for the shiny 24-carat gold front tooth. It was always rice cakes with Three-Eye, always tins of Typhone mushrooms, Santa Claus pineapple jam, Dana pork luncheon meat, jars and jars of pickles and the dry smell of rice sacks and small hillocks of white rice set in adult-waist-level buckets landscaping around them. They had rice around them the way we had trees. From Thailand, China, Australia and some even locally produced.

Three-Eye was Big Voice's best buddy. Then he also became my best buddy, which all made very good sense. I was the hunter. I had a rough and ready skill he admired, whereas he wasn't rough and ready. He was the birdman. Kept three birdcages hung up at the shop-front. Sometimes, when a customer entered he or she might be greeted with a, *'Getting rich, bro?'* while at other times it was a blatant, *'F— you!'* This of course gave the customer quite a shock, until they saw it was a bird speaking and not a person.

The story goes that Three-Eye and Big Voice had a disagreement at the Street of Singers about the colour of a parrot.

'It's bloody red!' Big Voice slammed, looming over the smaller boy. 'What are you – blind?'

'Of course not!' said Three-Eye, slamming just as hard. 'Colour blind, that's all!'

37

And that was how they became friends. But I think secretly, Big Voice desired to be like Three-Eye. Like most country bumpkins he didn't want to stay that way. He was the youngest of three sons but unlike Three-Eye, he didn't have an auspicious nickname and certainly didn't stand much of a chance in life. His father was a well-known heavy, an ex-coolie, so there was no '*Take it easy*' or '*Cool it*' attitude to the man. He could be calm one second then explosive the next, as if there were only two settings to his gauge. His quickfire temper was powerful enough to send his then nine-year-old son flying down a damp ditch all because he'd accidentally slipped in the rain and lost some groceries. Big Voice's sixty-pound body was picked up and thrown clear over a low wall. When you have a mean father like that, how are you supposed to get a decent start in life? Who is going to fund your tuition at uni? I hear in the States you can get a football scholarship by being big and tough, but not in HK. Big Voice seemed destined to be like his father, a labourer. Or worse, a gangster, and looking at him, in his sweaty vest with his big talk and his lack of interest in books, I couldn't help feeling his destiny was sealed.

In the multi-neon streets of Mong Kok, fortune-tellers throng using any means possible to cajole passers-by. In the famous old square, humans cleverly deploy animals of all sizes to do the forecasting. There are two reasons why this trade thrives: those who desperately want tomorrow's race results in advance and believe that the animals here have special powers, and the more realistic people who simply desire to see animals perform. A place like this, because it vows to answer

38

dreams, can tell you more about the character of a society or an individual than any diary or autobiography.

I remember how a small Indonesian macaque drew out a card with the shape of a mountain for Big Voice. Interpreted by its pipe-smoking handler as denoting a big future for Big Voice, this understandably made him howl with laughter, for he knew in his cynical way that there wasn't much chance of *that*. Next, the sprightly mynah bird picked out a playing card, the King of Hearts, which did nothing to alter Three-Eye's view of fortune-telling. Coming from a family in the cut-throat business of trading rice, I don't think there was anything that could convince his mercantile mind that this was money well spent. Round the corner, Ar-Fun chose the talking parrot which had a twenty-two-word vocabulary, but she was actually more interested in cradling the creature. In return for one of my hard-earned cents, I had asked a small green wren: 'When will I find my intelligence?' The bird hopped gentlemanly from its cage, selected a card, returned to its cage and I got told: 'Soon. In two years!' But most people, especially adults, came here for that one basic question: *When will I win the lottery?*

Then in late February, 1973, I had an even crazier question to ask: *'What are the chances of winning against the Supernatural?'*

TERRITORIALITY

There is a deserted village I have seen south-east of Tortoise Spring. Or was it north-east? In some ways it was almost the exact scale and dimension of our own. We came across it during a hunt last year, when it appeared to us from out of the mist like a wraith – white, sun-dried walls with eyes of hollowed black windows staring back. A million images conveyed. It made me suddenly realise that the demise of a place or persons doesn't always take on a sinister aspect. This place could once have looked as tranquil as Tortoise Spring. Could have died the same way.

We were, in reality, looking into a mirror: into the ruins we would soon become.

Here were the five of us. A condemned liar. A dog. A girl who couldn't talk. A boy who could see nothing without glasses. And myself, holding out a coin or a ten-dollar note, pointing to the picture of Queen Elizabeth II and saying, 'I came from her . . .'. My only claim to family status, my nationality. Instead of the words 'mother', 'father', I yelled 'Grandma!' Grandma, capable of clobbering a man with a broom, spoke her native Hakka tongue no matter if you were English or dog or duck. Could it be in her previous life she was a muscle-man and not a woman? Anyway, none of these were reputations to boast about. So how could anybody have listened to us?

LUNCHING OFF A DEAD CHICKEN

When World War Two ended in Asia, after years of Japanese oppression, places like Cambodia, Indonesia and Taiwan rooted out those hated individuals who had collaborated with the enemy. The more fortunate ones were beaten with hammers. However, in Hong Kong

40

there were no such persecutions. Some collaborators even went on to claim properties and buildings of the unfortunate dead, and later became rich. This was what locals would call 'lunching off a dead chicken'. And the Lohs had done that, for sure. They ate lots of 'dead chickens'. My translation is not 100 per cent accurate but I think it is close. Gaining from somebody else's misfortune, like vultures. In this, the Lohs were true professionals. The 'Werewolf' clan was so because of this history. They had overcome a time of imminent death and were no doubt *the* most professional Immortality Hunters we had ever seen. And now they had marked our territory.

I knew as well as Three-Eye, who never bade any-body Hello or Goodbye, just placed his hand suddenly on your shoulder to signal his presence, that once a predator claims its territory it will feed there as long as there is food. It will only leave when there is no more food, just as we will leave when we know a field has no grasshoppers.

PRESERVATION

19 May. Our first journey, moving away from the bor-der city of Sheung Shui and heading south towards the sea. A six-hour journey. Everyone was there except Echo, who barked us farewell as he chased our depart-ing truck: Big Voice, Three-Eye, Amber, young Ar-Fun and myself, along with seven buckets of turtles and tortoises. This was our expedition to reach sanctuary in a bid to save the remaining numbers of turtles from further possible theft. 'It's a sanctuary that's within a

temple of wells,' Three-Eye had told us, after hearing about the special temple from a transient rubbish collector he once met. 'A place built above a lake, and when you walk there, apparently it's almost like walking on water . . .'

Our one-hour train journey with live cargo presented us with numerous problems. Trying to find the girls an available seat, for a start, along with passengers wanting to buy the turtles from us (more for lunch than preservation), and trying to make deals. Every time the train rocked forward, water spilled from the buckets. Deciding to move to a space by the far window to get away from it all, I gingerly placed myself and the muddy turtles next to a well-groomed lady. With her lipstick and sunglasses, she was a real city sphinx. Fearing my muddy bucket would inconvenience her, I decided to once again move away. But as I began to leave my seat she turned her head, then grabbed me by the arm. 'Sit down!' she demanded. 'I am not contagious, you know!' Later I discovered she was no sphinx but quite a nice person, owned some kind of boutique. She gave me her business card and told me that if I ever needed a job, to give her a call in a few years' time. I thanked her kindly.

At 11 a.m. at Kowloon pier, we joined the harbour crowd by the famous white clock-tower. It was prime time. Hawkers paced the streets with sliced melon, sweet beancurd, and cooled fruit juices, all for a cent or two to forget the noonday heat. We saw police officers kick over a tray of mangos, the ground exploding in yellow. Holding Ar-Fun's six-year-old hand, I told her not to worry. 'That hawker obviously refused to pay a bribe . . .' Yet round the corner I could hear a different

42

story. *'Forgot your money? It's OK. You go home and get the fare. I'll wait here. I trust you.'* That was what taxi drivers were like in 1973. One of the better things to remember.

We found strange eggs for sale at Junk Island, dug out from hot salt and sand. The cooked, unpeeled egg was then sliced into two halves and in went the strange spice.

We were acting on our best behaviour while eating a couple of these eggs on the next ferry towards Cheung Chau island. Mad Dog would have approved of us. There were fewer passengers this time, and we were able to sit together. Ar-Fun was next to Big Voice and being asked by him whether the cheap marshmallows she was nibbling tasted any good. She winked at him and he winked back. Her bobbed-length hair was continually sent blowing across her eyes by the hot ocean gust. Three-Eye was stuck in a newspaper as usual, nudging my elbow with stuff like: 'Today's fire warning is yellow.' Meaning it hadn't rained for a long time and anything that was dry could and would catch fire. I was sitting next to Amber and slid unintentionally into her every time the ferry got pitched by the odd wave. We were checking out the map together on polished benches. She was showing me places she'd been to that, perhaps some day, when all this was over, we could all go and visit. I think that was the only moment on our long journey when we forgot there were seven buckets of turtles all gasping for a fresh change of water.

An hour later, Big Voice and I talked to a squeaky old man by the port of White Bones, in the shade of great camphor trees that once sheltered pirates and smugglers. He was an old Hoklo, an ex-fisherman and brag artist – a vice Big Voice knew well. Apparently he'd never heard of this 'temple of wells', not in all the years he'd been here. Three-Eye didn't believe him.

'The old man is firing blanks!'

We jumped on the next boat and then there were only six passengers, including us.

After what has to be the longest single journey I have ever undertaken in my life, we finally entered a rocky gateway marked out by the Chinese character for 'water' and found ourselves looking down on a clean open courtyard full of wells. Sensitive mimosa plants sprang from cracks in the pavings. Everything was suddenly so hazy and none of us seemed quite sure what to do next.

'I think we all could do with a drink,' someone said.

For a second my mind went blank, as if the strange beauty of this place had enraptured my senses. Only when I turned to my left did I notice Three-Eye, in his ebullient Hawaiian shirt with all the world's light refracted off him, especially his glasses, and his fringed hair whipped to one side by the breeze. 'We all could do with a drink . . .' he repeated, and I realised that for once, it was him and not Big Voice talking.

But it was Ar-Fun who made the first real move. Before anyone could stop her, she ventured down the flight of white steps and danced her way past the wells one after the other as if she'd known this place all her life. Amber quickly followed, her blue dress and dark hair trailing soundlessly behind. We watched the girls meet at the very far end of the courtyard where the cliff dropped narrowly into the sea and could tell by the Christ-like way they reached out, hats off and arms out, that there was a cool, fresh, smiling breeze no money could buy. We stood for what seemed like eternity, but may have only been a minute, watching them. Staring at the millions of tiny mirrors in the sea, endless crystal balls, the *zap zap* razors of light in our eyes and none of us saying a word. As if silence was sacred. But perhaps more so to see if anyone was around.

'The coast is clear,' mumbled Three-Eye, stalling, finally picking up the two buckets left by the girls. 'Nobody's around.' Looking at me and smiling, he said, 'Let's get it over with, shall we?' In his haste sounding more to me as if he was trying to sell another bag of rice rather than set free a few smelly turtles. Three-Eye was, incidentally, very good at selling patter and could judge his customers down to the last penny. *'Mrs Wong, you look rich today – why don't you take a tin of fried tuna? I can throw that in for half price, OK?'* That was how Three-Eye spoke at 31, San Shing Avenue, less than a few streets from our favourite drinks machine.

It was there, among the comforting valleys of rice that late one afternoon, Big Voice and I caught him napping, an abacus in one hand and homework in the other. He always preferred to sleep by day and stay awake at night. On this occasion, we carried out our all-time classic stunt. We painted both of his spectacle lenses red. Waited. And when he woke, fresh from baking afternoon dreams and saw the world as red, he flew chicken-head-first onto the open street screaming: *'Fire! Somebody put out the fire!'* Followed by laughter which went to the moon. All very tasteless, I have to confess. However, to catch a tail that was not meant to be caught . . . now, that's a rare egg. Very few mortals could have gone against the words of a Hoklo man and survived, as Three-Eye did that day. And it was he who, against all the odds and in a time of lies, believed what

45

a trash-collector said was true – that such a sacred place of wells did exist.

I nodded and relieved him of one of the buckets. The three of us took a step forward. It was as if we had come out of a drowning. We descended the stairs.

We had entered a new universe.

There was a time when freeing marine life was a national obsession, just like the way they free birds every year in the name of Buddha. Caged birds purchased from the Street of Singers at Hong Lok Street are taken to temples and sold, then later released as a show of kindness. Birds free in the air. Turtles free in the ocean. That was the belief. So only by being captured can you know freedom. Know life because of death.

At this moment, our turtles, poor creatures, hardly seemed alive. They didn't move. Their eyes were shut and their legs fully retracted. We approached the wells silently and placed down the buckets. An echo, redoubling emptiness, engulfed us: the sound of subterranean water filling the area. Around us we could see pagodas and willows and the odd unknown bird, but there was still no sign of people. Just the courtyard and its white wells. 'White as ivory.' As it should be, like Heaven. I picked up the first seemingly dead turtle, held it with both hands over the flicker of the lake beneath us. I could hear doubts coming from the group, from Three-Eye in particular, unsure whether the turtles could navigate deeper waters.

'I thought you said they can swim . . .' Big Voice complained, as if it was a business deal that hadn't turned out quite right.

The boy with the glasses just glared back at him.

'Are you an idiot? There's a deep ocean under this well. What if they can't swim that deep? Once we drop them into the well there's no way we can retrieve them again – and they may drown. Do you want that? There's a difference between knowing and doing, you know.'

A good point made.

But I wasn't paying attention. *My* point was, we had come this far. Oceans far. And right now there was only the sound of my own breathing echoing beneath a twelve-foot drop, and Amber's voice, her elbows leaning next to mine on the well parapet telling me to *do it*. 'They will be OK.' Her whisper blending in with the well's watery echo. Because she knew, just as I did, for the turtles this had to be where their story ended. There had to be a happy ending. There had to be. There has to be a place far from people and evil where this kind of wisdom can happen. And looking around me, at the brightness, the stone pagodas, the magical way Big Voice and Three-Eye had suddenly stopped blabbering, I was sure this was 'it'. I am a believer in resurrection. And here's why: when Grandma gave me the order to drown five unwanted kittens or not come home, I knew that I, Sundance, the catcher who saw the profession more as The Great Escape, had to believe in resurrection and rebirth, otherwise there was no earthly way I could have carried out such an order.

The object of life in my hands looked barely alive; then suddenly, as we knew it would, there it was, the most miraculous single movement we ever saw. Into the well our spirits fell, a blue, swimmers-filled well where thousands of others were like the creature I once held – but now diving, pushing deeper and wider into a liquid world. We watched the first one descend, lightning fast, till nothing more could be seen except the sea of traffic. It was finally home.

By the time all twenty-three were released, with a euphoric cheer for each turtle, floral blessings given by the girls and a special prayer in memory of Lord Baltimore, a small crowd had materialised from out of nowhere. We stood within this human light as long as we could. Even ate monastic jelly. We explained we were explorers and people laughed.

'You mean the five of you came *this* far?'

We nodded. Stayed another twenty minutes. Time enough to learn that not all monks are bald. And for the monks to learn about and be reasonably well-impressed by our desire for preservation.

'We are doing this not for the village but because we just love animals. Is that OK with you?' Everybody was still stuffing their mouths with cool jelly when the eldest septuagenarian monk, also the temple janitor, said yes, it was perfectly OK with him.

'And what about this pretty young lady here?' somebody else said, indicating Amber. After all, she was the centre of attention. You could see her radiance coming from a mile off. Those big eyes, flower-bud lips. As always, it was the opening Big Voice had been waiting for. He couldn't help himself. He just had to do it.

He said: 'That's *his* girlfriend,' disarmingly frank, finger in my direction. And I turtle-shrank after that. His outsized arms were suddenly around me and I cringed. I wanted to run, hide, sky-dive off the nearest cliff. My face was blushing red as a Chinese flag. But thank Bruce, city-smart Amber was fully in swing with the joke.

'Believe me, you could do a lot worse,' he continued, and winked, his chewing-gum breath close to my rosy

48

features. 'You—' But before he could finish, Amber leaned over my back, her fist forward and, smiling in grace, she tried giving him a dead arm.

'*Get lost!*'

But she missed. He dodged away, howling like a cat, and everyone laughed, even little Ar-Fun with her missing tooth and cheesy grin. Above us we could hear a plane whirl over and we all looked up and waved.

'A Spitfire?' My words were jumbled and muted, lost among the plane's chorus.

But Three-Eye, his chin up, an explorer's hand shielding himself from the sun's glare, confirmed it to be something else. 'It's a Vampire. You can tell by the twin-tailed fins.' And went on to clarify: 'HK Spitfires were de-commissioned in the fifties. Most were bulldozed off the runway into the sea. A few are still kept flying by veterans and collectors, but they're rare.'

I nodded. Not fully catching all of what he said, but I still gave him a nod. It seemed like the right thing to do. But Big Voice glumly asked the question I probably would have asked if he hadn't: 'What's de-commissioned?'

We finally left the Temple of Wells bang on 5 p.m., feeling that we had witnessed resurrection at first hand.

During the long journey home our discussion centred around the unknown bird species. We talked passionately about them, as the ocean churned sienna, sometimes so bright we had to avert our gaze. 'What's the name of this new species? Where else can it be found?' Three-Eye once thought he had found it, but as it turned out the bird already had a name. A common mistake. In the darkness when you discover people it's

49

the same. Give them your own name of choice first before they disappear, even though they may already have a perfectly rounded name.

I watched Amber, cuddled with a sleeping Ar-Fun near the front of the boat.

I watched Amber. My discovery.

FIELD OF HERBS

After a long evening's hunt is when I have my customary rest, my lie-down in the grassy hills, body stretched out lazily, listening to the buffaloes grazing nearby. It's a must. The day's work almost over as I relax in a panorama of herbs and light. The last time I counted, there were twenty odd herbs you could use as medicine, from Rosebud (for bronchitis) to Daniella (for poisoning rats). So I knew these fields well by mind and heart. Knew that Sundance wouldn't get disturbed here. I could be myself. Just the open pink sky and the *munch, munch, munch* of cows chewing grass.

This was how Amber found me, on our very first meeting: tattered, with bruised knees, a ripped straw hat covering my face, and hands full of flowers, looking about as useful as a left-over banana skin. Maybe, I can say now, that was what she liked about me. I was harmless, lyrical – the kind of schoolboy who couldn't say no. Couldn't say no to Big Voice asking for money, couldn't say no to Grandma telling me to break the law. Couldn't say no to a stranger like her, looking lost.

'Can I help you? Are you lost or something?' I quickly shot up, threw the flowers to one side and straightened my creased shorts. Stood to attention like

I would have done in class. And quickly found myself, in her vivid presence, silenced. I couldn't even move.

It might have been the finely bow-ribboned hat, fully haloed around her head, the brim the size of a double-decker wheel. Or the pale pink dress, plus matching sandals . . . yes, it might have been all of those. They were part of the enchantment. But the special character-istic that shone out of Amber was pure altruism. It was there in her eyes. Big. Magnificent. I was hooked.

'A-Afraid to walk alone in the d-dark?' I stammered. 'Yes? Passing the dark grove beyond here? So am I. I will see you home.'

But the truth was: I didn't need to pass any dark grove beyond here. I didn't have to go that way at all, it just felt like the right thing to do. Felt appropriate being caught out this way, caught out by an angel.

'Thank you.'

'You don't live here, do you?'

'No. Over there.'

'Ahh. The city.' I point, my eyes brightening. 'Then I will take you all the way. You see, this is my home. I am a *hunter*. I know this geography and I can guide you through.'

Big word. Cocky words. But they worked. So on the evening of 23 March, my dog Echo and I found our-selves walking with someone who had qualities akin to an angel. Either that, or she was genuinely lost, or plain crazy or a ghost. A bewildered spirit lost in the dark. Throughout our first encounter there wasn't much I could say. She gave me no name. No address. I wasn't at all sure what she was. The journey out of darkness and into the glittering lights was mute. Time seemed to stand still.

I remember telling Grandma this, as I needed to say something to explain why I had gone missing for over two hours, yet somehow she seemed oddly pleased. The wrinkles under her eyes turned watery, as if she was about to cry. 'Was she a nice girl?' I said I didn't know. I said I'd only just met her and didn't even know if I would ever see her again, or even whether she was real. The case of 'lonely spirits' seeking company from the living was not uncommon here. But Grandma went on to reassure me: 'If she was a ghost,' now standing up and straddling her giant troll feet toward the night door, opening it a crack to see if Echo was still sat in darkness, 'you wouldn't be squatting in that tub having a nice bath, would you now?'

I nodded. I couldn't have agreed more. She closed the door, slid the wooden bolt into place. Then I went to bed, *quick*. Real quick because I wasn't ready to tell her about my long eight-mile walk, which was no walk at all but more about hitching a lift from a Police Land Rover and being sat with two coppers on Jockey Club Road while my dog and I wolfed down fish-ball noodles next to a cool bottle of cream soda. That was our little secret. Because a man's got to have some privacy, right? Not that Grandma would have agreed. She would have barked, 'You are no man yet! You are still my grandson!' To most people the Closed Area may sound like some lost world but it isn't easy to leave the place without being spotted either by a searchlight from way above or the headlights of a police vehicle. Grandma didn't need to know everything. But she did need to know I was growing up fast. I was soon becoming a man. And as a man you had to do things with style.

You had to know how to impress, or maybe brag is the more appropriate word.

At 6.25 p.m. I could still see my way home. In the hazy distance, the smoke rose from village chimneys, and the echo of barking dogs gave the world shape, depth and acknowledgment of approaching forms, be it from the road or the hills, or animals that science has yet to name. Twenty minutes later, the world became complete darkness. Nothing could be seen, since there were no street-lamps or electric bulbs in the village. We called this time the Hour of the Snake. A time when Amber must depart promptly for the city.

HIDE AND SNEAK

What is a Snake really, you may ask. I will try to give you a simple, straightforward answer, but of course nothing's ever as simple as it seems. Snakes, with a capital S, were just normal people running across the border, trying to get out of The Big Amber in the hope they might one day find a better life in the numerous riches of Hong Kong. That was the official version. But I prefer the other version: the one that says they once might have been human, but in the darkness of the valley's eye, the sinuous way they moved showed differently. There was no way a man could move like that. So when seeing a Snake you always expected it to shift shape at any second – something I personally have yet to witness.

The Gurkhas wanted them badly, and there was even a cash bonus depending on how many they could catch. In the night hills they kept fires burning and dug ditches to play hide and seek with them. And when they did come, the fugitives would shed clothes like snakeskins, exchanging a Maoist jacket for a shirt – anything, as long as it removed all traces of the place they had come from. Most illegal immigrants were caught within the first few hours. Those who did make it to the city were either lucky or skilful, or had something special like a local guide, a SnakeHead.

SNAKEHEAD

I know that Big Voice, wherever he may be in the world today, would prefer me not to discuss any of this. So pardon me, my old mentor, bro. I would never say anything that would give you away. Never make a sound, just like certain insects that are smarter than the others.

By the time he was nine, this son of a pigeon-breeder no longer had a proper name. 'Blame Big Voice the Ghost! Get that scoundrel!' The words just stuck to him. By the time he was almost eleven, his voice and pilfering skills had matured sufficiently to make smuggling humans appear as simple as passing postal packages. During a night of rain and thunder, despite seachlights that could shine up a cat's eye, a young spectral SnakeHead could make his mark.

'This is the way fast money is made,' he told me. Neglecting to mention it was also a fast way to prison.

But against heroin, opium and the Aphrodisiac Industry, what was wrong with aiding someone's dream of freedom and expecting a gold tooth or ring in return? If you have never seen a constellation, you don't know what it's like to view the city at night. There *are*

54

angels. There *is* hope. Big Voice said that in reality, he was aiding hope. All he had to do was wait for the growl of somebody's dog – my dog Echo, whose sensory skills could differentiate between man or wolf. Then from around the moonlit corner he'd appear and whisper, 'What have you got?' That's when the five and a half mile journey began. Because that was all it took, five and a half miles to get out, hide and sneak past the police inside the boot of an Austin 1300 or under a false ID card. The only difference with this game from our game of 'hide and seek' was, when the would-be immigrants got caught, they were sent back over the border. Until 1967, grabbing legal documents was as simple as taking an evening stroll. There were then no SnakeHeads. Borderline was minimal and not electric.

Of course, Big Voice wasn't the only one playing the game. There was a host of others playing it too for all its worth, way advanced from him in years and experience, with contacts and bribes and telephone calls which went like: 'I've got your niece. $800 on delivery. Take it or leave it.' But of course he was cheaper. Just a daredevil, that's all. Because when you are no good at school, and know that you haven't got much of a future, what else can you do? Like me. I was like a violin virtuoso. I was good at the one thing. To catch

THE LOCUSTMAN

'I hear you are going after Werewolves . . .'

In the mornings, the village could sometimes sound like an ocean, thanks to multiple echoes trapped between the

55

valley walls. It was a perplexing phenomenon, unique to Tortoise Spring. I swear, if you stood still long enough in the silence, in the next few seconds you would feel the ocean, miraculously crashing its way towards you.

At morning there were the bicycle people. As they called out the name of their trade they added to the rhythm of the ocean. Casual symphonies produced by casual noises – a cicada, a clap, a moving wheel – coming through the light mist. In bed I could hear their signatures, blown through conch shells or rung through a brass bell or conveyed in more direct methods, by a yell. Foodsellers from the city arrived early when the air was cool. They pedalled in. And if the price was right Grandma would unfurl her cotton purse, but most of the time she was hard to please. The Fishman, Porkman, Beancurdman, Noodleman, Barley Sweetman all did their best. Throughout the day they would continue their symphonies till finally there was the last and perhaps most discreet symphony of all, the *tap tap tap* of the infamous Locustman.

They are no good to me dead!

They are no good to me without heads or legs!

A road. A dark iron billboard. Dusk. And along with these spoken words the evening was complete. For years and years, every day would conclude this way, with the arrival of Locustman laying out conditions which disqualified the amateur. People and animals moved around us in clusters. The chickens especially were forever in the way of the grasshopper man's path, and would only explode away at the last second. As his dawdling, plodding two-wheeled machine came to a heaving halt he would be pleased to see there were so many of us. A quick yank from his foot and his bicycle

56

went into parking mode. His first words were always, 'Has everybody eaten well this evening?'

Only the old were impressed by this ancient greeting. We, the professionals, we knew better. As the hustle for insects began, so would the ballad of laughing doves. Their chatter was not so much laughing but appropriate. The stick frame of a man beside his stick frame of a bicycle now in the process of getting what he came for, absurd insects as amazing dollar notes, fifteen miles into the unknown.

'I hear you're going after Werewolves . . .' he announced suddenly.

That evening there was a pause. Nobody seemed to move.

'What's it to you?' we said.

'I have come especially to help you.'

'What can you do?'

'I can get you The Man of the West Winds.'

'How much?'

'Give me twelve lizards in one evening.'

'*What?*'

'That is cheap, compared to what I am offering.'

'Where is he?'

'Don't know. But you should know *he* has no address.'

'But you know – right?'

'Maybe.'

'Why should we trust you?'

'You don't.'

'We can take care of ourselves.'

'Not this time.' He folded away his cloth moneybag and stepped back onto the two-wheel machine. It was heavy now. He was about to carry away a trapped insect universe.

'You see, little ladies and gentlemen, when you are up against *the* Supernatural, and I must add, I have never seen anybody challenge Supernaturals before – it's not simply a question of catching them. You have to understand the substance they are made of. In other words, you need to know the constitution. You need something better than a quick wrist . . .'

THE MAN OF THE WEST WINDS

In 1963 a group of workmen cutting a government road through San Uk village negligently bulldozed a nearby Ancestral Hall. The subsequent mayhem also damaged feng shui and almost certainly caused the supernatural death of one person. Compensation followed thereafter. There were similar cases elsewhere in Lantau, and in the New Territories, some cases involving the poor, hardworking cow. From as early as 1899, during Britain's acquiring of the New Territories, law and order, unlike in other regions, were slow to enter. The British presence was kept minimal. Local rituals remained secret.

So the Closed Area meant what it said. It was a private world, isolated from both politics and commerce, crucial elements in the protection of endangered species, which must include hermits and wise men. Years from now, journals and papers will report on birds and lizards previously considered extinct, species The Big Amber no longer has, discovered in Hong Kong thanks to its numerous sanctuaries. I won't say the Man of the West Winds was wise. I won't say he loved sanctuaries either. The truth is: the Man of the West Winds does not

58

exist. There is no such person. He is a figure of speech, a bogeyman. In the hills there are times when wild dogs are responsible for the desecration of fresh graves, and the locals will blame it on the Man of the West Winds.

The Locustman was implying that he could help us, yet he wouldn't say how. It was difficult to tell whose side he was on. Every time the shadow of his palm fell towards us we knew exactly what to expect: money. One became accustomed to these things and nothing else. So imagine the surprise when three acceptance certificates signed by the red seal of Loh fell towards us instead of money during the last few minutes of 26 March. Our names, along with 76 others on the qualifying list, were posted up on every noticeboard throughout the Closed Area. The reality: we were competing against somebody who had been personally trained by Bruce Lee, the master of Kung Fu. None of us wanted to believe this, especially not Big Voice. 'Bruce wouldn't train that son of a ———!!' he fumed. And who could argue against that?

In books you can locate information and perhaps even find ways in which you may alter your future. To become a sailor, you would look up nautical books, discover how to navigate dangerous waters and survive. There are no beginner's handbooks on werewolves. But as we true hunters know, if it bleeds, it can be killed.

DISCOVERY

Everyone has a secret ambition: to become an astronaut, actress, singer, empire-maker and even millionaire. I would not have called my ambition secret, to be an explorer-hunter. Truth was, I didn't even know if there was a living to be made from it, but it was my choice. Mine alone. And as that, it was natural that I should desire the makings of great discoveries, be it a new species of insect or a wholly undiscovered country, like the lost city in the Central Asian desert, found by Sir Aurel Stein in 1908, or Thylacine, the Tasmanian tiger, killed off by man in 1936 but believed by some to be still alive somewhere. Until the moment of actual discovery, of evidence, there is only theory, sightings, records and cave paintings.

As far back as I can remember, I have had this strange little skill in me which came out of a desire to touch, and gain knowledge of worlds I didn't understand. The translucence of a sunlit wing in a field, for instance. What made it shine, fly, attract attention? The one of a billion wings caught and held gently between my fingers, as I whispered, *'That's an interesting sound you're making. What are you?'*

With each new discovery it was important to proceed in an educated manner. My own procedure took place after school. I would walk through the playground and into the emerald classroom towards the man marking homework. The silence there was awesome. I'd then unravel an object to place in front of him, which through my years of finding and collecting, resulted in a number of items from small dangerous snakes to fragile herbs that could be an antidote. 'This is a sky horn.' I'd tell him, giving my theory, though knowing well I could be wrong.

'This is a bagworm.' Pointing to it in a book as he looked up from his desk. 'Anything else?'

Yes.

For years now, I've been finding eggs that are like nothing the world has ever seen. My theory is they are the property of the real thing, angels. If held up to the evening, these eggs are almost the colour of 24-carat gold. I know I could be laughed out of town for saying this, my reputation ruined. However, that's a chance I am willing to take.

I did see something, once. Just once. A moment like flash lightning. A fizzy bone-chilling vision of something benign – something no textbook has ever described. A winged beauty suddenly appeared from behind my shoulders, laced by the fire of dusk. And as I turned, it was gone. Where would things be, I have always wondered, if I saw it again?

The end of the world?

The last time I saw it they were bombing Vietnam. A terrorist explosion in Israel. Fish poisoned in Hong Kong, then a typhoon, the worst in history. And I was suffering from a near-fatal hornet sting, on the left side of my forehead. But still, my lifelong search for true angels should it end life altogether, then so be it. There will be a day when I can wear a penguin suit and announce it the way they do in London, Washington, Paris.

'It gives me great pleasure to announce the name of the new species. *Garrulax angelsis*.'

EVIDENCE

I have proudly placed before Mad Dog snakeskins twenty feet in length that had only been discarded seconds earlier by the reptile. I have, during nights of the wild boar, slept under straw and rain and stars along with Big Voice and my dog just to chase off hungry pigs hoping to raid Grandma's communal plot, and afterwards in the cream morning glow found a broken-off white tooth the size of a penknife. I have helped complete my tutor's long-cherished butterfly collection. I have even captured birds considered unavailable on the market. So my aim has always been the unnamed or the impossible. Therefore, would it not be appropriate to obtain evidence of the Supernatural?

DAY OF THE LOCUST MYTHOLOGY

When I woke and found Lord Baltimore gone, Echo barking over me, there were several imprints left in the soft mud. A tyre-track, some footprints, plus the paw-marks of the beast, a werewolf. Three hundred yards from the scene of the abduction.

I have always hoped that some kind of psychological profile of the bully could be given, based on this evidence. That their character could somehow be described in the way these things are dealt with in novels and movies. But it didn't happen that way. Even though this story is set in between two worlds, in between two opposing societies, it can never have in-betweens. You are either very young or very old. There are no middle-aged people. This is no halfway story. I am telling a tale which may or may not, according to individual tastes, have a happy ending. When you are up against a Werewolf clan, happiness doesn't come easy. Due to such incidental and uncontrollable forces of nature I have no other choice but for now, to go back to where it all made perfect sense.

III

The Sacred Swing

YOU CLIMB TREES because you want to reach heaven. When you fall, you almost get it. In no way have I ever tried to climb to heaven or any higher social ladder, and besides, falling off trees is no big deal since I've been falling out of them since birth. And I didn't mind the pain as long as Amber was around. I didn't mind at all. At the tall Australian tree planted by my great-grandfather more than a century ago, I climbed. I climbed trees for the simple reason everyone else did — to get my hands on their summer fruits. But that time was different.

Amber woke me and told me I had scared the life out of her. She had watched me tumble through the branches of Great-grandfather's tree, landing with a thud. I was out cold when she had hurriedly dragged me away from the arid sandy earth where I fell, and only then did I wake.

'I was certain you were dead,' she told me. 'So I moved you from that death spot. And now you are alive.'

I remember looking up, warily. A death spot? Seeing her head within the overexposed halo of sunlight, thinking, what did she mean? Still unsure whether I was hearing right. Did she mean there was an area in this world where, if you stood on it, you were likely to die? Is that a death spot? *Mmmm.* I was in no position to think about it.

As I lay half-dazed, the last thought in me before passing out again was: How can these not be the words of an angel?

RESURRECTION

The swing that was hooked to the big old eucalyptus tree just outside school was where we met almost every other evening. If there was no sign of her at the hunt, then later this was where she would be. It was a promise within birds and echoes. For we were both in love with the same thing: the pretence of flight.

It was the perfect co-ordination. Holding on, each hand on a rope, standing on the swing in mid-air face to face. You kneel. Then I kneel. You kneel again and I fall further back. And the same when I do it to you. Each time one of us 'curtsied' the forest got closer, and closer. It was 'a swoosh of senses'. A moment held to last light. We continued to hurl each other through avian space, till again and again I could see her framed against the silhouette of sky and leaves. Then suddenly we were too high and it was dangerous, and she began to scream as if she'd seen a ghost.

The shrill sound piercing the near-darkening forest.

I can't give a date. There was no telling how long the swing had been there or who first thought there should be one. Some years back, before the arrival of a new playground, it used to be quite popular. During breaks this was where most children would gather, and Mad Dog would watch from his window, drinking tea, as laughter swung high and low, making him worry as to whether the old ropes were safe. Being a busy hunter of grasshoppers, I never gave these things much attention. It was only in the New Year, when out of ancestral respect Grandma and I went to pray for protection against evil spirits and the White Lady, that we went anywhere near the swing, since it hung no less than ten yards from a god. The famous White Lady ghost was a beggar who had died of starvation many years before; she was supposed to haunt the classroom, but thanks to the presence of this nearby god her spectral vengeance only manifested itself about twice a month. Why was it called the Sacred Swing? Precisely because a god was watching. A stone deity. Thanks to the latter you could swing far into the darkness and remain unafraid, no matter how threatening the forest noises became. Every move you made towards heaven was blessed.

The swing was not the best place to meet some-body, but Amber didn't seem to mind. In fact, it was her preference. We only met there when it was late. When most people were sitting down to eat or pack-ing up for the night. Cows and Gurkhas idly going by. Leaves falling. I had been in the process of repairing the rope and not climbing for summer fruits, when I fell. It must have been at least a twenty-foot drop. So I should have been in heaven, until she gave me resurrection.

'You shouldn't have swung so hard. This isn't an airplane.'

One day, as a grown adult I will get up in the morn-ing, have breakfast and be ready to go to work. I'll slip into a jacket and then a pair of socks, then shoes, doing up the laces – and like a landmine she will come back to me.

67

'For you I will wear trousers and shoes,' I promised. 'For this swing we will look our best!'

As a village boy, naturally, I was born shoeless. Once home from school or from the city, my shoes were flung to one side, useless. Yet in the years to come, I knew that by the simple act of putting on a pair of shoes, I would think of Amber. Recall the joy of slipping into shoes knowing I was to make a short journey to see someone special. The best-dressed person memory can buy; the best-dressed person the village had ever seen. For that reason, people used to stare. A princess, in among the mud and buffaloes? What was she doing here? It couldn't be for the dancing boy, could it?

Don't think so.

Still, I introduced to her my world and my life. Led her into the fields' minor seductions of geography. A pleasure that was entirely mine. 'Allow me to take you,' I gestured, removing my battered straw hat. 'Allow me to take you to a place where you enter Zen wizardry, and where you suddenly lose all sense of identity, because somebody else is whispering to you in secret notes. And your one desire is to locate this singer, talker, seducer. It is like discovering a great romance.'

Those were my words. This may not be the answer to the question of why she came here, but it was close. I like to think so. For this was a place like no other and a game like no other, within a village lyrically named after a tortoise. However, Amber was happy to settle for the lonesome swing hooked up just outside school. In the twelve months I knew her, this simple rope and plank of wood was to become her everything. As important to her as the game was to me. She often said she wished she had been born here, among the chorus of leaves where a god, a stream, a school in the middle of nowhere was all any person could ever desire. An oasis of the heart. But doesn't all this sound a little bit too perfect? A place is how an individual perceives it. Gather the right elements and furniture and light, and anyone can feel at home. And Amber *did* perceive it. Her way. That's one thing the rich can always do better – make the right choices. I must have been her arm-chair. A real honour, of course. But then again, if you know where to look, the heart of any individual is not too difficult to find either.

It didn't matter where or what I was doing; if I saw the slightest stream of white or silver pulse, any possible sign that there might be an angel unseen before by man, I would pursue it further than a rainbow. In the name of science, in the name of alchemy. My own secret desire was to find it, perhaps even catch it for a single moment and tame it. Crazy as it may sound, that was how I felt, in the flow of the moment. And in a sweet innocent way, I am sure the moment was flowing well.

Things happen all too fast sometimes. It was a day or two after the night I had led Amber back through the city lights thinking it was the last I would see of her, when I spotted something small but bright, slicing through the village in the direction of school. At the time, what it looked like was the silver-blue streak of a Kingfisher, but much, much brighter. It blistered my eyes. I dropped everything and immediately gave chase. My dog followed. Then as we entered the cocoon of leaves to school, to our sudden surprise, there she was!

I stopped. My breathing was like a piston, up and down, in and out, full of running energy.

'Did you see an angel of light come through here?' I asked. My chest still panting away.

She looked at me calmly. I was all muddy and wet, wearing a holey vest. Then she said, 'My name is Amber. I would like to thank you for your company the other night. It was most charming.'

Don't angels always descend to earth dressed in beauty? And can't ghosts and demons appear equally radiant? I don't wish to describe her that way. I want none of her to be revealed and simplified and forgotten. Don't want to remember Big Voice calling her a 'rich princess' as if that was all she was. 'You can't take a city person into the game!' he boomed, not wanting her to join us. 'City people buy from us. They don't game themselves!' There was no point in arguing against that. But I had to persist, the same way I persisted when he turned down Ar-Fun, claiming she was too young and it would be unsafe. 'She hasn't even got a basket!' was his rather crude complaint against Amber.

'No,' I grumbled.

Reaching out, he scratched my head. 'Is she your girlfriend?' he nudged. 'Is she?'

Stopping in my tracks, I burst out, 'Yes! That's it! That's what she is.'

'Well, why didn't you say so?' he asked, throwing up his thick arms with an elated smile while I could only cringe at what I had just said, for how can a millionaire's daughter possibly be the girlfriend of a penniless farm boy?

During her first few weeks Amber wisely watched from behind, stuck close to Ar-Fun and listened intently as I intoned the game's folklore. 'Beware of the field's natural hazards,' I told her. And with my finger ninety degrees at the sky, I offered the following points.

- Always walk 10 feet in front of the marching flames.
- Never touch or eat anything, especially purple fruits.
- Green ferns can appear deeper than they look. Watch out for open mine-shafts covered over by dense ferns. They can be a mile deep.
- If lost, do not panic. Look for chickens and cows. They know the way home.
- Never kick anything that vaguely resembles a football; they are, in reality, wasp nests.
- Drink always from your flask. Although wild gooseberry and rose myrtle are just as drinkable. However, excessive intake of rose myrtle will result in rock-hard faeces, making toilet duties a true struggle.
- Wasp pupa is a regular source of rich nutrition.
- Always wear a brimmed hat (made of straw if possible).
- Be delicate with life. Respect all forms of life. For a missing leg will reduce half of a grasshopper's net value.
- Sun-baked herbs can induce a false sense of security as well as of serenity, a sea of hallucinogenic experiences. Experiences that can be as confounding as they are astounding.
- The basic act of picking up a stone may thwart dogs, but it can do little good against a wild boar. Your best luck charm is a dog. Failing that, run!
- If wearing a dress, beware of goose grass. Their seeds stick to cotton like glue.
- The truth is: all you will ever need is a hat and some early dreams, a basket to contain the catch and to

eagerly reach for it, like a star, high up in the green and blue was all you needed to qualify. With a desire to pounce! The greatest secret of the game.

Of course, if I'd had my way, I'd have worn nothing at all. No shoes or vest, let alone gloves. The need to communicate with life was greater. How can you touch with gloves and know whether something is alive or dead? How can you ensnare the legendary Grass Lizard other than with your own naked palm?

For most ordinary people, seeing a one hundred dollar note is what makes life worth living. Seeing a Grass Lizard surface among the deep lime ferns is, for any experienced hunter, much more than that. You cannot count on luck. The moment you have it in your sight the rule is: never blink or it will vanish. Pressing the head will ensure success. Pressing the tail, however, will break it from its already escaped body (such is a lizard's brilliant survival mechanism), and you will find that you have been fobbed off with a lifeless tail and nothing more.

'*I bet there is one other thing you can't catch,*' said a faraway voice.

'*Name it,*' I demanded.

'*A millionaire's daughter . . .*'

There were days when I went to the swing and she was not there, and the only thing that could save me was 'Sweet as Sweet' by Teresa Teng, courtesy of Polydor Records, Taiwan Inc. It was Amber's favourite song, and my goodness, couldn't you tell. She played it on tape all the time and even translated the Mandarin lyrics to me, singing, curling her tongue to the words,

'*She nee! She nee!*' meaning: '*It's you! It's you!*' followed by '*The one that's in my dreams . . .*' Then telling me from her point of view, 'It should have been sung by a man to a lady . . . because how can a lady say a man is *sweet?*'

I could see her point.

'But you are sweet,' she went on.

'Am I?' Turning my head, as she sat behind my bicycle the time when her taxi didn't show up. Pedalling her ten miles back towards the city lights.

'Like now. You're sweet, taking me home like this.'

'It's my pleasure,' was my regular reply.

A blossom. Thousands, one after the other. A hand scoops by, taking a blossom. Next, the hand swings back over a shoulder and hands the pink blossom to the girl sat on the back of a bicycle. A smile from her, then the boy riding on this same bicycle smiles also. Blossoms everywhere as they move though delicate light. Her petite face in this delicate light, in tune with the lyrics of the song. In perfect happiness.

Call me over-romantic, but whenever I hear that song, whenever it beatifies a street radio, that's what I see.

The wind was in our hair. The light dissolving somewhere, perhaps from behind us or from the shine of the handlebars or maybe not at all. The flapping of her luminous red sari, as if on the Sacred Swing, except the landscape was changing, every few minutes changing, and she was silent, no longer screaming. Till I took the sharp precipice left of Lo Wu and her grip tightened around my waist. Almost as tight as the night we shook hands and said goodbye for the last time. 12 June 1973.

The night of our final parting.

It was a scenario she often talked about. Leaving for New York, 'the mother of all cities'. And I would nod, half-looking at the sky and her, never certain what new birds or words might appear. She went to the Colony's most famous private school, the Heep Yun. She knew about the world and could speak five languages whereas I knew only about the game. Her parents, apparently, were big in the world of freight shipping. I don't know how Big Voice found out – he just knew. Even at his early age the Triad connection was strong. His future with the underworld was sealed. Just as her future with the international world was sealed. So it was only a matter of time before she left for good the place that Mad Dog had so honestly named as 'No Future'.

And New York, East Coast of America where she was due to join her parents and make a new home, had a future, a big future. Fast city, fast commerce. People walking miles faster than people here. What made her come this far back in time and place was anyone's guess. Tortoise Spring – the middle of nowhere, the complete opposite. Maybe that was it. Perhaps she saw our pastoral solitude as the right balance, to get some fresh air after the city pollution.

'Won't you come in?' she asked. We had reached a white wall and a gate with lamps on either side; a man opened up to let her in. This was the city opulence where she lived until June 1973. It was soon to be her eighth birthday party on 29 January, lavish with all manner of cakes, decor and respectable people, including her boyfriend Simon. And I was invited.

I told Grandma my shirt needed to be whiter for the occasion, my navy shorts ironed. 'What? Are you marrying her?' She looked at me from the corner of her head shawl, crouched down to wash cabbages. 'Splendid!' She looked serious. The only reason she agreed to press my evening attire was because of marriage. I protested. 'I am a hunter, Grandma! Not a husband!' Yet there was no running away from it. Flowers in hand. My head held high. The exuberance of walking through the village better-looking than usual. Posing as somebody else, and hearing the usual sniggers. *Who are those flowers for, bright boy? Who is the lucky girl?'* And immediately, I would proudly announce, 'I am off to see *Teng Lai Qwan!'* Meaning Teresa Teng. Which may have sounded amusing to them, but not to me. Grandma's maiden name was Teng also – Teng Sek Gal, the name she used before coming to Tortoise Spring. So I said to her, 'If your surname before you got married was Teng, then is it possible that you and Teresa Teng, Amber's number one idol, could be related?'

She was, as usual, nipping off the dried ends of her spring onions, getting them packed and ready for the 6.30 p.m. pickup. I had shown her Teresa's picture, the heavenly smile and peach face, telling her all I knew about her. I said, 'When Amber grows up she'll look just like that.'

'And why not?' Grandma replied, fudging her lips. 'We Tengs all came out of The Big Amber at one time or another.' At which point she looked almost proud. But I knew it wasn't so. Grandma was above such silly notions. She was too deeply into farming her prized gourds to concern herself with such trivial human cravings.

'But you don't look anything like Teresa,' I objected, and I wasn't being funny. If there was a comparison between the two, then Teresa had to be the complete opposite of Grandma. Teresa had a sweet, soothing voice whereas Grandma's voice was coarse. Teresa certainly did not have those big hands and ears and lips nor, dare I say, the age nor the brute strength. 'There's no resembl—'

She dragged me over before I could finish, then shoved my naked chest into a T-shirt. 'The sun is bad for you!' she chastised. 'And don't be cheeky! What do you know? I was beautiful once.'

Later on, she showed me her red wedding gown, all boxed up in a brown worn-out leather suitcase sealed by cobwebs, just to prove it. She told me that that was what Amber would have to wear also when I married her: even in this modern era, a traditional red wedding dress would bring good luck and prosperity.

'Grandma!' I cried, once again making my protest clear. 'Amber doesn't even like me!'

But, of course, that wasn't entirely true. For her eighth birthday, seeing she had received pretty things a boy like me could only lick his lips at, I'd asked her plainly, 'Is there anything you would like from *me*?'

'You?'

'Yes, *me*.' Pointing to myself. 'What would you like?' She turned to me, holding a small pebble in her hand. We were in the midst of playing hopscotch at the school playground. It was her turn to toss.

'You already know what I desire.'

'Do I?'

'Yes. You.'

'What, *me*?'

'Yes.'

My immediate response was of course, speechlessness. I was a little confused, lost for words.

76

'All I desire is you . . .' she went on, 'to show me your scar.'

'Oh. My scar,' I sighed, finally finding my voice.

'Yes.'

'Is that all?'

She tossed the pebble and winked me a smile, a lovely bunny-toothed smile, and whispered, 'YES, PLEASE!' Then she jumped forward, her pony-tail brushing hollow space. Both her feet landing with a well timed *clap*, followed by its echo.

'You touched the line!' I shouted. But she kept smiling, jumping and spinning 180 degrees all at once, quickly bouncing back through the playground silence and beating my previous effort so I had no other choice but to comply.

'Are your eyes closed?' I said, like it was an order rather than a question. And they were: she was already standing behind me with legs together, eyes tightly closed. When I was certain no one else was about, I pulled down my pants just past the tip of my bum and revealed to her my scar. Showed her the bite-mark left by one of my famous after-school canine encounters. In all honesty, it was a pleasure to show it off. After two years I was quite curious myself as to how the scar was healing, since there was no way I was able to see for myself, not even in the mirror.

'Is it still there?' I asked.

'I think so.'

'How does it look?'

'Not that bad.'

'What?'

'I mean . . .'

'Mean what?'

'Well, it doesn't look like a bite at all.'

'No?'

'In my opinion it looks like you've been kissed.'

'*Very* funny.' Hearing her giggles and finally getting the joke.

'Do you mind if I touch it?'

'Be my guest.'

And that she did also. It was a double honour. Amber touched my bottom! Blessed it – or more accurately, pinched it. '*Ouch!*' I gasped, feeling the precision of her fingernails. 'What did you do that for?' But there was no answer. Obviously she must have been having a private giggle at the sight of the place where the dogs had (and I so much prefer her expression) 'kissed' my schoolboy bottom.

Even though I am a person who has lived in the fantastic where it's all too easy to lose yourself and get distracted, you mustn't get me wrong. I *don't* subscribe to fairytale endings, like the pauper marrying the princess. The pauper is the pauper. The princess the princess. It's possible the pauper may one day discover treasure, but that's one day. Now is now. Catch that grasshopper, you get money. The world is a practical place.

She grabbed me by the arm, her grip desperate and fast.

'If you win Day of the Locust, you are dog meat. You know that?'

I said nothing. I wasn't ready to be dog meat. Yet she seemed to feel that might happen. She placed her mouth into my neck, losing the swing's momentum and her arms were suddenly worn tight around me in mid-air.

IV

Memoirs of a Hunter

DAY OF THE LOCUST
(past winners)

Year	Hoppers	Lizard	Winner
1913	27 oz	8 oz	Y.S. Loh
1923	19 oz	15 oz	O. Loh
1933	22 oz	7 oz	S.S. Loh/S. Lam
1944	9 oz	–	D. Loh
1953	25 oz	8 oz	E.A. Loh
1964	17 oz	10 oz	M.R. Loh

THE ONLY YEAR in which the date of Day of the Locust altered was in 1944, when the contest was delayed for nine months owing to the Nazi–Japanese Occupation of Hong Kong. In this period werewolf evil was baby's play by comparison. Yet this was a minor loss of face compared to 1933, the year which saw the Werewolf clan share first prize with an outsider, a name and person who has remained a fantastic mystery. In a region which has little or no change for hundreds of years, rituals and ceremonies are routine, not competitive. The only other mass games event was the Festival of Pau, or the Birthday of Ama, the female Buddha, which did, at times, result in bloodshed. Until 1807 there had never been a sports ritual belonging to one single clan.

When they come, they will come with others. The champions, the runners-up, the short-listed hunters from as far afield as Lamma Island and Stanley, bringing their weird giants and gods to a day where there can only be one great hunter. Throughout the Colony, monks from temples afar will begin pilgrimage till they reach the Closed Area where hunters of all styles will gather alongside the religious circus itself – the tiger dancers and sea beasts and chants that in-spell the blessings of gods.

From here on, the event will be out of the hands of the government, and it will have a life and law of its own.

From our Ancestral Hall records, 1908

RETIRED HUNTERS

A once-upon-a-time hunter. 'Not too long ago,' he muttered, 'I was like you. A locust hunter.'

'Yes, we know,' I told him. 'But now you are merely a shadow of your former self.' And he just chuckled.

We were at the iron billboard, Big Voice, Three-Eye, Echo and myself. We had been saying goodbye to an old-timer by the name of Firecracker. He was a retired hunter, someone I'd often see in the Sea of Whispers because grown-ups joining in were not unusual, for the chance to earn three or four times their normal daily rate meant that they came to play quite often. Their performance was quite impressive. But the older you get, the fewer risks you take. At my age I could go on for a whole day and think nothing of sunburn, dehydration or fatigue. It was of no concern. Yet the mystery of 1933 and of the dual win – that *was* a concern.

Seeing that Firecracker was about to emigrate to Canada, with his belongings and a little wren left to our care, we put to him the question: what *did* happen in 1933?

'There was a boy – about Sundance's age.'

'Where?' we asked. 'Where did he come from?'

'No idea. Until that day, no one had ever laid eyes on him.'

'A complete stranger?'

'Yes. I couldn't make out what he was. No one could.'

'Explain?'

'He was neither Oriental nor European.'

'You mean he didn't speak?'

'Oh yes, he spoke. He said he'd been hired by a secret client. He was a hired mercenary, if you like. But he wasn't cocky. He was good. So good, he was able to light a furnace right under the nose of a wolf and get away with it. Of course, if he had hung around and got caught, they would have broken his legs.'

There are some people who talk like they think you are *this* small, as if you don't know how many beans make five, but not old Firecracker. He didn't say, 'You shouldn't' or 'You'd better listen' or 'You should do this.' Firecracker knew we were serious. We weren't *just* playing with fire. This was big time. Big stakes. All he needed to say was, 'Don't hang around if you get caught lighting that fire . . .' Something we definitely hadn't planned on.

He was sat upon an upright suitcase waiting for a taxi, hunched over as if he was fishing. And with such early memories flashing by, he honestly did look as if he actually had a line in his hands and was peering into reflective waters. Another casualty added to the list of departures. Another goodbye. Whether his leaving was due to the death of Lord Baltimore was no longer relevant. People were leaving. It was a hard-skin fact. We were getting used to it. Firecracker's neat grey-white hair, white handkerchief and white shirt with his Parker pen in the top pocket were becoming less and less bright in the permeable orange glow of 6.46 p.m. Soon, his taxi would come, and the Man Who Spun Wild Yarns would have told his last yarn. For that was what his nickname 'Firecracker' meant – to tell an imaginative tale and make people believe it was true. And many had believed, including myself. I recall the number of times I've pelted pebbles at his window or thrown firecrackers into his living room making him dance (crimes I now willingly admit deserved punishment), yet somehow he'd never laid a finger on me. So why should I not believe him this time? Firecracker was a very nice man. And evidently a man who had no son, and who wanted a son, an heir to his name. Firecracker was that old-fashioned kind of man who thinks a boy child is the bee's knees: a son can be counted on to carry on the family name, look after the parents and so on and so forth, but lucky for him (we say) he ended up with three daughters instead. A man not too long ago, I remember, who lived with his wife and three athletic daughters in the house smothered by firecracker vines, close to the Sacred Swing. He had seen me when I was *this* big, before I had a herd or a dog. And yes, he had teased me with many a wild yarn: apples that fruit in the winter hills, a snakewoman who hunts people in tall grass, Chinese griffins, cow-foot-sized puddles that can drown a man, why pissing on an open fire will hurt, and how to recognise the drawn-out howls of a ghost with a dangling five-foot tongue! However, we did not believe this last tale of his to be a lie. He had evidence: a third-place medal that had been hanging on his wall for years and which proved he had actually been present on that big hot day back in 1933.

Seeing him leave, I knew I would miss him. His bronze-cast Day of the Locust runners-up medal was his only medal ever: it was a considerable achievement, especially for a man who couldn't read or write. He was the last of the retired hunters. Then like Houdini, as his taxi came rolling up the incline, he held out his illusionary empty palm and gave it to us. A parting gift. The bronze medal of 1933.

84

So in 1933, according to history, you could walk in from out of nowhere, come face to face and eventually level with a pack of werewolves. Almost outdo eight hundred years in a matter of twenty minutes (which was the actual length of the contest). A duration, we had discovered, that was timed by an ancient 15-foot twin water tower contraption which bled water from one tower into another empty tower till it floated up a candle which then ignited a series of fireworks. A great trick, if you knew how it was done.

In his corridor of doves Big Voice considered this phenomenon, mouth open, breathing and talking through it at the same time. We had been here all morning, as one by one, we transferred the dozen or so flightless chicks from the wooden wall of cages into two rattan carriers. After which, we intended to refill the cages with fresh hay. During this time, as Big Voice continually stressed, it was vital there should be no sign of any cats. It was about 11 a.m. We were at his house, a shack built from sheet metal and wood, twenty-three day-warmed paces from my place and walled in by pigeons that flew round and round, encircling the village as if they had no idea where they were going. Unlike us: we knew where we were going.

'Like a finger pointing to the *moooon*,' Big Voice twanged, once again confirming himself to be my own personal neighbourhood confidence guru, whose own undaunted faith in Bruce Lee was greater than all the teas of China. I enjoyed jingling along to his endless quotes, from the mindful yet riddled: '*How to express yourself honestly, as a human being*' to the simpler, cow *moo*ings of '*finger pointing to the moooon*'. Classic Bruce phrases while on the move or on the job, or as in this case, walking with baskets held against our chests, as if carrying laundry. Except that pigeons were heavier. I had about fifteen. They were heavy enough to make me walk funnily and sweat as badly as Bruce did in *The Way of the Dragon*. This was Big Voice's number one movie, and he regularly and generously provided us with endless anectodes, since not only was Bruce a 'heung ha lo' – a village bumpkin like we were – his character actually hailed from the New Territories and even walked around with a stern bucolic swagger. And some days when I woke up, all I had to do was run round the corner, look at Big Voice's lean face, his tanned skin, his naked arms always exposed to the harsh sun and his sweaty sheen, and I'd say to Grandma, 'Did you know Bruce Lee lived next door?' Though whether Bruce bet on horses, bought sweepstake tickets, played street poker or got himself (ironically) booted in the bum Bruce Lee-style by his own father, or whether he'd lose his temper if he lost a bet is questionable. Big Voice would smash the street table with his mallet fist then walk away as people stared, then minutes later, as if the devil had left him, he'd come back round, laughing it off as if it wasn't that bad at all. And who could blame him? Big Voice had just lost forty dollars, including some of his father's cash, made mostly from selling pigeons. And the hardest part, of course, was how to tell his father or how not to, what the hell happened to the rest of the cash.

But we survived. Big Voice survived. Do a song and dance and move on, because there is nothing else you can do.

Once a month in baggy shorts we would take to the city and join the party that is trade. Do some haggling while listening to the latest pop song from Sam Hui. Sam who is our very own workingman's Elvis. Honkers has never been a romantic place and I myself have never understood what all the love ballads and sad ballads and traditional ballads were doing here. All we had in Hong Kong was work: from the sun-blackened coolies at building sites to the street-level sweatshops where workers toil for less than a cent to the hour. Sam mused about work. 'It's Better To Be a Con Artist Than a King' was one. 'Without Water How Am I Going to Wash Tonight?' was another. A song about the misery of water rationing caused by another rainless summer. During the years 1963, 1967 and 1972 (1963 being the worst), four hours of water every four days was all you got. Everyone remembers the lines of humans stretching back mile after mile every morning from a single street tap. A bucket per HK city person if you were lucky, and don't even think about a bath or a date with your girlfriend expecting to smell like roses. That's what made Sam hip and cool to us the working-class heroes. You never sing a sad song as a sad song. You should sing it as something else. Sam could do that. It felt more like situation comedy. His lyrical irony – his philosophical irony – was what Big Voice could groove along to. Those ideals were right down his alley. Catchy tunes catering to all tastes. Lost a million? Ah, so what. It's not that bad, is it?

Maybe not. Not when you listen to Sam.

The depressive city madness was always around you like a damp kitchen cloth and all you had to counteract it were songbirds and Sam. Take any turn on a Saturday afternoon and there he'd be on the short-wave radio telling you about losers, winners, moneymakers and jazzmakers and the likelihood that those beggars sat at the steps of the local Ritz cinema were actually millionaires in disguise! Everybody looked busy, too busy perhaps at times to admire musical poetry. The restaurants, the snack bars sizzling with aromatic fried dough and congee, decked out with people, the English cafés too. Rubbish-collectors who would fine you a hundred dollars just for dropping a sweet wrapper. The police too looked busy, or were they? A crazy question, but a good one. The one question everybody would like to ask but prefers not to. But if I may, I would like a crack at it, though I know well Big Voice is perched on a better position to discuss it than I will ever be. However, I will give it a shot.

There is a law in the city to prevent disturbances at night, especially the level of noise from your next-door neighbour. The walls of city flats being about as thin as paper, any arguments, music, footsteps from above, all come through loud and clear. By midnight, most of the city should be in bed, preparing for the next gruelling day. Walk down any street, look up and you will see that all lights are out, except for the odd few. And those are the ones the cops look out for. Why? Because they're the ones where people are still up playing Mahjong, or gambling – which is illegal, by the way, both for the noise it generates and as a link to crime.

The cops are always eagle-eyed for this. They glance up, see the lit windows, go up and knock on the door and when it opens they say: 'Do you people know what time it is? Don't you realise you're causing a disturbance and keeping your neighbours awake?' The answer will be: 'Yes, officer. We do. And we didn't mean any harm. We'll be finishing soon.' Saying this, they'll be parting with the bribe at the same time – a sum anywhere between fifty to a hundred dollars, which is a fantastic kill for one night's work, on top of their monthly four-hundred-dollar police salary.

But as I said before, all this is not first-hand information. If you want top stories, Big Voice is your bird. He could sing to you things you wouldn't believe, that would make you laugh out loud. For example: what do you think a copper does when he gets told there's a robbery on Cameron Road? Go into action? More like *go in the opposite direction*. He would radio back saying he was nowhere near the crime scene when the truth was, he was standing right on it. The general view was: why put your neck on the line just for one lousy job?

My personal favourite was the searchlight operator based at the border. Oh yes, he did his duty, he shone the lights. Only he was using his foot whilst his hands were playing cards! All the time he was just pushing the handle of the beam left to right, and if he got tired he'd simply change to the other leg. Information like this could make smuggling people out of The Big Amber easier than eating raw cabbage. It was amazingly useful if, say, you were a SnakeHead like Big Voice. It was all about making a buck without sweating too hard. In the city, when you ran a business, as a fruitseller, cakeseller etc, it was all the same: you needed to know how to sweet-talk. 'I know, sir. I know. I can't sell on the pavement but I am just trying to make a living – you understand?' Money changes hands and the trading stays. Everyone is happy except the constitution of the law.

For us, from the back and beyond, we had no way of forking out the extra cash supplement to make the police turn a blind eye to crime. Besides, what rights did we have to complain about the theft of an absurd little thing like a tortoise?

For us small fry, trying to illegally flog a few pigeons, we had to run quickly. The streets looked tantalising, mouthwatering as long as you had money. But you had to be 'smart' to have money. Hawking pigeons was not the best gig. Dodging corrupt coppers was no great fun, until we grasped the upper hand and began selling exclusively to restaurants. It was a good move. It was straight and simple. They were regular neon places, with cooks and waiters who joked about our clothes and our bad haircuts . . . and then one night in late February, the jokes included one about some restaurant that had been selling native tortoise meat with dimensions matching that of Lord Baltimore. Big Voice and I froze. The very act of selling pigeons itself made my stomach dry and my face white. I was trembling and sick to the bone.

As Mad Uncle indicated, werewolves never lose. They are born to win. The stone Hall of Fame has always been in their name, with the only exception in 1933, when they shared a disgraced joint win and barely maintained 'face'. Near Loh town, a town named after its most famous family, there are thirty-nine blue granite obelisks lined symmetrically along the roadside. One name and one winner for each decade is carved into the rock. A proud family history. This is the kind of road a schoolboy like me would pass often, every time I got onto a city-bound truck to be precise. It is the kind of road that 'gleams' but you never get around to asking why it 'gleams' until it unexpectedly hits you on the head one day and becomes part of your destiny. What great empire and why? How much would a twenty-foot column like that cost today? It all stood, rather monolithically, like a walk towards some grand palace or the entrance to an emperor's tomb, depending on your point of view.

So late one Friday in February, the three of us decided we should take a closer look, once and for all. To make up our minds about the myth, the legend. We had gathered after school, still uniformed. Big Voice and I had come by bicycle while Three-Eye had obviously come by a floating Persian carpet as he was already there. The road stood numbly deserted, just a few trucks and cars and rural people skimming by. It was the time of the day when unbetrayed light can give a series of thirty-nine columns the visual impact its makers had in mind, a mythic quality. Line after horizontal line of shadows were thrown across a single white road panning back into a flat, intensively farmed landscape, so geometric and well-placed you could see it from miles away.

Big Voice was licking his lips compulsively, as if there was something tasty about this particular stone, or like a burned survivor who had just made it out of the desert and the first thing to greet him was a cocktail bar. The colour of the stone was very fine blue, almost turquoise, but of course it was the information he found tasty.

'I knew it!' he snapped, his right hand against the stone. 'Firecracker was right! They can be beaten!'

I nodded. And touched the stone also. It was smooth and strangely cold, even in this heat. But you could also tell its surface had been worn through rain, wind and time.

'You mean it was a draw,' confirmed Three-Eye, taking

91

off his glasses and wiping them. We looked over to where he was. 'We just have to make sure *we* don't do that. We have to make sure only one name goes in there. Get what I mean?'

We got what he meant. Both Big Voice and I were nodding like donkeys. But there was nothing new in what he said that we didn't already know. We were basically up against fire. Straight and simple.

PLAYING WITH FIRE

In any game, if you want to better your opponent you can bend the rules a little and cheat. If you're in a car race, for instance, you can get hold of a rocket and go supersonic. If, say, we wanted to bag more grasshoppers in faster time, we should deploy a similar philosophy. We should set fire to the whole field.

I don't know anyone who isn't scared of fire, and grasshoppers were no different. During a fire, they came springing out of the fields like a jack-in-a-box and all you had to do was walk in front of the smoke, reach out and catch them. You couldn't miss. However, there was one serious disadvantage. Fires are unpredictable and uncontrollable. You can stamp them out afterwards with bushes, but there's no guarantee that the flames are all extinguished. In daylight it's difficult to see the smallest flame, the tiniest cinder, and sometimes they can be overlooked and flare up again later. Just when you're about to hop into bed, it happens: midnight incandescence. The hills behind us lit up like a festival and the entire village about to go up in flames. It was *that* close. Thank heavens for the grove acting as a buffer, and later, for the fire engines screaming along, with the village headman ready to yank a few feathers.

'Who is responsible?' he bawled. 'Who was catching grasshoppers? You? You! Was it you, Big Voice? It was you, wasn't it? Don't lie!'

The only thing to do was keep nodding your head. *No, it wasn't me, sir.*

But no nodding of the head would save our skins once we started this fire. In any game there are always tantalising options. With real life there are few options you can take to get around a problem. Especially a monster one like this. There were no short cuts.

Three-Eye normally had all the answers. He was the All-Seeing-Eye and normally we looked to him to wise up. But his 'look' at this moment was vacant. His posture, without response. He was about twenty feet away from us, sitting with an elbow at each knee under the 1923 column and, not having his glasses on, looked baby-faced and helpless. This scared me. It scared me because he had nothing more to say from a mouth that was usually persistent with the nature of truth (as opposed to Big Voice's mouth which could well drive an unstoppable lorry). A bowl of orange jelly could come towards me and all I could think about was tasting it, yet he'd see the germridden fingernail mark dug into the jelly and wisely hint: *'Have you seen how dirty that woman's fingernails are?'* But there was no smart advice on that evening of February, 1973. Three-Eye went to the famous English language school, King George V. His English was, with the exception of Amber, the best among us. However, good English was not going to be an advantage against a Supernatural

93

empire. We came away with just a trivial fact, that the stones hadn't converted to Roman numerals until after 1933. They were still using the Chinese system until then.

I think we were all hypnotised and inspired by the stone-etched evidence, deep and permanent, that showed another name resided here when there was no possible way it could do so. For the first time ever. The equivalent would be of Mad Uncle becoming President of the USA. It had never happened before but here, in stone, was the proof that it could.

If you go there today, you'll still find this sublime Supernatural quality. There isn't anything else like it in HK. There are shrines a-plenty, and more eyes focused on the famed Bun Building Festival at Cheung Chau island than there are buddhas at the spectacular Temple of a Thousand Buddhas at Shatin, yet nothing comes close to the Locust Hall's uniqueness. Standing there, it isn't hard to imagine the winner walking down the ancient, shadowed avenue, the sunlight shutting on and off through the thirty-nine obelisks as he passes them, the crowds cheering him and knowing that his name will soon be immortalised in stone. How many roads are there in the world that can do *that* these days?

As we left, I couldn't help but stare one more time at the new blank obelisk erected less than a month ago. The bamboo scaffolding had yet to be removed, the stone yet to be marked, yet to be named. I began to wonder whether the 1933 joint winner had walked that way, or was he running like a fugitive, the crowds stoning him, calling him names and trying to kill him? I tried to imagine what the three of us would have done in that situation, had we won, but I couldn't. That was another hurdle, another story.

A SMALL NOTE ABOUT 'SUPERNATURALS'

I met Amber's parents once. It was at their city flat on Moldy Road near TST (Tsimshatsui). Until that meeting all I knew was that her father was from Pondicherry, in India, where she was also born, and that her mother was Chinese. They were home to pay a brief visit to their only daughter and I happened to be around the area selling pigeons that Saturday. I had promised to drop by, not knowing that Amber had planned the meeting.

As you may have gathered by now, Amber too was a Supernatural, but of a different kind. The good kind. Perhaps a bit too good to be true.

When she got me up to the fifteenth floor, where the interior and leather sofa looked like it had been plucked directly from out of a Lane Crawford showroom, I was even more surprised to find her boyfriend Simon. He was standing at the balcony and seemed far more interested in his binoculars than me. After all, he was the boyfriend – so who and what was I supposed to be?

Unlike Big Voice, who was always full of fire, I was the possessor of 100 per cent village-boy mentality. I was shy, held myself back and could sometimes be nervous in the presence of people. If I didn't know you it would be difficult for you to get to talk to me. I would stand or sit like a lampshade, in the hope that if I kept still long enough, no one would notice me; of course this is a technique useful during a good insect hunt but an utter waste of a bag of rice amongst people. Maybe if I had had a father and a mother I'd be normal, who can tell? But for about thirty-five minutes, that was how I was with Amber's mum. I hardly moved. Tried to be invisible. Just a few minutes ago, I had sold three dozen pigeons along Nathan Road and I was sweaty, feathery, and wore baggy shorts stained by droppings and sherbet. Not the way I would normally like to present myself to people. Her mother was seated regally on the sofa across from me, divided by a small coffee-table, and she was everything Amber had described to me. She was elegant, calm, wore a silver Shanghai dress and spoke in a serene voice that never altered in tone, and which gave me the feeling an earthquake could be near and she'd still sound cool. Amber sat on her mother's knees most of the time. The maid, Ama Chan, who had seen me on previous occasions, gave me a 7UP in a tall glass and I tried to say thanks but made only a dog's *woof*. But she smiled and appeared to understand. We were the same, you see. Working-class.

'So you are Sundance . . .' Her mother was smiling. About to drink tea.

'Yes.'

'Amber talks a lot about you.'

'Yes.'

'She says you make a good living by catching insects. Is that so?'

'Yes, mam.'

'She told me you intend to become a field biologist when you grow up. Is that true also?'

A field biologist? I paused, knitting my eyebrows as I do when I am perplexed. I had no idea what that was, but it sure didn't sound like a job with a lot of dough in it. I nodded anyway, out of reflex. And it seemed to convince her.

'Amber wants to become a doctor, don't you, dear? And Simon says he plans to be a lawyer. Doctors and lawyers go well together, don't you think?'

I said, 'Yes, mam,' while fidgeting idiotically with my drink. When I should have said, 'I don't think so.'

I knew this was none of my business. I knew it shouldn't matter. And by now even I was tired of my moans and groans. I am just a village boy, that's all. What else could I expect? What did I know about love? Love exists only in movies.

But afterwards, a few days later, I found myself asking Amber a totally out of the way question. 'How did I do?'

Her reply was: 'You did great. I think they like you.'

Isn't that the craziest of things? I mean: what was the point? Where was it all going to end? No good ending, that's for sure. Her parents couldn't possibly like me, not after that performance. Not after what they saw. No Sir Isaac Newton way. She would get it together with this Simon fellow eventually and all would be coming up roses full stop. Sometimes I just couldn't understand myself. Was I plain stupid? The girl was already with somebody! Didn't I get that? Did I have some sort of learning disability? They were the perfect match, just as her mother had said. Her parents were rich and so were his. Business partners too. Whereas I was nothing but this muddy boy who had a thing about grasshoppers and praying mantises and bare feet. I had had this illogical upbringing. I slept in a bed where the mosquito net had at least two praying mantises, and I was the one who put them there — and if you asked me why I'd say they were there to hunt night mosquitoes before they got me, but still, it is weird. Just as weird as my dislike of shoes and preference for bare feet — but then Amber herself never wore shoes either, only sandals — pink, white and orange ones, as long as her toes were revealed to light and air. I was sure when she got older, she'd paint them pink, red and violet just like the other girls. I knew one day she was going to be a princess. There was no way on earth or in heaven that she and I were going to work.

There was only one logical thing to do. I had to get her out of my system.

'I am sorry to have to tell you this, Amber. And I would never want to embarrass you in any way, you know that. But I just need to say I like you. I like you a lot.'

This was not done under any natural impulse, by the way, nor was it like my character to come straight out with things. It was Big Voice, of all people; it was his suggestion. 'You've got to tell that person your feelings for them,' he lectured, while feeding his pigeons. 'Unless you try, you just don't know what's going to happen.' Was he speaking from experience? Did he have a secret girlfriend? Had he messed it up somehow and now, even against his own beliefs, was advising me to believe in the impossible? He was an adaptable fellow, that's for sure. And let's not forget that character-building and self-belief and self-motivation were part of Bruce's philosophy, and maybe he was just trying them out on me to see if they worked.

But the craziest of craziest things was, they did. They worked.

'That's what I like about you,' she whispered. And smiled, with her shoulder next to mine. A smile only a smart city person could do. Direct, not held back, not shy. Then she rounded it off with a remark only a being of her perfection could make. 'I like your honesty.'

I don't know what girls will be like in the future, but

98

that's what they were like in 1973. Beautiful, kind and er . . . rich. Or at least the ones were who looked to medicine as a future career.

I never thought that by simply writing about myself it could be a kind of confidence therapy. The bad points seeming not that bad when set in perspective. The negatives actually a positive. How socially low you ranked yourself when in fact you were as good as the next man if not better. Or that somebody could be extremely fond of you – but you were simply too slow-witted to believe your luck.

We sat on the iron billboard, happy. Wishing it could stay this way. The iron billboard was where it all happened. Notices of the week's going rate for fruit and vegetables, meetings, events, gossip about who was going to get what and when. This one object, painted in jet black and set into concrete, would always remind me of Tortoise Spring and why? Because this was where you hung around for a ride to the city or to see who and what was coming or going. The mountains wrapped themselves around the village like maidens reclined by a river, and only by standing next to or on top of the billboard could you see this, the undulations like hips and thighs. A vantage point where it all happened. The valley breeze ruffled her hair, the city and its lights shone in the distance, and I just couldn't believe what I was hearing. She was saying 'I like you too!' Imagine what else she might have said if I had slipped in '*I love*' instead of '*I like* . . .!'

'You're going to find it this time, aren't you?' Meaning the answer to why Lord Baltimore was gone.

'Yes,' I told her, 'I am going to find it.'

'Then what?'

'Then everything will be OK.'

'You're an optimist.'

'What's an optimist?'

'Like your nickname. Sundance.'

I think I can talk about her now. As I continue to sit here, as if I was still in class, as if there were still students around – but there are none. The school's been semi-closed for two weeks now and it won't be long before they cut off power. The fire alarm, the sockets, the fans, the lights, will all be dead. But it's not like I need them, as I am writing the whole thing under the natural light of three sullen windows. But I do need the clock. The silent, almost inaudible ticking of the electric clock installed last year along with a few telephone lines, dead ahead on the wall above the blackboard. Should that stop working, then I'd be lost, wouldn't know where I am – although this might be a good thing. Then time might stand still and I wouldn't have to think about anything or do anything. Wouldn't have to think about Day of the Locust.

Bravo!

But then . . . I suddenly remember I *do* have a watch. It's been on my wrist since I began writing this memoir. It's quite a decent one too. A Walt Disney one, with Mickey Mouse himself stood at the centre pointing out the hour and minutes. He's promised to tell me the reality of time no matter where I am (as long as I wind him up every morning). Yet it's strange because I can't seem to bring myself to trust him, no matter how big his smile or how jolly he may look. To have a watch is a sign of maturity. Time to wake up, time to go to work, time to get married, time to find a new flat and start a family then get old. Time to die. This is the one tricky moment no watch or clock can tell you, tell you when is it going to happen? It will just happen. Like the electricity that's going to be turned off, I know inevitably it's going to happen. It's only a matter of time. Till then, I must keep writing my story as if there's some kind of wisdom to be gained from doing so. There is nothing else left to do. There's nobody left to play with or talk to. No teacher here to teach. Just three students remain, including myself, but I am the only one who has turned up for lessons. Even Mad Dog is absent.

BORN TO MAKE A STAND

At the age of ten months, I was already on my feet and walking. A remarkable feat, that still makes me proud to this day. I was standing on my own two feet! Indeed, for me, it was remarkable. But with this achievement came also the dogged and unremarkable unwillingness to come back down. I do not know why, but I simply would not crawl on all fours like a normal one-year-old baby. This, as Grandma remembered, had its disadvantages. While most infants when faced with the same predicament, had the initiative to crawl down a set of stairs on their hands and feet, bottom-end first, of course, I, because of my inability to crawl, could not come down the stairs without tumbling head first like a Ferris wheel. Instead I would maroon myself at the top of the stairs, with my wobbly, fleshy baby knees looking lost and helpless, till Grandma came up to retrieve me. And precisely it was this noble service that Grandma virtually carried out for me on the night of the great mountain fire of 1964. The trees behind the house were burning and crackling with destructive rage and threatening the entire terrace. All the other children – and it is only fair to argue on my behalf that these children were a few months older and wiser than I was – they crawled down the stairs and over any obstacles such as a door lintel, easily navigated by crawling up and over till they were out of danger and towards the safety of their mother's arms. I, on the other hand, had to be rescued by the strong caring arms of Grandma. It was not long after this that my neighbours became concerned. My stubbornness soon came under scrutiny. 'Is the boy retarded? Why does he not crawl like the other babies?'

Thus, with my 'uprightness' there were disadvantages and I suppose, in people's eyes, zero commonsense. However, Grandma blessed it all, nevertheless.

My 'uprightness' continued throughout my youth. School was always an obstacle. Last year there were twenty-seven students, meaning twenty-seven grades Mad Dog had to sign and hand out annually, ranked numerically so if you came first then you were the best and brightest student of that year of 1972, or on the other hand if you came twenty-first, then you were twenty-first dumbest potato out of the twenty-seven students in that year. Last year, it was me who came twenty-first. And I should consider myself lucky I didn't come last.

In my childhood, my teachers were dragonflies, lantern flies, fire flies, robber flies, singing cicadas, honey bees, worker bees, tiger beetles, click beetles, lacewings, ant lions, praying mantises, house swifts, wrens, citrine wagtails, mountain bulbuls, waxwings, Siberian

thrushes, warblers, finches, red buntings, munias, ful-
vettas, starlings, from rosy ones to common ones to
endless lists of other exotic buntings and the ever
cheap, cheerful and popular Yellow-Fronted Canary
singing till the cows came home and beyond. My
teachers were many. But it was Mad Dog who tutored
me in the ways of the human world. Standing upright
in class was a joy to me. I did not mind his militaristic
rules, my hand raised in silence for long periods before I
would be excused to the latrines. And neither did I mind
the running and skipping and push-ups and squats, in
fact, anything I would and will do, as long as he did not
make me crawl. To this day, he never has. In my reasoning, with all my after-school activities, my double zeros
at mathematics and history, plus my detentions, how
could I have attained a grade of 21? But grade 21 had
spared me the torment of going on all fours with
shame. It was, without a doubt in my daydreaming
mind, kind and generous of my tutor. I did not deserve
to be twenty-first. I will explain. Like a lot of people,
Mad Dog felt divinely blessed when in the presence of
Grandma, whom he referred to as 'Grandma Teng', and
it would not have been decent at all to confirm that a
saint had been bringing up a certified idiot!

A LIFE OF DOUBLE MEANINGS

I live in a land where I have experienced that a word, or
a series of words, can have double meanings, and sometimes even treble and quadruple meanings. Not to
mention, the confusion of meanings. Take for instance
the following examples:

1. 'Pigeon Eye'. Anyone who has lots of money in HK will have 'Pigeon Eye'; they will look down on other people as if they are above and better than their fellow human beings. My first-hand experience with this meaning came at the Kowloon train station, ticket office window number 3, where hung a portrait of the Queen wearing her Coronation gown. Amber and I were queuing next to a raggedy beggar whose unwashed stench was so overpowering, nobody could queue with a straight face. But she did. She did not in any manner or remark look down on this poor beggar. This proved Amber did not have 'Pigeon Eye'.

2. 'Soaking Up Oil'. What are the intentions of a man when he takes a girl out on a date to the back seats of the local cinema? It is resolutely NOT soaking up oil on a frying pan! This expression can be heard at the end of each working day around a phalanx of men casually ruminating on their plans for the evening. And like number 1, it applies not to me.

3. 'Stir-frying an Oily Fish' does not mean you are about to be treated to a nice meal, nor does 'Stir-frying Green Pepper and Black Beans' have any connection with a frying pan. It rather comically dictates that 'YOU ARE FIRED!' No explanation has ever been given why such 'stir-frying' activity could have someone end up being dismissed from their employment.

4. 'Blow Up' is to be confounded, stammering, your chest so puffed up with hot air, or bad emotional

vibes you have inhaled from the person who has wronged you, that you are absolutely lost for words. This happens a lot when you are a grown-up.

5. 'Eight Lady'. This is perhaps *the* most perplexing saying. In Cantonese, the word 'eight' normally rhymes with 'Get Rich' – a number very often seen on the private registration plates of Rolls-Royces. How it can be used in reference to a gossiping woman, like the English expression 'nosey cow', and not mean a very rich lady is perplexing. This is indeed an empirical number with treble meanings.

6. 'Wax Gourd and Beancurd' expresses the fragility of human life. A wax gourd melon is hairy and ribbed, almost like a human being. I have watched Grandma handle them with great care. This fruit grows suspended in mid-air and takes four to five months to fully mature, quite a long time compared to other fruits. It is Grandma's cream of crops and is always in demand during the hot seasons. Wax gourds are popular in soups and stews. And it is precisely because of their sheer size and weight that they break open, fissure easily with the slightest tumble. With the descriptive addition of beancurd, so fine, soft and fragile, the delicacy of the meaning is at zenith. 'If my sister comes to any Wax Gourd and Beancurd . . . I will hold you responsible!' as they say in the movies.

7. 'Slam Chicken'. The references to chickens, good and bad, are endless. I presume, since a chicken

pecks the earth continually in search of a good bite, it has a purpose to its (slam-like) pokings. However, apply this action to a tall, standing human being, should he or she bring their head as close to the ground and at such rapidity as a chicken would peck, and you will find their head could well end up in a terrible collision with the ground. To use against somebody, this was the curse to end all curses. And to prove my point, Mad Dog had categorised this to be a swearword, and never have I dared utter it during class. Only at the horrid individual responsible for Lord Baltimore's death.

8. 'Three Plus Six' adds up to the total of nine; 'nine' also has a treble meaning. This number too, is found regularly on the license plates of well-to-do people because in phonetic terms it rhymes with 'a long time'; therefore, if you are rich, having many nines may bless you with longevity of life as well as money. But of course, 'Three Plus Six' has nothing to do with longevity. During one of his most famous street brawls where he was outnumbered four to three, Big Voice came across his first '3 + 6' sign. It was a red, hand-painted shop sign hung above a rough-and-ready street diner. As dog eating is forbidden in HK, diligent traders have found wicked alternatives. '3 + 6' was a coded advertisement for places serving dog meat. Even though Big Voice was outnumbered during what he felt was his finest hour, I am pleased to tell, on his behalf, that he and his two friends came out victorious. So victorious, he told me, with such sparring might,

he jumped ten feet into mid-air and with one full-throttled kick, brought the dog-meat sign crashing to the ground in pieces. But in terms of reality, I have to question: is a ten-foot, anti-gravitational Superman leap into the sky humanly possible? Or was it simply Big Voice's infamous mouth and memory getting the better of him?

SMALL BUT POWERFUL?

On the path walked daily a thousand times you will find – if you look hard enough – one that is invisible to the naked eye yet has the power of a lion. Fall down its quicksand and unwittingly you'll become another one of its victims.

Once upon a time I was a happy, ordinary child. When people called my name, I'd answer right away like a nine year old should. But latterly I had been strolling through the village looking darker and leaner. Voiceless. Wearing my hat so I would appear even darker against the harsh sunlight. In the direction of the 6.25 p.m. sunset, my small shadow pulled and stretched behind me, seeming almost to disappear. As if it was too thin, too small to see. The insect of a person.

The ant lion is a tiny, aphid-like bug that lives within a small sandy pit and has, for its size, a large mandible which it uses to flick/shoot sand at and seize its prey, which could be anything from an ant to a small spider. But its ingenuity is its sandy funnel-shaped pit which

*drains downward just like quicksand, and once the prey
begins to lose grip and slide down the inner side of the
pit, its destiny inevitably belongs to the ant lion.*

I pointed this out to Amber, saying, 'Something amazing will happen here one day, and I hope to be here when it does.' We knelt over the microscopic lair. I was describing it as 'a place of small wonders,' unaware that she had been making notes of my exact words on paper. Her bare bony knees rested on my squashed and battered hat. The one courtesy I must bestow. My red carpet to her.

'Promise to let me know when it does happen, Sundance?'

I used to think city folks hated muddy places, creepy crawlies and insect bites, but I guess she was the one exception. Maybe her years spent in India had conditioned her and had also made her eyes sapphire blue, or more likely her religious faith was so strong there was nothing she couldn't overcome. But still, I avoided taking her through shaded woods or places where something (a leech, gnat, spider) might take a bite out of her. They could take a bite out of me and I wouldn't mind. My blood might even poison them! I like to think. But Amber Ar-Wan Shyamalan was not a species to complain. She just wrote. A bite on the back of her thigh as I applied the Tiger Balm cream and she just wrote. A blush on her smiling cheeks and she'd still write. She noted down everything – and I mean everything. Orchids, dragonflies, lantern flies. Things you couldn't find in the city. She had this diary she carried with her which, during blue isolated moments, I have seen. It never left her side. A little pink book. Once I even saw a pencil drawing she did of me, page 254, 15 September. Never knew I could look so serious. My hat shaded over my eyes while sitting hunkered, arms wrapped round my knees. But there was also the realisation it was me she laboured over. Her diary, right? A person's private thoughts. The heart. And it was not Simon she chose to draw in her heart but the locust hunter. That was truly something to think about. No matter what.

'I like that drawing you did of me and Echo, by the way,' I said. 'I like it a lot.'

'You do?'

I nodded. Looking at the opened book on her lap.

'That's how I will remember you. In these pages.' Then she placed her hand on my shoulder, and gave me a paper flower folded from her pages.

'The truth is,' she told me, 'you are very brave. Who else would dare challenge the rich? Rich against the rich, perhaps. If you were in my shoes it would be perfect. They could crush you like peanuts. But nothing scares you. Right?'

Then the taxi came. And she left. The silence of birds and thought surrounded me.

THE GHOST PLANE

Do you believe in ghosts? Well, out here everybody seems to. And on a clear night you can hear it in the distance: the whirl of a phantom engine as it struggles to climb air but of course, its destiny is always to crash. I remember when I first heard it, thinking it was no big thing, that it was just a standard reconnaissance flight, a squadron on patrol or something, until Big Voice bashed against my door at midnight screaming at the top of his voice: 'That's it, man! That's the GHOST!' Never thinking he could be so superstitious, sweat all over him. This drone may have meant 'GHOST' to him, but to others I knew, to people like Grandma who came cursing up at the sky's nothingness, I could tell it evoked memories of a more direct terror. Japanese fighters swarming in to bomb Hong Kong in 1941.

But then, you hear a lot of things out here. Rumours of extinct animals, of phantom machines. And if the truth is what you desire, there was only one light source: Mad Dog. I pitched this question to him during morning break the following day and, as I expected, he came up a winner.

'There's no possible way it could have been fighters,' he said matter-of-factly, standing in the playground with children swirling around him. 'Because,' and he liked this word, this fifty-five-year old ex-Corporal with thinning hair and glasses, whose fair complexion belied his true age, 'Because fighters don't fly close to the border in case The Big Amber, who are edgy about us spying on them, take a few pot-shots at our planes.'

This answer certainly spruced up my day. A simple answer to a perplexing mystery – I like that. Besides (if I may add), I've only ever seen Scout helicopters. They can sometimes be seen landing near the metallic tower. You hear them three minutes before you see them. They sound like the warping of sheet metal, different from the silkier hum of propeller planes, I am sure.

The wreckage from the *Empire of the Sun* has been lodged between a Camphor for more than thirty-five years now, sections of the Japanese fuselage embedded

110

in a cursed forest where lost wanderers were found days later, alive but with their mouths filled with locusts.

We all walked towards the wreck on the evening of 4 April with the idea of mastering our fear of ghosts.

Big Voice reckoned, 'Ghosts can't do much to you.' Then he smiled. 'They may squeeze the breath out of you, but that's all.' And by his tone I was certain that this remark was in reference to his father, who, having first arrived in HK and with nowhere to stay, took refuge in an old mansion and during the night got held down by an unseen force.

I could find nothing to say to this. As the youngest and most inexperienced I truly needed to know '*what*' I was going up against. In other words, I had to be following in the unreal footsteps of Bruce. Had to do more than just survive a daily gauntlet of bite-happy dogs or the possibility of getting spooked by the White Lady's whisper, 'Help me . . .' when in detention at school. There had to be a magic potion somewhere, some special kind of Kung Fu training or formula or secret weapon – a silver bullet, perhaps. A trick or a crucifix which could enable a mere mortal to contest werewolves. Big Voice reckoned sleeping on cursed earth might help.

'I'll see you tomorrow,' I said, turning to Amber. Looking for a sign of approval for this half-baked scheme. But she said nothing, her walking silhouette outlined by the evening river.

As time passes by, things change. The people. The environment. I don't know if it was my absence at the taxi or my absence at the Sacred Swing, but the girl from the big city was no longer talking. She used to be someone who treasured moments. When walking with

111

her to the taxi she would ask good, peculiar questions. 'Buffaloes work hard, don't they?' As if stalling. Young Ar-Fun would be ready to wave wildly. And Echo ready to pursue her departing Jaguar. And I, of course, always had homework.

Her school, the Heep Yun, was over an hour's drive from Sheung Shui, plus another twenty-five minutes to get to Tortoise Spring. So when she came to see us she was always late. But of course to her, coming here was a great romance. Every time I saw her, it was always at the Sacred Swing. Her back would sometimes be turned to me. As I walked over the roasted leaves, slowly making my presence known to her, she would spin round to face me and clearly I would notice the little red Hindu dot, so perfectly placed between her eyebrows.

Most of the villagers were indoors by this time, either cooking or eating, and only the animals remained visible. So when she stepped from her taxi, she'd be greeted by a village without motion, as if painted. Only moments later to be away from it all, wrapped in the orange atmosphere of evening like the many evenings before. Her destination being the Sacred Swing near the heart of a small forest. To wait there specially, for a boy and his animals, near the circumference of darkness.

THE HERD BOY

I have worked with animals all my life. I know well their character and emotions and how to respond to their needs. With herding there is a different appeal –

of idleness. I could spend hours lying in the grass. Just what you need at the end of the day. I have ridden buffaloes all my life and have found the technique to be somewhat different from riding horses. Under normal circumstances, a buffalo will never stray from duty. It might, during the ploughing process, munch some straw or somebody else's cabbage. It might even think it can get away with it. But once it detects another male rival – life, work, ownership no longer have any meaning. They interlock. They must do territorial battle.

Two years ago, as a less experienced rider, instead of de-saddling intuitively, I did a crazy thing. I thought I could control the animal beneath me. Well, I was wrong. And for that, I was dislodged, went flying headfirst into the mud as the bucking bronco made its territorial charge. I was eventually unplugged out of the mud (since my head was virtually planted into the ground like one of Grandma's crops) by this cynical old man who happened to pass by. A funny tremble came from his voice, as if he was about to cry with laughter but couldn't because there was no telling if I was alive or dead. '*Hey, boy! Are you OK?*' he asked, wiping the mud cake from my face to reveal two eyes and a mouth.

Amber found this story quite funny. 'And what did you say?'

'I said I was just fine, thank you. Then I limped home.' That was the honest truth. I did go home. Cleaned myself up, then went straight back to work, helping Grandma chase a few ducks gone haywire. All of which was within a good day's work, even if it included falling from your buffalo and recounting your theatrical fall for the pleasure of seeing someone laugh.

'Is there no way you can stop the battle?'

'No way. Buffaloes have free will.'

I rode behind her, careful with her red sari that was tinged with gold. The buffalo we rode upon I'd ensured beforehand was well and truly scrubbed with soap. My nose comfortably embedded within the honeysuckle of her hair.

ENTER THE FLYER

It amazes me sometimes, it honestly does, the fact that I am still alive. There are some people in the village who have lived to well over a hundred. That's more than nine times my lifetime, and if I can achieve even a third of that, I will die a happy ape. Getting bumped off out here is all too easy. Danger is everywhere. Three stings in the head from a blue hornet is all it takes. The brain goes into a seizure and that's it – game over. Or what about getting gored by a peeved-off bull? You should have seen Big Voice last spring – the dent on the back of his thigh: he was unable to sit down for weeks. I'd imagine the impact of such an encounter must have sent him flying over a bush or a fence. But of course for the veteran Big Voice, it was not an event entirely new to him. He'd been butt-marked many a times by his father eons before a land-lording bull ever came near him.

But it happens, even to the best of us.

There was Three-Eye and his legendary fencing match with a snake. None of us can forget this, least of all me. I had no idea of the danger spearing my way till my friend in his school specs skipped up in front of me, and with a cane in his hand, began to joust with a snake that was about to strike at me. The snake was aggressive, lunging at me with its fangs, just like a sword, which it had every right to do. We were within its territory and perhaps even its nest. Yet Three-Eye blocked every blow. Just like Zorro. This happened near the grassy border next to The Big Amber, virtually within view of the English watchtower. The Egyptian-style raised neck, its berry-red eyes contrasting beautifully with its light snake green (almost camouflaged) head and body, charging at me full speed. And suddenly city boy Three-Eye, demonstrating a panache we never thought he had, turned swashbuckler. As the reptile homed in for the big strike he caught it brilliantly in the mouth. Then angled down his cane and jabbed it out of action the way you'd jab a spade into soil. Leaving its head, whatever state it was in, wedged and held into the ground with the stick.

Later on, he admitted to us that he was not too fond of snakes. 'I don't like them,' he said, full stop. Lucky for me.

As far as most people who came to his shop were concerned, there was only one boss, his mother. She was always at the shop, sweet-talking the customers. 'Here are those two pretty-looking boys again!' she'd tease, meaning me and Big Voice, and on occasions Big Voice and I have turned our heads from left and right and asked 'Where?' just to be in tune with her humour.

The family had a cat, like all good businesses do, to keep down the rat population. It was ginger, it was a lot smaller than a common tabby, almost puny. 'We paid for her,' Three-Eye would say, and point to the cat, picking her up by the scruff of the neck and forever claiming that here was the 'gladiator' of all cats. This often got people giggling once they saw the cat was so small. 'See how she lifts her paws when I do this?' he'd say. 'See how she retracts her legs? That's the sign of a good rat-catcher.' Words of an educated person? I reckon so. And whether the story he kept telling about the king rat, about the size of a cat, a cat-killer, is to be believed, I still can't say, since his mother didn't let him keep the rat's carcass as evidence. But until they found this ginger moggie, all previous cats had had a lifespan of a few days only. Most were discovered the next morning stone dead, with their throat mauled and bitten into. Imagine that! Apparently the king rat was so overwhelming, no ordinary moggie could survive its wrath, and each night Three-Eye prayed in vain at the small Buddha statue in the hope that the new cat might stand a chance of survival. Until, of course, along came little Ginger. A smart cat. Not *dead* smart but ultra-smart. As the story goes, during her first night, Ginger pretended to be dead, lay in wait for King Rat. When the huge rodent turned up among the barricaded sacks of rice and saw what looked like a dead cat, it got curious and decided to go up for a closer inspection. This was where it made its first and last mistake. Ginger saw the opening and swiftly seized King Rat's jugular vein, eventually killing King Rat by bleeding him in familiar cat-hunting fashion.

'Hurrah!' we'd shout, every time Three-Eye retold us his favourite cat tale. Like me, it would not be wrong to label him a 'crazy animal lover'. But to say he and I were alike would be wrong. We were both raised by powerful women, yes, but that was where our similarities ended. He also had two sisters and a father, except the latter wasn't much of a father because he just sat upstairs and said nothing. He didn't go out. He didn't see anybody. He was blind. Had been blinded, would you believe it, by a snake. And as I understand it, it was all his own tragic fault, and maybe that was the reason why he was always sat up there, silent, feeling sorry for himself.

Not many people in this world like snakes, and his father belonged to that category. The man's main hobby, aside from gambling, was nailing live snakes to a great old banyan tree, maybe to show he did not fear them. Consequently, he earned himself the nickname 'Snakeheart'. When Three-Eye was just one year old, his father caught a black Cobra. The family were living in Yeun Long at the time, a big rural canvas of a place which farmed and supplied a large percentage of the Colony's vegetables, its landmass making up most of what is the New Territories. Cobras are known to spit venom, but his father didn't care. He was Snakeheart.

You don't have to go out specially looking for snakes. Sometimes they can appear just like the wind, and let me tell you it's a waste of time trying to warn people. I have personally seen snakes longer than a minibus slither into a house through a crack in the wall and tried in vain to warn the householder, but would they listen? No. It was the old story of the boy crying wolf. Nobody believes you.

That was where Three-Eye's father found the Cobra, either near or about to enter their house, and he caught it. He wasn't afraid of snakes, remember. He held the Cobra firmly by its neck against the tree bark at eye-level – the one thing you shouldn't do, the last thing you should do. Either he didn't know or he didn't care that a Cobra can spit as far as eight feet. If he did, then he would have known he was well within firing range. But maybe he didn't. He was about to nail his seventy-ninth snake and after he was through, he planned to skin it and wash the skin to let it dry and then go indoors for the day's last meal. He could smell it being cooked, the sizzle of garlic and ginger.

Three-Eye's father cannot have conceived that in the space of a few seconds he would never see his family again. I mean: they were just a few steps away inside the house. Not far at all. The last image he saw as a late summer dragonfly whizzed by must have been his left hand holding a rusty nail pressed against the snake's neck. Then just as the hammer descended, so did his destiny as a spray of darkness came down over his eyes like a fiery curtain.

I have always concluded that a blind man with no eyes, having a son with an extra eye – Three-Eye – explained itself rather well. Three-Eye never talked about his father. Father was a sacred subject with him, and I suppose it would be the same with me if I had one.

Grandma used to tease me on this subject. 'You were not conceived by a local,' she'd say. 'Your father is the Boss.' And she pointed to the metallic watchtower with the Union Jack sailing over it five hundred yards north of the border. Grandma never joked, not even when picking out the tiny red lice crawling under my testicles that I often picked up from scaling trees. An Englishman is your father, she was implying. But which one? Tilting my head, I stared at her huge hands, probably the biggest pair of hands I'd ever seen on a woman. Then one day, in between thirst and the need

118

for a glass of glittering water, it happened. Someone walked up to me through the mirage and said: 'I am your father.' And handed me the much-needed glass. And what did I do? I couldn't understand a donkey word he was saying. Couldn't understand English. I simply drank down, hard.

It must be the oldest wish in the book, for a fatherless child to have a father. Maybe even a rich one. Living in a posh city apartment as a rich boy, wearing smart clothes, strutting around the streets buying anything and everything and not going to school, instead just going on computer games and driving simulators . . . and coming home at the end of the day to find your father drunk, stoned out of his brains. He's actually an alcoholic! *Yikes!* No. Maybe I am happier as I am. Maybe a dad should just remain a wish, after all. Whatever, like everyone else in the world, I know I have a father somewhere. I know I was born of man just like I know what beauty is. But until that day, the moment the English soldier came up to us and stretched out his hand over the low wall of the watchtower, saying the words I didn't understand then, which I do understand now, it was again one of those things that for a boy my age never seemed that important.

I was just into catching things and that was all. Out here this was how you learned to communicate. The uniqueness of each creature and plant, the feelings that evolve when one makes contact. Every time I touch a click beetle, every time I see one, there is an innate picture which accompanies its existence. A colour of the world it carries, a scent and a scenery and even a taste which defies description. I cannot talk about it, only hint at its aerosol of noises, of the travelling hands,

119

but no more, for a poet is somebody else and I am a hunter. Sensibility has never been a part of my book.

Yet sensible I was. For instance, many years back, while on the way home from school, I was coaxed by a group of teenage girls into trying 'nail varnish'. What with my round eyes and roly-poly cherry cheeks, I surely would have passed for a boy doll. They had pulled me over onto their teenage knees and quickly went about painting my nails and toenails red, which I certainly would not let them do again today. I'd go up to Big Voice, reach up and pull down the tag behind his holey vest to check he was wearing the right size and tell him it was OK and he'd nod. Notify Grandma how she'd just missed the man who wanted to sell her a big-eyed fish for tonight's meal, or tell her about the stray duckling I pursued through the paddy, in return for mud pasted all over my face and shorts. I was that kind of child. Not serious. Not heavy. Just enjoying the moment. Just to be well-behaved around people was everything.

Perhaps this is an orphan's psychosis, always hoping that someone from a nameless crowd may claim me as a son or a brother (which Big Voice already has). I just lived with Grandma and that was it. Full stop. No history. Then one day somebody comes up to you and turns your world upside down by telling you 'I am your father.' Yet you can't understand the information he was giving you because you cannot understand English.

He might have been a Sergeant, a Captain. Might have been an ace, a flyer, like Steve McQueen. 'He was a flyer,' said Three-Eye, as if it was the truth. And I like to think so, to think he was right. That would be grand. He might have been pulling my leg also but I hope he wasn't. Why would anyone want to do that? The man must have seen something in me. Maybe a resemblance somewhere? The idea of an English father, and a pilot, a flying ace! Boy, just saying it sounds exotic and cool, if fanciful, because if you took a look at me you wouldn't think I had any English heritage at all. Mad Uncle's ancestry was part-Scottish and Amber was part-Indian, yet they didn't look anything less than Oriental. Look around HK society and only the best, cleverest cats (like Sam and Bruce) marry outside the system. If people knew you had an Englishman for a father you'd no longer be just a locusthunter herd-boy loser, a nobody, you'd be more than a somebody. You'd be unique.

I remember he had on a cap, an RAF peaked cap, which meant he must have flown something, a chopper or a fighter jet, even. I remember he was very light-skinned unlike us locals. Big Voice has always wondered why there are, 'Lots of beautiful American and English ladies all over HK.' Yet so far he hasn't seen one that isn't a pearl. *'Do you know why?'* Our heads turned towards Three-Eye, watching him polish his framed photo of himself and his gladiator cat that so many people find amusing. 'They send only the pretty ones over.' A nod from him as if to say: 'Wise up!'

That, we did.

We began to learn English furiously day and night. I tackled it as if it were a crab snapping at my fingers, and when gripped, I would beg for Big Voice's assistance to release me and he, in return, would end up being comically gripped. Beginning with Mad Dog, or with any Englishman or soldier we saw on the street or in the hills and just practised our conversation skills

121

with them. All, of course, were most obliging. Most of all, we used movies, listening to their dialogues again and again, trying to tune into Steve's accent, the McQueen way he does it: 'Job jest not walk owt hah?' Repeating those words 'job' and 'work' again then again. Then again. 'Job just didn't work out, huh?' after seeing the abridged version of *The Great Escape* which rolled for three weeks at the Majestic near TST. It took a while, but we got there in the end.

I began with the most important word of all, 'father'. If only we had known 'father', then all would have been roses and I would have raised my right hand to the watchtower soldier, yelling: 'Yes! Here I am! I am your longlost son!' But I didn't know English then, not the way I do now, easygoing and natural in my speech. Knowing a few swearwords, I am able to translate 'Ho Sien San' into 'Mr Noble' then into a more laughable 'Mr No Balls!'

So there you have it. My reason for wanting to speak English. Crazy? I told you it was. I told you it'd probably put a smile on you. Of all the dumb things that have happened so far, this has to rank as the dumbest. But at least it put me on the road to wrestle with the crab that is English. It got me talking and writing my story of mild-mannered woe, and maybe someday, that English pilot might even come across this story somewhere. It's not impossible. Is it?

A good clean start in life is everything. A good start to a New Year, a good head start to a horse race and a good start to a journey. What do you think? You believe in that? I don't know. Never questioned it until that day. Not like Big Voice. To him, where you are born and when, and where you live, do matter.

122

'If I was living in the city full-time like Three-Eye,' he quipped, a drink in his hand as usual, for that was how he liked to talk, with some kind of 'liquid', like Bruce did. 'If I was like him, lived the city, breathed the city, knew people in the city, ate it and talked it every day, I reckon my head would be working eighty-eight miles per hour and not twenty-two as it is here in Tortoise Spring. Definitely. No doubt about it.'

Amen.

And he did try. Believe me. Sometimes I wouldn't see him for weeks and when he did turn up he'd come walking into a village of smoking chimneys in a new Hawaiian shirt and flared jeans, and right away I'd know what had happened. He was a new man. He had bunked off school and taken a few weeks of working vacation. And the location? Where else but the big fat city of Kowloon.

'I worked for this man named Li Kai Shing,' he'd proudly announce. There was always a name, he was into detail. 'Yeah. Making plastic flowers.'

'Yeah?'

'*Yeah.*'

Looking at each other and smiling, a quick nod from him, the style of nod which said, *Take a tip from me, boy. I know better.*

'Was there any sign of Bruce?' I asked. Meaning the King of Kung Fu. And I wasn't taking the mickey, because it's not unusual to bump into somebody famous in a small place like Honkers. This kind of thing happened all the time. And Bruce was the biggest HK phenomenon ever. His lean face was on the cover of every HK magazine and newsstand, and he was even venerated as a living god by some tribe in Malaysia.

Big Voice shook his head, flattened his lips, defiant. Then he took another swig of Coke and I did the same, followed his every move as we sat fishing off the unrailed bridge coming out of Tortoise Spring. The bottle's end parting from my lips making that familiar *pop!*

'Maybe next time, then?'

'Maybe.'

The best thing that's ever happened to Big Voice, and he'll probably tell you this himself, happened in the big city. It was there he met God, met Bruce – coming down the stairs of a Kowloon restaurant, or so he told us. Ecstatic as ever, he quickly introduced himself. Told Bruce where he was from and promptly played a coin trick on Bruce made famous by the master himself, whereupon the great man smiled and told him in English, 'You got style, man!'

That one-dollar coin touched by Bruce now hung around his neck, drilled with a hole so he could thread a string through. It was his lucky charm.

'I'll teach you how to do that trick one day,' he said. 'I'll show you how to open a bottle without an opener, like Bruce. I'll show you how you can do anything you want, OK? But don't flunk school, man. Whatever you do, don't ever do that!' Shaking his head and finger. 'Get yourself a good education so no heavies can push you around, understand? Remember that. I'll be real proud of you once you get into uni . . .' Then he put his wet callused hand on the back of my neck. *'Real proud.'*

Big Voice was only thirteen when he said that. But it was the vocal verisimilitude, sounding like he had lived a whole life. It is at moments like that you know you are not with just 'any' friend, but a 'say dong', a blood brother. A brother you know you'll never have but wished you had. The place was never the same without him. Mr Wiser-up picked me up, cared enough. A bottle luminated by sunlight didn't taste the same without him there. Even a truck ride didn't feel the same. I don't remember telling anyone this and I don't think he will either, but we used to bathe together in the same blue plastic tub. Sat naked and face to face when I was four and he was eight, with Grandma asking us whether we needed more hot water. It may sound girlish now but it didn't then. It's almost six years now, since I've known him. It's a long time to know somebody. I think of all the things he taught me and all the insects we caught together. I don't know if a true blood brother would do half the things he's done for me. Would he, for instance, show me how to wipe my own bottom in the middle of nowhere using a certain type of insect-free leaf? And would he kick through smouldering rubbish just to find me a few plastic superheroes before they got burned out of recognition? Or would he think twice before picking the red lice (and you have to excuse my sordid repetition) from under my scrotum the way Grandma did? He may have been something of a thug, out there in the big wide world, but he was still human and a true believer in *heng-day*, meaning 'brothers'. I always get a genuine thrill when turning that evening corner past the reassuring coo of pigeons to find him sat eating, his boiled egg planted cosily atop the white rice much the way an egg is planted within a nest. There was always something 'happening' with Big Voice. He was the youngest of three and probably the most immature, because he still hung around with a shrimp like me. His mother was small, stood less

125

than five foot tall yet could still work as hard as Grandma. I've seen her carry heavy buckets of water, huge bundles of dried branches and think it amazing a woman of her size was so capable. The tin shack they lived in, when everybody else around the village lived inside proper solid houses, told you not only were they *struggling* but also they weren't part of the clannage. They were like me – outsider, guest, rogue. They were *given* a space by the village council to stay and erect that unhappy tin shack, and when his mother first saw what her future was, she couldn't stop crying for three days. Yet I've never seen a woman with a happier smile. I think that was another reason why we got on so well. Big Voice had no real name or status either. He didn't owe the village anything, nor did the village want him particularly, yet he was defending the place. The one person with enough bottle in him to call it 'outrage' when the clan themselves were too scared or just too passive or simply couldn't give a monkey's. Crazy or what? A lost cause from the start. We stood to gain nothing. Suicidal is a better word.

He had taken a two-month apprenticeship in making dim sum at one of the busiest and biggest restaurants in Kowloon – The Noble Crown, number 525 on Nathan Road where he had his revelatory encounter with Bruce, but then there are no un-busy restaurants in Kowloon. He had slept in rough, cramped dormitories alongside the heavies, got the wooden leg of his stretcher kicked over and he himself rolled over just because he was some new punk kid come to learn dim sum and the heavies thought he should know that. You got up at five in the morning each day, and if you didn't, the cook would bring down a bucket of water over your bed, which also meant you were fired! Big Voice would never go into another noodle café and look at a wanton or a dim sum the same way again, not without thinking about the discipline involved in shaping them. He could do those things and probably a lot more. Perhaps to prove to himself he was 'somebody'. That he wasn't just the son of the fiercest, meanest and poorest bull in the village, so fierce and mean, a haunted house would no longer be haunted should his father decide to enter. He was able to make it on the outside for real, all by himself, and not look like cow fodder. Although the jobs he had taken so far weren't high on skill or intelligence, he was no zombie, no thin-beef, no third-rate character.

He once told me he spoke to a man who was perhaps the one person who other men, even the heavies, wouldn't have the guts to go up and talk to: the night-soil man. In the city where most flats still have no sanitation, night-times is the time when they must leave out their night-soil buckets to be collected. And in the heat – well, you can imagine the stink. Round about midnight, the night-soil collector will appear with his truck dawdling almost to a silence under the orange light of the street. And that was when Big Voice bumped into him, whether by chance or intention, I can't say, though no doubt most people would prefer to think it was by chance. He stopped the man and asked a question few people in HK would have dared or have bothered asking.

'Do you like smelling shit?'

What kind of thin-beef would ask a question like that? What kind of a thug would bother? Some curiosity in him must have made him brave enough to ask this. Was it some kind of inner desire to understand humanity, or am I talking shit myself?

The night-soil man didn't find the question absurd at all. He answered the question immediately. 'Do you think a man working at the abattoir likes to kill pigs?' he asked in return.

And Big Voice must have said no. Tried to explain his curiosity while standing on Kennedy Town Praya in flared jeans and wearing a silver belt buckle embellished in the shape of two crossing guns. Obviously needing to hold his nose from time to time (which is understandable). He told me the night-soil collectors used Leyland trucks which had rear canvas roofing, not unlike the ones that picked us up during the day when we would ride shotgun (I think that's what they call it), hanging out of one side of the truck's canvas frame like a starfish with the wind in your face and the oncoming traffic just a few inches from your outstretched fingers, and him shouting, 'You're doin' good!' So by day they used these trucks to pick up people and vegetables, and by night, according to Big Voice, it was possible they used them to . . . need I say more?

My friend may not make it as President of the USA. He probably won't even make it out as a decent citizen, yet he was no bad egg. Meeting somebody can change your destiny. Nobody, even if you are not superstitious, can disagree on that. It might have intrigued him, the way I was so good at snatching grasshoppers – the same way somebody can be a chess genius at an early age, and he might have stayed with me for that reason alone. Consciously or unconsciously, he did use me. I lent him cash and he never returned it, though whenever he came back after one of his 'vacations' he always brought me something. A story as well as a half-chilled drink. Anyone who can remember to get you a drink in a place like this deserves to be remembered for the rest of your life. Just like Amber.

> *In the streets two cents a drink,*
> *A few million for a Rolls-Royce,*
> *But less than a cent for Michelia.*
> *Smell like paradise or own a Rolls –*
> *Which would you choose?*

She wanted to know what my favourite flower was. A trick question, this. I was never particular, but she was watching me through the amber light. So I thought about it.

'Not a flower, an angel.' When I should have said it was her, or maybe I should just have said what was in my heart and not in my head, attempting to be clever.

The school is silent around me now. Blades of light are turning gold, almost horizontal across my pen and wrist. I am certain, if I'd said it then, it would have made her more happy, carried more sunlight into the picture – not that she was in any way *un*happy. But I am sure if I had said the truth, it would have helped. Because even as an angel, she did have her darker moments.

ANGELS CRY, DON'T THEY?

In the thirteen months I knew Amber, I saw her cry three times. A strange thing to remember, I know. The first time was 15 February, the day after Lord

Baltimore's disappearance. On that day, we did no hunting, no joking and no swearing because everything around us had changed, had darkened. There was no mistaking it. I sensed it. Big Voice sensed it. Echo in particular sensed it. His wet nose quivering strangely, he halted in places he would not normally halt. From the grey light across my bare arms to the complete and controlled stillness in the trees, the mood *was* different. Even the birds were. I saw a group of swallows head west but didn't see their return. In the ponds there were no crabs or fish. I stood waiting for Amber at the usual spot, by the iron billboard round about six-ish. When her Jaguar came I stepped up and opened her door.

'Thanks,' she said, her left leg appearing first, with rosy sandals. But she could tell from my glum expression that something was up.

'You OK?'

I said nothing. Neither a yes or a no. I took her hand, and asked her to follow me, which she happily did. I led her to the half-wrecked Ancestral Hall situated within the old village fort where the granite-based buildings were at least three hundred years old. Inside the old hall, now with the caved-in roof swept to one side, there was a plate of greens left by Ar-Fun. On the partially destroyed wooden table with three legs standing lay lettuce, turnips and Chinese Kale. We stood at the doorway. She took one look at this and knew right away what it meant. They were Lord Baltimore's favourite foods. And they were being offered to her departed spirit.

Amber said nothing. She didn't ask me how had it happened, or who was responsible. City people didn't need to do this. She slowly went down on her knees and started to cry. I don't know how long for. I didn't have a watch then. I was more worried that she might scrape her bare knees with all the splinters and grit that was lying around.

Sunlight came down over us through leaves and the broken roof. A dead silence. A deader calm.

Finally she announced, 'I don't want to go to the brook any more.'

I nodded. I could understand what she meant. The brook was creepy, and without Lord Baltimore it would be *very* creepy. I knelt beside her and watched the tears roll down her cheeks then hit the dry ground which greedily swallowed every drop. I thought I should be crying too, but I didn't. Though I was sure I would later, even if it was years later. We didn't do anything that evening. Seeing somebody cry is the hardest thing in life. No matter how tough you think you are, it affects you.

There are three kinds of tears I have seen so far. True tears, false tears and death tears. True tears are pure and work on their own. But oddly, death tears and false tears seem to work together. And here's why.

On 30 March I came home after school to find Grandma sat with almost the entire neighbourhood. It turned out that the eighty-nine-year-old woman with the Russian hat had died and funerary arrangements were being prepared. She was apparently quite rich. Her late husband had earned his fortune by running some kind of general hardware store in Jamaica.

As usual I came running home with my dog just after four, throwing down my schoolbag and shoes to one side then pouring myself a drink of sour cold tea. Long hot summers and all you had was cold sour tea, and that is no way fair, is it now? As I gulped it down I couldn't help but eavesdrop on the conversation taking place.

'It's going to be long. Her family would want it that way.'

'At least a week.'

'What? That short?'

'Have you got the *nam mor lo's* address?'

'You mean the one that's from Yuen Long?'

'No expenses spared.'

Like I said, I listened unintentionally. I wasn't even interested. I had my attention on my dog, admiring Echo's huge front biceps, thinking they looked almost human. But of course it was his erect ears and great smile that put him above human beings. I stood no more than three foot above him yet he still gave me that same good-natured white-teeth smile only he could do, his weatherproof trademark. The ears occasionally forked back in response to some unnameable noise he may have just picked up from behind the wild hills. Like generations of guard dogs before him, he ate our after-dinner scraps and knew that his place was at the front door and never inside – and that went for anybody else he was unfamiliar with.

But I should have been paying attention. I should have. The *nam mor lo*, as I was to find out, was a kind of rituals man, exorcist, counsellor of the spirit world or con artist, depending on what you believe in. But didn't they say one week was *short*? A wake lasting for a whole week was suppose to be *short*? To me, it ended up feeling more like a year. I immediately volunteered for detention at school, not wanting to go home, because I wasn't able to sleep. You see, before the body is buried, there must be nightly laments, actual crying (and

132

there's nothing more spine-chilling than a lady wailing at night), a sad piety to appease and send the soul on its way and only by crying, even fake crying, will the deceased understand he or she is 'no more' and therefore move on to the next world, and if there is no crying the soul may well remain in our world as a ghost, still seeking that lament.

Like I said, I couldn't sleep a wink. The wake was only two doors away, and knowing that a deceased, unsmiling body lay adorned in scary ancient attire sent shivers down my spine no matter how hot the night was. Also, the thought of that's how *I* could look, once werewolves were through with me, with my own for-ever-sleeping face, no longer able to wake up to the first light of dawn and whistle at the metallic tower perched some five hundred yards away, knowing well I'd only get a response from my dog and no one else, or worse still Grandma's attempt at faking tears as I lay looking pompous, sounding as if she was calling for her ducks to come home from the rice-fields rather than an attempt to appease my departed soul, really *did it* for me.

I began to scream.

I held my ears and screamed and screamed like a little Miss Muffet after seeing the lanky spider drop wriggling before her, a continuous scream as if some-how I was trying to outdo the miserable fake crying and the gongs that went with the women's loud grief. I just kept screaming away till the lights came back on in the house and the shadow of Grandma loomed over me, yanking aside the mosquito net and saying, 'What's the matter? Can't you see I am busy?'

Yeah. Busy two doors away with the monks, the exorcists and the dead. Yeah. Busy with the dead. I don't know how she could stand it. But she was a living saint herself, right? To her, death was just the next stage. A progression. I remember her sauntering up to a neighbour's son after his mother (who was an old friend of Grandma's) had been buried, hands behind her back, asking him, not solemn at all: 'Is she on her way?' And when the man dressed in full white, for white is the colour of Chinese mourning, nodded, she held his arm gently and said, 'Good boy. You did well. She will be proud of you.' And I am sure her simple words must have made him feel better, as if death was no big deal, just like going on a long business trip away, that's all. The same way she made me feel better by sitting on the edge of my bed casually saying, 'Can't you see I am busy?' her tanned and lined face looking almost sympathetic, as if she could understand why a boy of my age was screaming like a rooster. She put her massive finger against my face and told me to keep my mouth shut and go to sleep or else. But the deal was only struck when she agreed to leave the lights on.

It's absurd. It's crazy to think the career you choose is also the path you choose towards your own destiny. If you choose to be a policeman, it's possible you'll face death every day – unless of course you're a bent copper. But who's to say a man working in a safe office environment won't get burned to death in a multi-storey fire or die in a commuter train crash or get buried alive in a landslide? Or a child walking down a street get knocked down by a Humber Sceptre or jump from his apartment window because he can't handle the pressure of over-schooling?

At the time I never could have imagined my chosen career would put me in danger. But I didn't choose it for the obvious reasons, for self-satisfaction or greed. No. It actually came out of a necessity, came out of compassion.

ORIGINS OF A HUNTER

The reason why I became a hunter went something like this . . .

It was August, 1971. My regular journey home from school always took me past three things: the gauntlet of angry dogs, the calm pond with crabs, and finally, a terrace of working people. I'd walk through with my usual interaction, depending on the manner of their interaction. I was no God's gift hunter then, didn't walk like one or look like one. I was just a common farm boy making his way home with his newly acquired puppy, with all the time in the world until Grandma pointed a finger in my direction.

'You know what you have to do this evening, don't you?' She held out a bag. There were five small kittens inside, eyes tight shut, no more than few days old.

Given this circumstance, there are several things a child could say or do. Laugh or cry, sing or run. But all I could do was shake my head, step back, serious. 'No way. I won't do it.'

'But you have no choice!' she stamped. 'We cannot afford to feed them! You know that.'

And I was left with the sad bag in my hand, unable to say another word. The world silent around me. Finding it difficult to move. Finding it difficult in all honesty to be my casual old self.

I cannot deny that I love cats. In Tom & Jerry cartoons, cats go after mice – but has anyone actually seen how they dispose of their catch? I have. I came home one sunny day and witnessed it with my own eyes. My own tabby had the mouse's rear end going halfway into his mouth. You just can't comprehend that kind of thing until you see it happen. It's like a furnace being lit right under you. And suddenly . . . you know it is all true. And you say, 'Thanks, cat! Thanks for the revelation!' Whispering these words, kneeling down to my new-found revelation in the hope that no one was listening in case they thought I was nuts. So you can understand why I was more than upset when, one fine day, I came home to find my personal revelation gone, bagged off, and sold to the Bagman, the devil himself. All for a measly one cent, as if the cat was just nothing. So to ask me to kill, not just one, but *five* kittens whose father was my personal revelation, was downright unthinkable.

We must have wandered around the fields for hours, Big Voice and I, trying to find an alternative, an answer to mercy killing. But 1971 was not a good year for answers. I was young and without any independence or power. There was only guilt, sadness and confusion as I held the first kitten. About to let it go, we thought, in the kindest way possible. By drowning. Big Voice muttering, 'Sorry,' as it wriggled worm-like, as I let go. The one of many lives that fell from my hands at the small concrete dam fifteen minutes west of the village because it was merciful killing. It had to be done. There was no other way. Was there?

Bubbles kept rising up from the kitten's mouth and we knelt like immovable rocks. A closed face struggling eternal in pain as its body sank deeper and deeper into an oblivion of leeches, and all we could do was kneel like useless rocks. Just watching, helpless. Watching my own hand lift the second cat, then the third, the reprise of pain and sinking to death. Just kneeling with this emotional wound, trying to believe it was merciful killing. But was it?

'The tearless child,' Grandma called me. Believing I was devoid of tears because, as she told it, when she supposedly 'found' me nine years ago she found a baby neglected, his nappy unchanged (which left a scar I have to this day) and yet I was, apparently *'a silent, adamant baby without a single tear'* but sometimes, unknown to Grandma, even I can have my inconsistencies.

We must have stayed underwater for at least a minute, in a swim of tears and spidery weeds. Going down at least seven times each, deep enough to feel the water turn cold, coming up only for air or only if we found something. Hanging onto the concrete bank of the dam, tired, drained. Swearing things like: 'I don't want to do this again!' 'You won't!' *'Promise me?'* 'Guarantee it!'

We had to talk that way for a while, just to feel sane, till I became convinced that only money and not wisdom, physical strength or religion could have made a difference. Our hands were still squeezing belly water from the two we rescued when Big Voice pulled another leech from my neck. Like chewing gum it was.

'A locust hunter you say?' I asked.

His yet-to-be-Brucey head nodding under five recently appeared stars as we talked our way back home through the darkness.

'. . . and you can do as you please?' I persisted.

'As you please.'

'I can have independence? Can keep these cats alive?'

'You bet.' And he took a swipe at the air as if catching something.

'Sounds too good to be true.'

'You game?'

'You bet.'

Girls won't matter. Marriage, money, retirement won't matter. Once I get there, the game will provide.

'The game will bring you everything!' he yelled.

And without sounding like a believer, it did.

THE BOUNTY

Our expedition was five miles east of Robin's Nest when perhaps by accident Three-Eye disturbed a wasp nest. The paper wasp, *Polistes olivaceus*. A species no man was meant to disturb. I say 'perhaps' when it was surely deliberate. Sometimes during the hunt, thirst can be relieved by items you come across, like wild berries, rosebuds or red juicy Emblias, the most thirst-quenching of all berries. Other delicacies can include a wasp nest. Look for the white pupa in the shape of rice. Toast them over a small fire. Perhaps that was on his mind when he took the plunge, and supposedly discovered half-buried treasure. 'It was just lying there,' he said, still dazed by his own good fortune. 'Next to the wasp nest.' In between the aromatic ferns.

THE COLONEL

Three people were waiting by the iron billboard, their eyes wide open, thinking they were going to be rich.

'Maybe even as rich as your girlfriend!' screamed Big Voice.

'No. Even richer!' cried Three-Eye.

'She's not my girlfriend!' I protested. But they weren't listening. They were money mad.

'What, are you nuts? You don't open a bird shop, you open a restaurant. That's where the real money is made!'

During a last moment of light, with the mountains dark yet the sky clearly lit, the evening over our skin like fine silk, he had cupped in his hands what appeared to be nuggets of pure gold but which, as it later turned out, were in fact brass blanks.

Ask any farmer and he'll tell you he can smell perfume from the rice fields, but you can't. Ask him if he can distinguish between the sound of a gunshot and thunder and he'll look up, straight into your eyes and say, 'You mean the Colonel?'

Since 1954 the Closed Area police force has been led by an old Englishman. We knew him as the Colonel. The dog hunter.

'Is that your dog? Next time, sonny, ensure he's tied up, will you?'

The Colonel and darkness stood before us at 8.25 p.m. He was a giant of a man, bearded and uniformed, and he always carried a rifle. He was not kidding. Usually when the Colonel makes thunder, something has to die. Dogs with rabies, quarrelsome hogs and, until 1952, the odd man-eating tiger. It was very unusual for him to leave without a dead boar or dog in the back of his Land Rover. But it could happen.

The gold nuggets slid into the barrel of his revolver like a trick. And like a good trick, it worked. There was thunder, *BOOM!* Except miraculously, nothing was dead. 'These, my young friends,' he said, with not a trace of irony in his voice, 'are what we call blank cartridges.' And also, if my memory serves me well, although I don't want it to, three blank and dumbfounded human faces – those of me and my two friends.

Sometimes, if not all the time, twilight or the Hour of the Snake can play tricks and jokes: as if you never saw that silver birch or ravine, but I did. Blanks as gold, girls as angels and humans as werewolves, it was just another regular illusion. Once this happens the only thing left to do is make *mooing* noises during a head-wrestling contest which is what happened then: me and Three-Eye against our overpowering leader.

'Ha ha! And you thought you were rich!'

But the fooling around was short-lived.

THE MENACE

Take the initiative, be alert, and you will be praised. *You're a smart boy, right?* The Colonel was perhaps the most stylish talker of them all. He pioneered this method of talk. Then in April 1973 a voice from somewhere else told me I could be even smarter.

Your nickname is Sundance. Right?

I was standing in the doorway of our house, my right foot over the granite step and my right hand holding onto school paraphernalia as if it was welded to my body. I had just reached home, and my late afternoon shadow was thrown through the doorway as I stood there, not knowing whether I was dreaming. Talking figures, a smoky room. Sweat pouring down my arms.

140

There were two men, werewolf emissaries, it turned out. There was no telling how long they had been in our house or how they had got inside. They were sat in the centre of the dark room far from the oblong light of the main doors. I smelled strong tobacco smoke as I walked in.

Your nickname is Sundance. We have heard much about you, heard you are supposed to be the best. Perhaps even too good for your own good, but we can also see you are a smart boy. Right?

Afterwards, I stood in the doorway for about ten minutes, with no memory of seeing anyone leave or walk past me, just like the way I have no memory of Lord Baltimore's abduction. Light can play tricks, we all know that, but objects disappearing is another matter. There should have been something – a tortoise, some talking men. But where? You can search heaven and earth. Light and darkness. And find nothing.

The future was looking dangerous.

THE DRUG

A collection of herbs lies on a desk inside a room the way the room lies within a swirling city. There is a man sitting in front of us, a grumpy old man, a distant relative. Someone we have been coming back to as far back as memory can recall; it was within his aromatic alcove and no less than six months old that I was claimed and collected as a mysterious parcel from England. Soaked in the scent of herbs, Ficus, Rosa, when Grandma carried me away. And since that first baptism, time and time again I have returned. Even when there was no problem I still came and slouched over glass cabinets guessing at their contents and usage. Asking them and myself whether resurrection is possible.

As a younger man, he fed Coca Cola to a sick buffalo whose symptom was bloating of the belly, and for this he was nicknamed 'Mad'. In the top left drawer of his desk you will find crushed beetles while in the other, a deadly serpent, guarding what we have always believed to be the resurrectionist potion. Mad Uncle often kept his right arm over this drawer, had rolled up his sleeves, always wearing a dark Chinese robe. Muttering as he wrote.

'They can't cheat. The counting of locusts will be done in the open on 21 June. There will be government officials present. Millions/Brilliant was born in the year of the Ox, and this year is Ox, so they believe there's no way he can lose. Why then, would they cheat?'

'How do you know?'

'Bah!' he fumed. His eyes, instead of turning beady and sarcastic like some adults, turned big and wide. 'Think you are the only great locust hunter around here? In the time before motorcars I not only hunted insects but hunted cures for snakebites. Remember the time I sent you to hunt crickets? Told you it had to be pairs otherwise it wouldn't work. I have retrieved eggs science has yet to name.'

There was the usual pause as he loudly sipped tea, then swivelled left on his wheelchair, indicating for me to fetch something on the far shelf. It was Monday afternoon and the place looked almost tranquil. The chequered floor had been newly polished, the red shop sign realigned. The cycle repair shop and dried seafood seller and all the other shops across the road looked realigned and washed too. Especially the barbers. They seemed to be doing brisk business, and why not, with every man wanting a Bruce. Go in, and if you're between a certain acceptable age limit the barber will ask: 'Is it a Bruce?' You nod and five minutes later you get exactly that, a Ferrari streamlined bowl head. But since I was not a susceptible age, my haircuts always came away close to a bald monk, so avoiding the barbers was a must, yet no matter how bad the trim, Grandma and other ladies around the village would still confess: 'Ooh, you do look handsome!'

Lots of things had been happening around us by this time. The world was changing, moving on, shifting towards a new era both personal and international. In Central District there was a building called the Conrad where an open room was created without people or walls or windows, all because (according to the knowledge of the day) it had been blocking the mystical energy flow of feng shui. There were new stamps of the Queen and Phil. Her Majesty is seated next to a phoenix while Phil stands by a dragon. There were also, to my surprise, stamps of our forever suffering, ever reliable brown cow.

Meanwhile Big Voice had gleefully been telling us how he became a 'true hero' after single-handedly saving a lady from two muggers trying to nab her purse. 'I just dived in,' he said, swinging his fist. 'I yelled.' And he demonstrated for us his by now famous Bruce (cat killing chicken) yell 'Waa-saa!' A yell so authentic, it no doubt impressed the lady he saved immensely. Her eyes widening like a china plate as the muggers fled leaving him to stand like one pure knight in shining armour.

Three-Eye had checked in at the small opticians next door to Mad Uncle's and got told his eye-sight was not improving. On the street, almost every radio seemed to be playing 'Ghost, Horse and Twin Stars' by Sam. And listening to him you could almost believe he sang the truth, as if the internal workings of a complex culture *can* be explained away through one cool spangling tune.

Closer along the street's decadence I could hear the casual flip-flop of slippers come and go, voices vaguely echo in the knowledge of a completely new one-hundred-dollar note and a forthcoming visit by the Queen. Then suddenly, all these crisp sounds were drowned out by the rumble of a monstrous passing truck.

We were on half-term from school, with plans to buy Japanese comics and Fanta from the refrigerated oasis from around the corner. More importantly, I was there to collect Grandma's mail via Mad Uncle, as the village had no postal service.

'This visit to you,' said Mad Uncle, coming back in from his mental drift to drink more tea, just to clear his throat, 'was to size you up. Put the frighteners on you. It is in their interests to know who and what they will be up against and, perhaps, decide whether it will be worthwhile bribing you. Since they saw you and left nothing, there is no doubt they know you by character better than you think. This looks to me to be more than a game now. They have waited ten years to win, and they will do anything to carry on the tradition. Better expect another visit. Expect Millions/Brilliant himself. And soon . . .'

Well, guess what? He couldn't have been more right.

THE WARNING

As I've said before, the worst thing that's ever happened to me was being stung in the head by a hornet. It felt like my skull was being electrically drilled. So bad I was out of action for days. But I guess there's always room for improvement.

On 20 May at 4.56 p.m. (a day my right thumb will never forget as long as I live), I came home like a walking wreck. Grandma, sweeping the courtyard, the chickens pecking around her, took one look at me and yelled: 'AhhhhhhMeeeerrrrrr!' The longest Hakka yelp I've ever heard.

'Who hit you?'

'No one,' I blurted, wincing from my injuries. 'I walked into a branch.'

'Right! Looks to me like you fell off a mountain!'

She could always tell. There was no hiding it from Grandma.

I had been in detention, copying out more text, my scrawling Chinese characters as usual having the appearance of road-kill. I was the only lucky one in detention that day. And why? I'd been caught daydreaming, what else? I was by myself. Mad Dog, as always, was somewhere else – at Uncle Wu's place probably, to talk about the school's future, which of course, was non-existent. In the shadowy classroom solitude you could hear every whisper. Every small note produced by the soft rubbing of a few dozen or so swaying bamboos and in particular, footsteps making their way towards you through the unswept playground. The place was certifiably haunted, everybody knew that, so detention was to be avoided like razor-blades. So far I had yet to see anything to prove it one way or the other. Until now.

He was standing right before me. Suddenly. There was no warning.

A real Supernatural.

There had been no approaching footsteps and no voices. Nothing. I looked up from my desk to check the time and he was *there*. Sunglasses, a respectable school shirt, tie and jacket (even in this heat) and a watch.

He was just *there*.

You know how people say: 'Don't take this too personally. We all just want to make a living, right?' Or in my case: 'This is nothing personal, we simply want some justice. A plaster for the wound you've caused. Is that too much to ask?' This was how I put it to the man, nicely, gently, in a civilised way. But still, he took it too personally.

The desk went into the air and was instantly smashed into fifty odd pieces. I didn't even get a chance to see whether he did it with his leg or fist as my arm had gone up to shield myself from the flying debris and splinters. But I was lucky, as in every story that's ever made it to the end you need a little luck to get by. I came away with just a small cut across my forehead, but was more worried about the destroyed desk than anything else, and with good reason. I mean, how was I to explain it to Mad Dog? How could such a well-dressed paragon behave like this? A respectable student from a respectable school . . . how could he say the words he was saying, which I omit to write down for the reason of obscenity. This is supposed to be a story intelligence and grace. I am trying to appeal to the imagination, and any signs of bad language or violence should not

146

come into play because the world has enough of that already. Unlike urban city schools where bullying was nothing new, here at Tortoise Spring it was unknown. But then this wasn't bullying.

He stood close to the blackboard, hands behind his back, looking straight ahead as if there was nobody else in the room but himself. And perhaps that was true. I was nobody. I didn't matter.

That day, 20 May, I found myself suddenly face to face with the future. It was no longer just a date on the calendar, 21 June 1973, far away in the bordered distance, but here – *now* – blood-red real, a hurricane. And to admit I felt fear was not something to be ashamed of. I am not and never have been a bad loser. The purpose of the visit was to dish out fear – and it worked.

'YOU ARE NOTHING. YOU'VE GOT NO NAME, NO MONEY, NO PARENTS. YOU'RE A NOBODY, LIVING WITH SOME OLD HAG AND YOU THINK YOU CAN BE SOMEBODY? JUST TAKE A LOOK AT YOURSELF! I WOULDN'T HIRE YOU TO WIPE MY ASS!'

It's obvious to anybody that when you are in a position of power, say with a gun in your hand, there's no need to raise your voice or get angry. But did he have to bring my parents into it and get all personal? There were many bad things he could have said – about the red lice that kept hanging off my private parts or the canine toothmarks on my bum or better still, my retarded attempts at maths, eating double zeros every time, but no. He just couldn't leave it alone. Couldn't simply beat the beans out of me and forget about it. He had to bring in the personal, bring Grandma into it, too, and that is no way fair, is it now? A lack of respect for my folks is one thing, but no respect for a saint? That was going too far.

Maybe, without even knowing it, I had already turned into a grown man, because words were beginning to matter. Words were getting to me like never before. Words which had never meant a thing to me in class or on the streets were starting to cut me like a razor. And sincerely, deep inside, I don't think I liked what this was doing to me.

Big Voice once said that when a dangerous predator is less than a few feet away from you, running is out of the question. Turning your back to run is the worst action you can take. So I didn't run. I stood my ground, and that was how I ended up getting my first fat lip.

I was jerked up by my shirt collar and smacked straight in the mouth. I fell back, like a lob-sided scarecrow against a desk two desks behind my own. I fell clumsily, my head jarring backwards, and crashed down faster than a ton of bricks. I lay there against the desk leg looking both surprised and stunned, to say the least. And not just by the stars and cartoon birds I was seeing. He had actually knocked me twice in the face with one single blow! Gave me a black eye as well as a fat lip. And for the next three weeks I'd have to go plodding around looking like I'd survived a train crash. *What happened to you?* I was in a train crash. *Ha, ha, ha.* I lay on the floor with a face like a tropical sunrise, thinking, Wow! That was fast! Lord, that was so fast it didn't seem to hurt!

But it *was* going to hurt, *bad*. And had I known it was going to hurt that bad I would surely have dragged my sorry-looking vegetated state out of there *fast*. No matter what Big Voice may have said.

But I didn't. I stayed. Though I would have much preferred to be 'standing' at the least, but neither was I 'crawling' in order to save myself. My characteristic refusal to back down forced me to suffer whatever was coming my way with the defenceless innocence of a newborn lamb. For that's what I am and was. A lamb. To the slaughter. You can only be who you are. And the werewolf *was* 'somebody'. A bully boy. A make-you-feel-small man. An insect-crushing, turtles-and-junkie-bashing Superman. Meaning he was invincible. But I would never have guessed in all my years, that this was how a turtle-basher would have looked, with sun-glasses, that scooped-back hair, hands behind his back, and walking like it was just another day. The tap of his expensive well-polished shoes, which I couldn't hear before, now sounded off clearly. I could only watch. Do nothing but watch. I could see more blood to come, more bad weather ahead. I could see nothing and every-thing at once. I could—

The honest truth was: I don't think I knew what I was watching. There were too many constellations around me now, still too many Milky Ways. Two other shadows came up from behind as my destroyed face fell to one side. I thought they were about to plough into me but they didn't, not yet. The second time I was picked up it was not by the shirt collar but by my neck, the way a ventriloquist would pick up his talking dummy. Except this dummy had nothing to say. This dummy wasn't able or allowed to talk or even breathe. The dummy knew this partnership was about to end in tears.

There's a part of me that is always waiting for Big Voice and Three-Eye to turn up and help, as if they were just behind me in the field or just around the corner of the city comic-stand, the way they did when the red-eyed grass snake came for me, or when I accidentally kicked into a beehive and they yelled, *'Duck!'* and miraculously, the bees went over me and I was spared a few hundred stings. We looked out for each other this way. We stuck together, in fights, in everything. Not one of us ever dared buy an individual drink, it was always two or three, that was how it worked. We always sorted things out when there was a disagreement. 'Take it easy, all right! Don't do anything crazy!' 'No! *You* take it easy! I am COOL!' 'I am COOL too! I am cooler than you!' 'OK then, so why don't you take it easy?' But that didn't happen this time. Big Voice and Three-Eye were'nt there to support me, and that was when the world became a dark, dark place.

I should have screamed. But I did no such thing. Not after what he said about Grandma. But I am sure, if I had screamed, somebody would have answered. At least, I am pretty sure my dog would have.

They did it by putting my right thumb in between the ramming path of two desks and simply drove one into the other. They held me down and had a white string noosed around my thumb. The string was then pulled down 90 degrees which kept my thumb in position at the edge of the desk while the other desk made violent, almost clinical contact. I thought I was going to hear my own bones crack, like eggshells, or the sound Echo makes when he chews his way through a white bone after it's been boiled for soup. But there was nothing of the sort. Only the wooden, hollow bang of two desks in collision, followed by pain which for me reached a whole new dimension. No teacher or wise sage could ever have warned me about such a pain in this world or the next.

I was left on the floor in ruins, too broken to scream and too shocked to watch them walk away and get into a Triumph TR6 parked at the village centre, then to see how they blasted off, raking up fumes and dirt and flying roosters. There were more important matters to contend with now, like: how was I ever going to catch another insect again? Where was the next drink going to come from? And the big one: how was I to enter Day of the Locust with no thumb?

For many, many minutes, I sat unmoving, shaking feverishly, considering these facts. The painful truth. Not yet knowing that soon I would find myself staring at other people's thumbs, at how they held a basket or a set of keys, or gave the thumbs-up sign. I'd stare at what they could do that I couldn't, since my own thumb was useless, swathed in a plaster cast and bandages. It was as if this event had somehow changed me. Somehow poured cement into me.

When I finally got to my feet, my right hand automatically cradled itself against my belly. I stood up because I felt it was necessary to straighten the desks and chairs back into their original position, an impromptu attempt to tidy up the mess. But then, hadn't I just been roughed up? Didn't I have a broken thumb? And yet I was more concerned about Mad Dog's reaction, should he enter and see the chaos than about myself. I couldn't find the broom so in the end I kicked all the bits into one pile. I sat down again at 4.45, according to the clock on the wall, but on my own chair this time. The silence around me was awesome. The pain still unbearable, but hey, I am the boy who got stung in the head, remember? But still, it did take me ten minutes to do what can normally be done in three.

I felt as if I had been in a train crash. Taking another deep breath, I looked at my thumb, which had bulged into mega proportions in a matter of minutes, like a multi-coloured moth pupa about to break open and hatch.

How was I ever going to catch another grasshopper now?

I just didn't know.

I closed my eyes, blew out all the air from my puffed red cheeks and thought to myself: My thumb's a goner for sure. It was game over.

I slumped there, with my shattered thumb, shattered desk, pieces everywhere, in the awesome silence. And you know what? Mad Dog didn't even ask what had happened. He came back, bandaged me up, put a sling on my arm, discharged me and cleaned up the whole mess himself. And if that wasn't amazing then I don't know what is. I could say it was his job. He taught, he looked out for us. Looked out for *me*. That time he took the class on a day trip to HK's only zoo at Li Chi Kok and I threw up all over the seat of the minibus, he just cleaned it up with a cloth and with minimal fuss. Just like the way he cleaned up that broken desk. No questions. No complaints. I like that in a man, don't you? Cool, dutiful, minding his own business.

The following day he called me over during break and held out his hand, and naturally when somebody does that to me, I shake it. I shook his right hand awkwardly using my left hand. He looked at me ominously for a moment, then said, 'Same grip,' and sat down. And as he sat down the level of noise from the playground behind me suddenly seemed to drop, like there was a hush, making the place seem hollow. 'You had the same grip when you came here nine years ago and you'll have the same grip when you leave,' he said, which could only have meant he once held me as a toddler and discovered my one unique talent, a firm grip. 'In life you must do what you have to do and don't let anyone else tell you otherwise. Understand? I won't wish you bad luck. But I won't wish you good luck either.' Then he waved me away. And went back to marking homework.

If I had to recall one image of Mad Dog for future reference, then that would be it – the waving away. He was famous for it. When coming and going from the village he could always be seen doing it. 'Hello!' or 'Bye, bye!' The movements of course would be different but only marginally. His limping wife always linked to his right arm, at about 8.30 a.m. or 6 p.m., he'd be coming and going just like everybody else, on the back of a Leyland truck more used to carrying vegetables than people, and with only two foldable planks of wood for seating; all late arrivals had to stand grasping a rope as the truck discoed you left to right. I'd be there sometimes, to see them go, then wave to them as the truck thudded off, his wife still holding the basket containing their daily provision of food and rice that you could smell being cooked round about noon.

I think I can understand why a teacher's goodbye can be strange sometimes. Anyone who's been to a good school will know what I mean. They bring you up like their own. Tell you what not to do in society and what you should do. How you should help an old lady across a busy street and why you shouldn't buy spicy giblets from a man with a cigarette in his mouth. All that care and attention they put into you just so they can say goodbye one day as if they didn't care.

Do you believe that? Any other year I wouldn't have thought much of what he said, but this was the last year. The last of everything. It's possible desks can self-destruct and he had seen it all before. After all, he was a man who fought both Japanese and Communists and had lost his first wife and child, all without too much complaint. But there was no doubt in my mind that he meant Day of the Locust. He knew about werewolves, and about wars. He knew my mind was never in class. Always out there, in the rich hills, in the juicy offerings of the big city. He knew about a lot of things, even our little plan to go up against werewolves in the name of Lord Baltimore. He was a teacher, after all, so how could he not know?

THE FIX-UP

'I know this stinks,' Mad Uncle said, applying dry, pungent herbs. 'The more unpleasant the smell, the better it is for you. Get it?' He grinned at me, a bearded grin so reassuring, I had to nod.

This was the second time I had been fussed over, baby-style, in twenty-four hours. The night before, Grandma had temporarily patched me up using one of my old vests. Grandma had this habit of keeping everything, throwing nothing away, not even a Coke bottle or plastic ice-cream cup. She had her own box of

154

potions hidden away in a cupboard built into the wall, used as a kind of food store before the days of refrigerators. But now Mad Uncle had taken over. The mixture didn't smell as bad as he said. I was kept at the shop for over an hour so the rock-hard hospital plaster cast could set and dry. Like most pharmacies at the time, P.O.T. stocked virtually everything, from Western antibiotics to Eastern antlers. Mad Uncle himself, he was more into beetles. And I should know, I supplied him. 'Asthma? No problem. Try this beetle mixture. What? Mosquito bites? Here. Smear this on – beetle scent. Works every time . . .' And whether it worked or not was not the point, the point was the fun: it was fun collecting beetles, each one coming to you in colours as different as the rainbow. In fact, I wouldn't call it collecting, almost a cruise because they are slow movers, in particular the Longhorn with its antennae that are twice the length of its body, growing up to 7 cm to become what is translated as 'the biggest little mountain cow there is'.

Mad Uncle was conventionally unconventional in some sense. Or how else would he have earned his nickname? The plaster cast was like a white mitten. My thumb was set at a near permanent two o'clock position, leaving just the four fingers exposed. Grandma was with me, but thankfully not in her *sploshy* wellies. She asked her brother tentatively, in a tone only a caring sister could know how to use, 'Will it heal?'

I believe my wound was what doctors call a minor fracture, in between the knuckle and the joint. Mad Uncle said the break was reasonably clean. 'Nicely done.' And without his potently active herbs (patented only to him) healing would normally take two months. But now, nodding his chin, his lips pursed in certainty. 'Less than three weeks.'

What? I looked up. That quick?

'You don't trust me?' Reading off my dull expression. 'I have fixed you up since you were *this* big and you don't trust me? Bah! Don't you kids have any filial respect? Bah!'

He turned away, comically annoyed as usual, and went back to his patients who were mostly children, like myself.

Grandma left to proceed with her shopping. Grandma, with her baggy strides and rattan basket. The image of her haggling her way through old and worn yet comforting labyrinthine alleys was already flashing through my mind before she'd even left Mad Uncle's. 'Wait for me here!' she had instructed, as if she was going to be some time among the dried fish and radishes and pickles.

Time stood still. The city silenced. The electric fan above me silenced. I felt as if I were in a dream. My eyes lazily and surely started to close. When I opened them again, it was 4.32. The old clock above Mad Uncle's head was going *tick tick tick*. Four thirty-two. Prime time. People coming home from work. People in need of healing. People in need of my uncle's attention at 7, Tsun Fu Street, directly opposite from Lau's Bookstore thinly shaded against the harsh light. This was where schoolchildren gathered among wooden panels folding out onto the street that held comics of all shapes and order. With Japanese UltraMan, SuperFly, and Ding Dong the Miracle Cat being the most abundant and fun. Yet 'Old Master Q' at 1 cent, was the most real and

surreal of all the Honkers home-grown comics. The
heads downcast in reading, the joy on faces was something I knew all too well.

I must have dozed off on my uncle's desk for about
thirty minutes. A sleep so soothing to my olfactory
senses, it could only have happened at a herbalist. The
breath of the fan's shadow across my skin as I inhaled
sixteen times per minute next to his work and wooden
pipe and boxed aroma, and his patients with their arms
resting upon my uncle's desk, glaring mutt-like at my
sleeping face lurched on the same desk and asking my
uncle: 'Is this your nephew? The parcel baby?'

'Yes. He has grown, hasn't he?' Mad Uncle replied in
his customary mumble. I rubbed my eyes. I looked up at
him. I looked around myself. There was a small room of
people. I stretched, and yawned. This must be the one
place with all the answers in the world, I said to myself.
So spread the word. All the answers in the world.

The next time I looked up it was 4.50. And the
fourth time after that it was nearing 5.00, till it was
5.14. Time, for me to be on the train, Kowloon-bound
to meet Amber.

SAD ANGEL

When she saw my new face, saw the state I was in, the
bruised eye and split lip and the artificial white hand,
she actually fell against me crying. It was the second
time I'd seen her cry. And not the last.

'Sundance . . . What have they done to you?'

She had been to the dentist and was all set to meet
me at the nameless rough and ready noodle stall on

157

Temple Street. As its name implies, the street had a temple but there were no monks, only a caretaker. The place had been made famous by its one-hundred-year-old Banyan where, late in the evening, singers and Kung Fu men bashing at their own heads with bricks would gather and entertain people under the cool shade of this luxurious open-armed tree. I did on several occasions go in myself, walking under its all-encompassing branches to light a few incense sticks. Just doing it because Amber did. For fun.

It was supposed to be just like any other day in the city. We'd meet and hang out and the city was ours. She swerved her way towards me at 6.39 p.m., according to the chrome Rolex dial from across the street. As always she was the first to wave, crossing over from the other side and waving to me with the sun in her palm while trying to determine the speed of a red Hillman, but knowing well that in less than twenty minutes there wouldn't be a single car in sight. The street would have closed and instead of cars, the road would have turned into a market, selling fake watches, Red Cock soap which, as far as I know, was *the* only cheap soap in HK, used for everything, from washing your socks to washing (if not destroying) your hair and good skin, and of course the usual craggy-voiced fortune-tellers and singing, swearing con artists trying to flog you that miracle drug to turn you into a sex-appealing superman. This time of the day was what people would call the street's 'Happy Hour'.

But that day, Amber's jubilation lasted only until the final twenty yards, when her expression suddenly changed and the burst of tears that followed was so sudden and furious it near enough made me cry too, just seeing the state she was in. Of course there was no way on earth I was going to cry, not for myself and absolutely not in front of Amber. Only drowned cats do that. And I was determined to stay afloat.

She stood five foot from the table and me and was crying reservedly, like a well-behaved school pupil would cry after being told her terminally ill father had just died and was finally free of pain. Both her palms like an opened book were held against her crying face. Still trying to control the uncontrollable that is emotion, as if somehow she knew the train crash was a bad lie even before I opened my mouth. But the truth is: I couldn't lie to her about Lord Baltimore's murder then and I certainly couldn't lie to her now. I had to tell the truth. Don't I always?

'Yes. They got me,' I said, a beat. 'But it's OK. Honest.' I held onto both her arms as if in an attempt to shake her away from tears. 'Mad Uncle said the fracture is clean and I'll be back to normal in no time. So you don't have to worry. It's OK. Yes, it honestly is.' But she was inconsolable. The more I tried, the further her wet marble-like face pressed against me till her tears began permeating through my white shirt that had been so carefully ironed by Grandma. And soon, in a matter of minutes with the traffic and people roaring around us, a somewhat brusque yet benign voice sounded from out of nowhere.

'What seems to be the problem, young lady?'

I looked up. It was the cook at the noodle stall, a lean man in his forties. I didn't know his name but he knew we were regulars and also we were two sweet-looking youngsters in trouble. I presume, from the point of view of an adult, this was just too irresistible to ignore.

'Someone giving you a hard time? You tell me and I'll sort him out. Just point, OK?'

He towered above us. A Jolly Green Giant. A lot taller than Big Voice, I was sure. Miles taller, if not a future projection of him. But he wasn't the only one; there were others there too. I saw a traffic warden, and you know what they say about them: just wave two ten-dollar bills in their face and the ticket will be in shreds in seconds. That simple. A housewife was behind me with a Golden Thread fish in her basket. And next to her I noticed a trendy-looking girl with flaming red flares and apple-shaped sunglasses, and to her immediate left was an office girl in yellow and an old man hawking some chickens. It was an interesting street assortment, as if the whole of HK was there from all walks of life and occupation, from the very top of the ladder to the very bottom, encircling us in an amphitheatre of faces. Yet no matter how different they were as people, they all wore the same expression, had the same question: Why is this girl crying against this boy?

I heard the cook repeat his proposal. 'Just point, OK?'

I looked at Amber, but she wasn't pointing at anything. Her face was still buried against my chest and she only managed a short negative nod. And kept nodding till he could find nothing more to say. I had feared that he would lay the blame on me, pull me up to see if I'd been teasing her, but one closer look at my battered features changed his mind completely.

He backed away. Then came another voice; this time it belonged to a lady with a bundled coiffure, looking almost identical to Three-Eye's mother. She had her hand on Amber's back and in a soft massaging motion she hummed, 'Come, come. Stop crying, now. Be a good girl.' And maybe it was the way she warbled that made Amber look up and see the commotion she was causing and feel bad about it. 'Oh, what a pretty little flower you are!' she purred, gazing down at Amber. 'Here. Let's wipe away those tears first.' Then, setting aside her glance momentarily she saw me, which understandably made her jump. 'What happened to you!?'

I said I had been in a train crash.

'*Choy-gaw-lay-merh!*' she hoarsed, pulling back, exclaiming blasphemy. Thanks to her, the crowd began to disperse around us like smoke, as if her words had dispelled them. Everyone went quickly back to what they were doing before, either catching the next bus home or going to meet friends at a restaurant or heading off to work as a night watchman in one of the millions of offices that never seem to close. The street quickly falling back into its usual six-ish pace with ease. The intermission was over.

I saw the cook knocking around looking awkward, then before finally backing away behind the gas stove, he said to me, 'Why don't you two have some beancurd dessert? Made it specially this morning.'

Made it specially this morning.

I didn't care if he'd made it a week ago! I said OK, it was a deal. To tell you the truth, I was enjoying this. Yes, I was. I was enjoying it flat out. Not Amber's tears, of course, but the fact that normal, everyday people were going out of their way just to give us that extra 2 per cent. And boy oh boy, I felt like a king. I wasted no time. I gave the man the quickest nod of the day, knowing there was nothing Amber liked better than a dessert. After what had happened so far, I sure could do with one too.

161

The warbling lady, I was to find out, was the owner of the noodle stall. We sat down on her stools where she made us feel like a pair of exotic birds. 'My, the two of you go so well together.'

We said nothing to that. Especially me. When the dessert came I asked if I could have a little more syrup. The first scoop in the mouth was indescribable. The delicate texture disintegrating on my tongue like a beautiful wish; even with my stinging lip it still tasted like heaven. But it wasn't easy to stay poker-faced. I did wince a couple of times. And maybe Amber didn't like seeing me in pain, or she was struck by my clumsy use of my left hand. The wave of tears soon came back to her, like race horses.

'What have you done now?' complained the noodle-stall lady.

'Nothing,' I protested. She seemed sure it was all my fault somehow. But that wasn't the point here. The point was: *What would an angel's tears taste like?* Of syrup? Honey?

A weird question, but nevertheless, a good one. What *would* an angel's tears taste like?

At my age you get some illogical thoughts, sometimes so silly you feel like one of those strange little insects that prefer to drink other animal's moisture or tears, and you'd never dare tell these thoughts to anybody, except on paper, and at that precise moment that was what came into my head. The taste of an angel's tears. But *why* she was crying so much that day I wouldn't like to say, not just yet. This is not the time. Though I was certain that those tears weren't all for me.

The best thing I did was to show her that pain can have its funny side. I made her look at my plaster cast in detail, stare at it till her watery eyes saw sense and slowly (as I knew it would) her former self returned.

'Oh! What a charmer you are!' exclaimed the noodle-stall lady, walking back up, bending down with both hands on her knees. 'What does it say?'

On the back of the plaster I had written in capital letters, using my left hand: YOUR TEARS TASTE BETTER THAN SYRUP AND HONEY.

I remember we both laughed about it, the corniest phrase of the day. But I cannot remember if she laughed right away or whether it was a slow subtle realisation of a smile. I was too occupied with the street's 7 p.m. senses bursting into life around me and also, in warding off the noodle-stall lady. She was annoyed because I couldn't bring myself to tell her what I had written. She was shouting across the tables, 'Just because you know English you youngsters think you're something . . .'

I didn't say anything. I never answered back. My goodness! I was just too reserved!

THE BAIT

'Are you OK? Nothing broken?'

'*Narrr*. It was easy.'

'And?'

'It was just like Mad Uncle said. It was good – except he almost killed me.'

Which was no lie. When you're supposed to be the hero there's a lot of stress you have to take. Suddenly people think you're indestructible – you can fly, wear red underpants on the outside and can knock the socks off anybody.

I was trying hard to smile, tried to shrug off the pain. But I only felt the wound on my lip rip open with a sharp sting.

In the city and in life there's only pressure. Big, bad, rotten-egg pressure. It's a universal truth. The pressure to keep cool while under great stress is something you have to learn how to do in a small compressed place like HK. Losing your head is not going to get you anywhere. It's better to say, 'Hell, it was easy!' while swigging back a Coke or, 'Easier than eating raw cabbage,' which I can do with great ease – and did.

I could not honestly tell at the time whether Big Voice was capable of tackling a werewolf hand to hand or not, but he knew if he wasn't careful, he could very well be next. They could seek him out the same way they sought me out. He was taking no chances. There was a squint in his eyes when he paid for a second 7UP bottle at Fat Man's, a tin shack oasis at TakWuling and a few paces from the Locust Hall of Fame that sold almost as much as the city but was five miles closer. He yanked open the bottle against the side of the fridge, but I was pretty sure he could have done it with one push of his thumb, because he was *strong*. He drank the entire bottle in one go and sighed, 'Arrrhhh . . .' Like it was some kind of reward to take a second drink, as if he knew a trick or two that nobody else did. Like there was no way we could lose.

THE WEAPON

At the place where water gushes in between two rocks, two rocks green with flowers and ferns surrounding a

164

small yet torrential waterfall, I am told a weapon will emerge, wrapped and boxed tightly in plastic. A kind of Excalibur waiting to be claimed. Just left there dangling from a dark thin chain below a thirty-foot watery drop.

The Werewolf Slayer.

I watched him haul it up inch by inch. The rust of wet chains passing through his hands like mud till eventually there appeared a colder metal, unveiled, de-mummified from the oil and plastic: the ultimate weapon, a Colt 45, identical to the Colonel's. Perhaps it was his. Perhaps the Colonel left it on the seat of his Land Rover one day while conversing with Mad Dog and *he* happened to walk by. Took it. And now, way up by the falls instead of in the Colonel's holster it will stay. Proudly spinning the gun, he told us it was *the* only weapon to use against a werewolf.

'No kidding?' exclaimed Three-Eye, ripping off his glasses, coming up to take a closer look. 'Holy mother of —!' or something like it. I didn't catch all of what he said because of the constant crashing of water. We said a lot of things but the one thing we didn't say was, 'Where did you get it?' There was no point in asking a bad question and getting a bad answer. Besides, I knew for a solid fact there was only one policeman in these parts who owned a silver Colt 45.

We watched with an explorer's exulted interest as he flicked out the revolving barrel, expecting to see Three-Eye's prized gold nugget but to our disappointment, there was none. The gun was empty.

The church by the sea dated back to 1898, was put together just as roads were about to enter the Closed Area. There is a crucifix there, inside that church, made of pure silver. 'The legend says only bullets made from a silver crucifix can kill werewolves,' we whispered to each other.

On 22 May we found ourselves walking towards the church, across the straight but isolated Shau Tau Kok Road in the late afternoon, and began a shuffle past the shoreline and the tiny bird island known as A Chau. The church stood among banyans and the clear blue ocean. It was the furthest point you could go without a special permit.

The priest at Puk Hok Lam, on seeing us enter, four sunburned statues, approached us and before offering us water asked if Echo would be so good as to remain outside. We explained our desire to purchase that large crucifix hung high at the far end of the church beyond the pews and he smiled. We explained again, but how can it be explained? There were werewolves out there and people were turning a blind eye. And I have lived in their eye. Otherwise how can one explain Lord Baltimore's disappearance? Then eventual cannibalism? Only with the Supernatural, said Mad Uncle, can a life as innocent and precious disappear from right under your eyes. In times like this, only one thing can apply. Believe in Supernaturals. Believe in silver bullets.

That expedition bought back three thumb-sized crucifixes. All for under twenty dollars, their religious powers genuine, touched and blessed by a holy man. About a week later Big Voice had them melted down and there emerged a bullet made out of the purest silver known to man.

GOD'S SPOTLIGHT

Grandma and I had been packing up for the day's end. It was the hour where 'anything is possible', the moment where darkness enters light, in between closing up the shed and pegging down the cow. We were at the point of penning in the animals for the night when the moon fell upon us like God's spotlight.

It had rolled in from the obfuscating hills as if it was alive and searching; panning in from the far left to the far right in a refined study of shadow and form, shadows which might turn out to be a Snake or some sad nocturnal animal petrified of light. Till it fell like grace, upon houses whose faces were like surprised youngsters. This was until you realised it was no moon, no planet, but the search beam, coming from the metallic watchtower. Like God's spotlight telling you it was time to confess your sins, time to do a song and dance act, time to be on stage.

We stood within this light, which to Grandma was no big deal. She was well-used to it. We were still hacking away at last-minute duties when the light found us. In Grandma's big hands she held two stray ducklings, their webbed feet yanking wildly. She didn't acknowledge the beam. She was *busy*. She stepped away hurriedly but I remained. I was holding my hat, had been using it to persuade the animals into their pens. I positioned myself directly before God's brilliant whiteness. Felt the aura intensify around me, dwarfing my body into nothingness. Felt as if God had found me, had even recognised me as His son. I raised my hat to shield myself from being blinded. Then I waved. I placed together my finger and thumb, making the sign OK, shouting: 'Everything's A OK, Dad! Thanks!'

MR TWILIGHT

In 1951 he swam through sharks and nearly lost a leg. In 1954 he floated over on a net of ping-pong balls but was caught and was later deported. The truth is, he'd been deported more times than the ping-pongs needed to keep him afloat. Then finally in 1956, his persistence and determination paid off and he made it into the dream lights of Hong Kong. Ten years later, from out of nothing, no possession or riches, he became a respected citizen and millionaire.

At the Street of Singers deep in the big-city heart of Kowloon there was a man by the name of Mr Twilight. A bird-admiring regular. A retired millionaire. 'For that locust I can spoon you a better price. For that lizard I could award you a medal.' Words of a millionaire? There was no way of telling. He had approached us wisely and simply, with no car or special attire. When he first came to us, all the way into Tortoise Spring, he appeared more like the angelic version of the Locustman. 'You a locust hunter?' To his question I said yes. It was obvious from the wasp-shaped paraphernalia that hung diagonally across our shoulders. It was late one Saturday afternoon. There was a net of red dragonflies as he stood against the blue sky. He had explained that 'fresh' commodity could only be obtained this far from civilisation, and of course we told him he was right.

People disappear by the second, all because of money. You walk into a café one day and it looks quite normal, then the next day it is closed, or under new ownership. It happens. You'd think nobody in their right mind could put so much on stocks and shares, feverishly gambling everything they have. Savings, property, business. First, they invest ten dollars. Win. Then a further hundred dollars. Win. Till eventually their entire business and family fortune are at stake. Then they lose it all. And these are people who are supposed to be in their right minds.

But to walk the way Mr Twilight walked, way ahead of others in speed and thinking, must have made him a millionaire. And quite often, when arriving at the Street of Singers, as part of our pun of hello, we would attempt to coax it out of him.

'How does a winner become a winner?'

I had won a few games. Got myself noticed a few times, but that hardly qualifies as great success. However, getting out of The Big Amber does. Once you have seen what is there: the dusty roads and scatters of water, the snail-pace of life and the children who would jump up and down in the hazy distance to let us know they had heard our calls, you could see why people wanted to escape.

'There is a possibility,' I said to Grandma, 'that one day I may not be around to protect you. You see, I may have made an enemy of somebody incredibly big. Know what I am saying?'

But she did not respond. And even if she had done so, it was likely to be along the lines of: '*You* protect *me*? I'd like to see that!' As the days went by I saw her forever wading through a watery field of rice, always joined by her animals. I talked to her, followed by Echo and the herd, but her mouth remained shut, as if she was sleepwalking. Then days later, in the courtyard after laying out the husked rice seedlings under sunlight in their millions, she started to sleepwalk again. This time a more passive sleepwalk. I watched her, tried to follow her. Every step seemed a therapeutic move. Her bare sole almost like leather as it trod over the even harder grains of husk. There are five stages in the production cycle of the rice plant. Here, Grandma demonstrated the last stage, the drying of the individual grains of rice. To walk where she walked, one's sole had to be clean and without footwear. A dirty foot or a shod foot is of course forbidden, is punishable, unless you are an angel or an insect or the odd werewolf. Those were the exceptions.

'They' had walked fully shod where no shod mortal should have walked. At the village centre they had left their parked Triumph and aroused local curiosity. In this last settlement before the lost realms of The Big Amber where only the hypnotic would go and not the rich and wealthy, why were they here? But Grandma told the werewolves nothing. In fact, she never said much at all.

The rest of the evening and during the meal she would ask nothing. I strolled back out to the courtyard and left her at the dining table. A habit of mine. It was important to end the day this way. The animals all around me. Counting their numbers. Listening for anything irregular.

THE BAGMAN

There is a way a sack or a bag can go over a dog's head no matter how fierce the animal. And once fully inside, powerless, the growl will turn into a sad squeal.

The Colonel was the dog hunter. He was not named that for nothing. His aim was to destroy strays, the rabies-infected dogs frothing at the mouth. That was what he was *supposed* to do.

When I realised what had happened, it was already minutes too late. Echo was gone, and the only thing left to do was run like mad. Try again to attempt the impossible. Resurrection.

We aimed south-west towards the old short-cut we knew, tore through three sweat-soaked villages and seven shrines, kept cutting through farmed fields for time and speed. Kept thinking this was the repeat of some bad nightmare, which it was. The same route, same fading landscape, same situation as on the evening of 14 February, minutes after Lord Baltimore's abduction. Except that time, we were pursuing a car. This time it was a bicycle. You lose once and the thought always stays. We lost Lord Baltimore and there was no way we could lose Echo. That couldn't be allowed.

When we saw the checkpoint, saw all the trucks, minibuses and people lining up before the barrier, our legs and lungs were finished. The Bagman had already made it through. In fact, he was already fifty yards clean through and headed for the city. Headed, it seemed, for the slaughterhouse.

As an experienced hunter I can tell you a thing or two about hunting. About a clear sky, about climate and the psychology of thunder, because when there is thunder the world stops. Birds, people, trucks, death. A bicycle fifty yards away. Some men can perform great tricks with dangerous weapons, and the Colonel, to Tortoise Spring, was a tricks artist. At the right time and the right place the Colonel saw something was wrong and

171

pulled out his revolver, fired at heaven and in so doing stopped the Bagman and contrariwise also saved what he should have hunted. By chance or by destiny, it is difficult to say. Things happen as they happen. A miracle. Echo fell back out of the sack and into my arms as if nothing had happened. Licking joyously at my sweaty cheeks and forehead to the point where I had to shout '*OK! That's enough! Stop that!*' As if there was no memory of a sack or a chase or the Bagman. As if he could appreciate at that moment in time, the three of us keeled over on the road from exhaustion, that he was probably *the* luckiest dog in this whole wide world.

Thunder can do that, has the power of resurrection.

We had done it! The Bagman rode away empty, for a change. Perhaps it was because of werewolves or perhaps it was more about territoriality. Whichever, it was getting too personal. We shook hands with the Colonel and he grinned. 'Transporting a dog in a bag is an offence,' he told us, which indeed was good to hear, yet he also gravely reminded me to: 'Keep that bloody dog tied up or else suffer the consequences.'

I have never felt that close to the Colonel. Guns frighten me the same way gunfire and helicopters frighten dogs. Though that was a new revolver I saw. No doubt about it. No nickel-plated Colt 45 Peacemaker but something plain and ordinary.

WATER

Water is indestructible. Water is immortal. It can evaporate before your very eyes but is never gone. Only recycled, reincarnated, again and again.

Bruce says you have to be water. 'Be formless, shape-less like water.'

A superior being can never be held, as Bruce demonstrated when he fought Chuck Norris at Rome's Coliseum in *The Way of the Dragon*. An unforgettable battle, both legendary in scope and psychology. At the beginning of the duel, Bruce, the smaller man, seems no match for his Goliath of an opponent. He is knocked flat to the ground at least three times by Chuck – until, of course, he transforms his body and thinking, and becomes 'water'. And suddenly, his wet marble skin stretches and gleams the way a brimming, shimmering river would when under clear moonlight. Thereafter, Chuck is unable to get near him. Cannot touch him. Because he is now fluid. Adaptable. Flowing.

So, *'Be water, my friend . . .'*

GRANDMA

I am standing naked in the mirror. As my eyes gradually become accustomed to the room's bleakness, I see the sheen of skinny arms and legs. I see they are actually tanned brown, the tan coming to a stop just a little way above the knees (up to where my baggy shorts are). And from the hands, it goes up almost up to the shoulders, where occasionally there are sleeves. I see this in my reflection. The reflection of my own puny nine-year-old body. All my back and the middle of my chest and belly areas are white. Like a white dog who had just dipped below belly-level through a pool of mud.

All the other women, like Grandma for example, go around wearing large rattan brims shaped like Polo

mints, and some city folks go as far as carrying para-
sols, but Big Voice and I, we liked going around
stripped naked to the waist. We were crazy. We
weren't scared of the scorching sun like they were. We
weren't scared of death. To be honest: we weren't growing up at all. And how could we? How can you face
reality when you still wish to climb trees and swing off
them? This was a question first put to us by Mad
Uncle. Some people called it 'immature', or 'childish
behaviour'. Well, we said, maybe you're right. So
afterwards we'd go right back and swing again and
again until the branch *cracked!* And then we'd land
back on earth, *hard*.

There were too many things you shouldn't do, too
many taboos. 'Why do you keep rubbing at your eyes?'
they would say. 'You've seen something you shouldn't
have, haven't you?' Like two dogs making out, or a few
girls swimming naked at the river south of Grandma's
plot. Images our young inexperienced minds couldn't
possibly cope with. I know girls don't have carrots (certainly not retractable ones as I once thought!), and I
know also why they giggle sheepishly at mine every
time I run forward to take a watery dive, but nevertheless, that is not going to stop me from making that
same dive again.

Big Voice is asking, am I ready? 'Sure,' I reply. He
nods. Then I nod. His tongue tips forward. Then, on a
count of three, we lift the giant rock at the centre of a
waterless December pond, quickly throwing it to one
side to discover a hibernating snake. The poor snake,
obviously in a state of shock, can only thrash about
confused, much less attack anyone. 'There's a snake!
Help me!' we shout, then bolt off. And indeed, the

chance of getting bitten cannot be outruled – but is that any reason to stop? There are certain risks you have to take. There's no point in stopping and thinking. It's what's called risk taking. No risk, no returns.

I am looking at myself in almost darkness. There is a small wedge of light from the double doors. Looking at myself, I am asking these questions, thinking as Bruce had intoned, '*Be water, my friend.*' Formless, nothing can stop you; you are soft yet you can wear away rocks and sweep away mountains but, looking at my own puniness, breathing in and holding up my ribbed chest, no matter how long I hold my breath (underwater) I cannot ever be 'water'. Can never be like Bruce. A puff of wind could knock me over. Yes. It's that bad.

I shout: 'Hey you! Yes! *You*! You nobody! Girly dancing boy! You think you are good enough to go up against an empire? YOU? Ha, ha, hah, hah, ha! Why don't you just take a good look at yourself? Yes, why don't you? DO YOU READ ME? Do you get what I am saying? Do you?'

Then Grandma pushes through the doors, and there is light . . .

INSPIRATION

There were days when a coarse hand used to grab me by the neck, and I'd turn around and see Grandma, a saint, insisting I should wear something against the scorching sun. Then there were the days when other hands grabbed me from behind and I'd turn around and see beautiful women. A city person. A sales manager, bank clerk, beauty pageant winners. Their hands shimmering with nail varnish and almost as mysteriously smooth as Amber's, full of gifts and expensive '7 Stars and Moon' cakes. All of them wishing to see Grandma. Ask them why and they'd say the usual. 'She was my once-upon-a-time saviour.' Then I would remember their once-upon-a-time raggedness, when they scared the trousers off me by appearing from out of a bush or a dark evening tree and I'd scarper back to inform Grandma; when they had no nail varnish and no perfume and no great smiles; when they were Snakes and I was a few inches shorter and stared at them like a severely spooked hound.

How many people has she saved? I couldn't tell. She couldn't tell. Smiling faces would appear and call her name, sometimes even call my name, comment on my good looks, and Grandma would pause, not because I was not 'good-looking' but she would try somehow to figure out who they were. It seemed as if most of what is now HK had passed through her hands at one time or another, aided by her kindness. And when they return, now no longer illegal but a working citizen of a free country, their first desire is to hug and thank her. They remember her small gestures. A bowl of rice, a map. The motherly protection she gave against predatory men who saw them as nothing more than an object of want, and on one particular occasion I can remember, thunderous, she forced open a door with the help of our beloved buffalo. Saved the girl and quickly did away with the sinner. So yes, she could take on any man. And with bravado. But did Grandma understand what a teary-eyed emotional embrace was? No way. No need, she'd say. But all the same, she is the most well-hugged person I have ever known. Magnanimously waving them off into the sunset, making sure the girl was safely on her way before moving herself. Words were minimal with Grandma. She embraced a saintly silence. Before darkness she would stand in the courtyard trying to receive all things around her.

Was it human kindness or a higher identity? Or was it simply that she loved people? She was a follower of self-sufficiency, something a widow would know best. She often warned me about the day when she might no longer come home. 'Remember that old widow over there?' She pointed. 'The other day she was sat over some spring onions. One minute she was talking. Then the next minute she was gone. I could go the same way. In that same position.'

But I would say, 'That's if the police don't get you first.'

To Grandma, I will always be just a schoolboy. A herd boy. Someone who penned in furry livestock and herded semi-aquatic animals. Day of the Locust meant nothing to her. Nor did Lord Baltimore. Her interests were too abstract to comprehend. She did not seem to be attuned to a world we knew. She tugged at her shawl. She picked at her onions. She said something about a bird in the distance. 'That young girl there,' in reference to Amber. 'Is she staying the night? If she is, she can sleep with you.'

My eyes squinted under the intense glare. 'No, Grandma.'

I explained that Amber was no ordinary person. Amber was no ordinary being. She was first class. Yet to Grandma, these were just details. Her only concerns were people, and cabbages. I don't think I can ever remember seeing Grandma look tired. In fact, I don't believe she had any expressions! She was wedded in 1925 at the age of sixteen to a part-farmer, part-pharmacist, which explains why Mad Uncle is in the occupation he is in today: influenced by the brother-in-law. In those days, Grandma would say, always jabbing with her torpedo right-hand finger, arranged marriages were the norm. Nobody got married any other way. You had no choice. I came into all this too late to know Grandad, but from the mug-shot of him hanging on the wall next to Grandma's I gather he was quite a thin man. Too thin to have stayed vegetarian, and that was what cut his life short. He was only fifty-one when he died. On his deathbed, nutrient deficient, the doctor had suggested force-feeding him a chunk of meat yet even in his semi-conscious state Grandad bellowed that he'd rather drop dead than eat meat. And in a way that was how he accomplished his destiny, as a purist, a man who had turned to Buddhism after marriage and four children, which I didn't know you could do.

So at the ripe early age of fifty-two Grandma was made a widow and found herself left with a daughter and a son who both, within a space of two years, were to marry and move away for ever – and I do believe it was those years after World War Two and the Japanese occupation of HK that she first learned the true meaning of independence. Being her own woman.

By the time I came to her she was sleeping less than five hours a night. Up at the first cock-crow of dawn at 4 a.m., three hours before I'd come tumbling down sixteen purple hollow wooden stairs for school. At four in the morning, every day, seven days a week, with the air still moist and fresh she'd come out of her partitioned room downstairs that had one window, and from upstairs where I slept I would hear her pull open those doors of Genesis, huge and squeaky and a good ten feet high. As you've probably gathered, my bed was upstairs where there were two other beds once slept on by her four children and I took the one by the rear window. This looked more like a prison as there was no glass, only green iron bars that harked far back into sea bandit days which even Grandma wouldn't be able to talk about.

All the houses looked about the same as the next one. All had ceramic roofing, two or three front windows and of course hand-painted murals just below the eaves, depicting mostly wise men and landscapes from a bygone age of poems and maidens. All had a mezzanine upstairs where you could look down over the balustrades to see who and what was coming through the front door. There was a lived-in, used feel to the place, with wellies, buckets and plastic bags.

The only exception was the village headman, who had tiled floors – and what a luxury that was. His house was the best place to stake out during the New Year and shout 'Kung hay fat choy!' because you knew he had a lot of dough. His interior was bright and colourful, unlike ours, which was dark and dull, full of spiders and geckos, and when it rained, leaking beams – and when it wasn't leaking, Grandma would be stamping on the floor as if she was going psycho. Then I'd walk up and realise she'd just squashed a pernicious-looking centipede notorious for 'expressing' a lethal squirt of urine. This was the only time you'd hear her swear or spit – apart from when I made my old joke about following in Grandad's footsteps as a part-time monk.

'*Poyh! Derksat!*' she'd spat, meaning a kind of blasphemy, her right hand raised at me in a mock gesture to strike. 'Don't you dare! I didn't bring you up so you could shave your head and shy away from women!'

I've always wondered what she meant by that, as if it was the worst thing I could do to her. (The other thing that sincerely got her goat was my bed being full of my friends the praying mantises.) The shaving of the head bit was obvious, but the shying away . . . I reckon it could have been in reference to Grandad. Maybe he no longer undressed in front of her or something or had spent more time devoted to his mantras. Who knows? Maybe he'd still be around today, had he not become vegetarian when he entered Buddhism. I think Grandma could tolerate a stone statue but not her husband as an effigy. She was too practical for that.

But then, I've seen her tolerate what I could in no way tolerate. Some of her precious ducklings got strangled by this girl wearing two pigtails who at the time I didn't know was Ar-Fun; she didn't know me and she certainly didn't understand that you cannot squeeze a small duck's neck like a plush doll. It was a complete massacre. At least a dozen fluffy yellow bun-sized dots lay one after the other along the courtyard, a trail of death. But instead of giving the perpetrator (who by now was crying like a sinner) a good hiding, Grandma sat her down on her own knees and fed her 'Rabbit' brand sweets, and both my good self and my mutt, with all our fine humanitarian intentions, got boldly told to 'Clear off!'

I think I've made my final point about Grandma here. People mattered – above all else. But she was never clingy, no Koala bear. The day I leave she'll probably just give me a nod and that'll be it. Like saying, 'OK, you're dismissed.' But I *will* miss her. Miss the fried vermicelli with ham she leaves me after school! The Colonel will miss her, lowering his shotgun and graciously accepting her cabbage and free chicken. He, like Mad Dog, was another 'admirer'. Somehow they seemed to get on well, with some kind of archaic sign language between the two of them. Being a true English gentleman, it was unlikely he'd ever consider it worthwhile placing a sixty-something-year-old woman in jail. Not for aiding Snakes. Not the way she did it, free. He saw no point in further reducing an already decimated population.

Towards the end of May, 1973, the village had been reduced to a mere twenty souls, from a healthy hundred plus. It was part of the chain reaction. Day by day, Mad Dog and his wife would arrive and find one face less in the classroom. Drop a pencil; hear the echo, like a well. Birds swooping through opened windows were no longer noticed. Closure was imminent, as Amber and I continued our idyllic swing towards the process of separation.

THE SYMPTOM

'There's nothing like a fight,' Big Voice mused, excitement on his face. 'You go in, full flow. It keeps you high and it just keeps going that way and never seems to stop. I can remember my first real fight. Yeah . . .' He paused, looking away, breathing in with another, '*Yeah* . . .'

His Brucey head was aimed at heaven, mouth open as usual, relishing, hinging on the thrills and impact of such a memory. 'My first fight was not that long ago. There were these four dudes, probably druggies, who thought they were big-timers. They were not much older than me, not any wiser. They used to come thundering into the restaurant kicking past chairs and tables, swearing, smoking, acting like they owned the place and of course the boss didn't take kindly to that. But what could he do? There's no way you can start trouble in your own place, right? You can't smash up your own place, just like Bruce couldn't start any trouble at the restaurant in *The Way of the Dragon*. So one day the boss gave us thirty dollars each and told us to, "Follow them. Pick a good spot. Teach them a lesson." So we did. We tailed them down a narrow street along the joy-houses, saw them sat out at a rough, on-street diner. It was a "three plus six" diner. They were smoking and talking hot air and eating dog meat. The swines! With one leg up on the stool as usual, still full of themselves. And man, the next few seconds for me was one pure roller-coaster ride. It was my first real fight, you see. And you could say, that's when I got addicted.

'Of course I felt sorry for them after the beating. The dog-eater I pummelled was pleading to me on the ground, hands together, face bloodied, eyes swollen for weeks to come. "*Forgive me, Bro! I'm so sorry! Please forgive me.*" Yeah, maybe I did feel a little sorry for the scum, kneeling down to me like that. I would gladly have knocked him a few more times just for eating dog meat, and for giving me hell back at the restaurant, but it seemed he'd learned his lesson. But it *was* boss! Felt like a million! Three of us against four! You should have seen it. It truly stung! And it was no cowboy showdown, you know, not like the movies. The four of them, sat on long wooden stools around a foldable pink Formica table top, eating. We didn't give them a chance. We stormed in.' He grinned at the memory.

'I smacked the first dude right on the cranium, then gave him a quick left hook. He rolled back over the stool faster than Humpty Dumpty, his head hitting the ground, hard. And it's funny, all that training I got from my dad, from my Kung Fu uncle back in The Big Amber, all that posture and stance and discipline – yet when the moment came for the real thing, I let rip the clumsiest punch you have ever seen! His head just axed forward into his bowl and he got a face full of boiling noodles! I had to control my laughter. It was superbly funny!'

His head was cocked now, and he was laughing almost at the top of his voice, long and hard, slapping his right knee.

'And that was my first fight. Over in less than a minute. Can you believe that? I couldn't.'

I could. Sometimes even cross-eyed liars and losers can have their day.

'But just remember . . .' And then he raised his right finger, the no joking finger. 'By day, he is almost human.' Meaning Millions/Brilliant. 'Almost. He goes to school. He sits through class, except he leaves in a Triumph TR6. But by night he is something else. A Supernatural.' He turned away and rubbed his nose just as the fishing line made the familiar *splosh* on the surface of the pond. 'You need to see him by night to get a true idea of your opponent.'

And so I did. In a way.

The next morning I came downstairs to find Grandma bending down as if she were picking up stones, but when I got closer to where she was, at the animal pen, to my shock they weren't stones but decapitated chicken heads.

Grandma was actually picking up chicken heads!

'WAH!' I exclaimed, the toothbrush almost bouncing out of my own hand, standing legs apart in my pyjamas, mouth still frothing full of toothpaste as I blurted out some words which vaguely resembled: 'What happened?'

'Mongoose,' she replied, and picked up the last dried and bloodied head, dropping it into a plastic bucket.

'Mongoose?'

'Or a wildcat.'

And maybe it was. Maybe there was a simple explanation. I gargled down some water and spat 88 m.p.h. to my left as if I was shooting off more than just toothpaste. I was standing in front of what should have been our animal pen, two chicken sheds and a lemon tree, some kind of harmony, but now it was a war zone. I stopped Grandma to take a peek and yes, the heads were badly torn, as if jaws had grabbed them and thrashed the body around before the head was completely severed, plus the neck skin's condition also suggested it had been torn away like ripped fabric. So Grandma did have a good point – maybe it was a mongoose or a wild cat, or it may even have been a dhole – a skinny feral dog which can sometimes slip into a discarded straw raincoat and go walking around in it, masquerading as a human until you throw a few stones to break the spell. But I wasn't convinced. I mean, how could a simple animal come in through the night and cause so much havoc without us hearing a sound, either from our neighbours or from Echo? I wasn't buying it.

And I wasn't waving at the watchtower. I guess, the real truth was: nothing was OK any more.

THE DIAGNOSIS

They say you can either dance or do Kung Fu. The two disciplines are arguably quite similar. Great martial arts people, Kung Fu masters, often began their life in dance as well as Kung Fu. It's just a matter of choice which way you eventually go. I chose to stay with dance. Or maybe I should say it just happened that way. Three-Eye said he was never too sure which way he would go. As for Big Voice, his choice was unnervingly obvious.

'I know you are a dancer,' he said to me, twirling his knife, 'but sometimes you've got to fight. And that time is now.'

So he began to teach me step-by-step about strategy and about how one responds to assault. Yet it wasn't the same. I couldn't handle a knife the way he could, or make a knife-handle and sheaf from out of an ordinary leather belt, because he was that tricky calibre of a person who copied Bruce Lee's art of fighting on the rooftops of skyscrapers, where in accordance with the rules and conditions the loser must be thrown off the edge by the victor. And because of this element of danger it can be said something 'smart' could be learned from all this, because there was no second chance.

This was how he lived. Fast. Knife-edge. Go to any of the basket-ball pitches in the Western District, wait till it's quiet at about 8 p.m. and you'll see it happen. Two vans drive up and bang, from within them will spring two gangs both armed with knives, choppers, rusty chains, anything as long as it can inflict damage.

He said he'd take me there but I didn't need convincing.

'They'll keep trying to break you,' he warned, a multi-coloured bruise above his left eye caused two days ago at the start of a street fight when he was kicked as he bent down to tie up his lace. My attention focused on this bruise when I said, 'I know.'

I know that every place and every creature has something similar to a backbone, and once that bone is broken, everything falls apart. Everything else can fall away from me – the guiding stars, the compass moths, the taste hanging from trees – but I cannot be broken. The worst they could do is put the knife in me but they won't, because I know, at least I *think* I know, a boy like me is not worth the effort of killing.

'See this? This is the barrel of a canon. And you are standing in front of it. When it fires, it will hit you. That is what you are doing. You are the target. The Loh are the canon.'

There was the old village fort, where the earliest foundation of a village settlement was laid and ironically, the first to be abandoned. Behind the measly walls, doors remain broken, pots smashed and items rearranged as sunlight enters through cracks revealing, more visibly, other forgotten rituals. Wedding palanquins, winnowing machines, drums, gongs, and the old eighteenth-century canon. A canon still aimed at history, towards the sky of 1832, a time of pirates and looters.

I had been looking into its dark barrel, shouting into it, wanting to hear the echo. One of the wise voices had been showing me this. He used to be a robed man who ran a tuckshop round the corner.

'Have you got anywhere to go after all this is over?' he asked me. 'You could go back to England.'

In 1965 Grandma stepped off the back of a distant truck and began a two-mile walk under the noonday sun carrying groceries in one hand and a cradle in the other. She wore a kind of farming hat, like a parasol and was walking passively close to the border which then had only faint demarcations. Her destination a village. A lost corner. Home.

She walked down the usual slow depression with vines and leaves walked over countless times that will always trigger the memory of her first day, as does everything else she passes, her wooden bridal carriage cruising in, shouldered by four men on dusty sunbaked earth, followed by an array of colour and musical people. She was only sixteen. And sad to leave her family, sad to hear her kid brother protest: 'Why are they taking my sister?' and sadder still to hear, 'Hope you live as long as the Great Wall!' She recalled the goodbye ballads that were sung by her childhood friends during her departure from her home village of Crane's Nest fifty odd miles south-east of Tortoise Spring. It was a clear day, the trees were younger, the waters like crystals, seeming like mist now, her life before marriage and before the place named after a tortoise. And today was a clear day. And she could see there was a wedding.

There were about fifty families living in Tortoise Spring in 1965. The population was healthy that year. Over two hundred people moved through the seasons; every small ritual and celebration obediently observed. For instance, the Moon Cake Festival required a colossal balloon, about the size of a house, fuelled by fire. The preparation was intricate. Weeks of construction, ribbing the frame with paper and bamboo, till it was finally launched before a circle of people during mid-September of each year. Where, in phenomenal darkness, you walked the village with nothing more than the glow of a cosy little festive lantern. All that simply to celebrate some cakes.

Normally it would be impolite to leave a wedding, but Grandma had a mission. She needed three things from the city – salt and sugar – things she couldn't grow herself. The other item, a cradle containing an orphan, had been handed to her from out of nowhere by her younger brother, Mad Uncle. 'Don't ask any questions. Just take it and go,' he'd said, waving her away, knowing she couldn't refuse. She was a lonely widow, after all. The child's grip like a vice on her finger, as if he needed her.

I was told the first place I came to touch was school, which at the time had been turned into a kitchen. The high leaves that would have normally sheltered a laughing playground instead sheltered tables of San Miguel beer and lobsters in the school made sacred by a god. For once its tense classroom was transformed. Mad Dog transformed. No longer a stern teacher but a drinker, toasting everyone's good health. But nothing was to prepare me, years later, for the transformation of the summer nights.

CLASSROOM CINEMA

Some time ago I made a short journey during sleep. There were fiery mountains that hovered. I was going somewhere – a wedding at midnight. There was a road laid by lost ancestors, forbidden people behind distorted trees. As the vehicle moved on, shaking my sleeping body, it revealed before my eyes a secret landscape. I found myself very still, unable to ask questions. There were mountains burning around us because of light. I was going to a wedding, but where?

Cinema was like that, especially at midnight. You knew, as you stepped towards school, that it was no longer school. It was something else. The dark room of tables and chairs cocooned by both hanging and fallen leaves where a playground lay carpeted in sand and the odd unclaimed marble were all waiting for the ultimate baptism, an entertainer, carried in some nights not by coincidence but by the hum of Land Rovers. These were immaculately armoured men, who would come to us through the mist, install a projector where Mad Dog took his tea break, as far back as the classroom could go and almost against the wardrobe of books and medals. No prior posters or ads were needed for the event. We would hear rumours in the air. *A Bruce movie tonight.* 'OK.' *The usual place.* 'OK.' But sleep was always more in your mind than cinema. At the end of a long working day, the last place you'd expect to go was back to school.

Classroom cinema was unique. I could watch TV and see Steve Austin trounce some impossible robot, but TV is just a small box. I could walk into a big city cinema and see Steve McQueen almost make it over the Swiss border and almost believe it, even though he didn't. Yet out here I could watch that same movie then walk back into the village silence and believe anything. Continue the magic in my own personal little way

189

undisturbed by anything; I could even imagine making the jump myself.

However the place I'd be desperate to escape from wouldn't be Germany, it'd be The Big Amber, because everybody I'd ever met from there seemed to want to get out. All my aims in the past were to get away from class, the blackboard, the rigid posture adopted for maths. Never once did I look back after the four o'clock bell. Never once considered that I could return there for the possibility of escape.

The show, as advertised, began at midnight and anyone was welcome. Once the movie jumped into life, the night was gone. On the cream wall where the blackboard would have stood in daylight, the transformation was complete. Light, mono music, pictures. Depending on the length of movie there might be an intermission, a moment which gave the audience the chance to remember they were no longer in a desert or a war but a classroom, just a few hundred yards from The Big Amber where, it seemed, no light could penetrate.

I came, and just like everybody else, I was after the spectacular. A new religion. Perhaps even to pick up a few Americanised slang expressions. Perhaps even seeking that hypnotic imbalance not unlike what we experienced in the fields. You tuned in, then tuned into somewhere else. In the end, that was what usually happened. Dream. Hauled away either by Grandma or a face I don't remember as the film rolled its final credits. The audience disbanding at 3 a.m. The very, very late hours of darkness.

Going to a midnight film show was like going to a wedding: you knew beforehand that there would be a union of music, colour and excitement. What you didn't know was whether it was dream or cinema. You could only remember sleep. All happening at the most uncanny time of day.

Classroom cinema came to an end on 2 May, 1973. The last showing was *Pinocchio*. As we sat for this première, something had already changed. Big Voice was no longer his old self. In the past, whenever he saw a mirror or his own reflection against a shop window he would stop and strike his customary Brucey pose. Throw two rapid side punches whilst observing his own reflection, often getting observed by others too, passers-by amused by his antics. Pulling down the pink below his eye perhaps to check his own physical perfection, the way Bruce so comically did in *The Way of the Dragon* – the only film which he starred in, wrote, directed and for which he arranged the fight scenes. According to Big Voice, it was the BEST Bruce Lee movie ever because the character he played was the closest to Bruce the person as you'll ever get. I think they call this sort of thing a Tour De Force. 'Long Live Bruce!' he'd shout. Often timing it and shouting it directly outside Mao's place, just to annoy Mao who we all suspected was the vile poisoner of several dogs. And 'Long Live Bruce' sounded light years better than 'Long live *you know who*.' But Big Voice was doing less of such things these days. Darkness, after all, was his active time. Why should he be here watching a children's film or pretend he was the King of Kung Fu when he could be making fast money? Nothing lasts for ever. Such is wisdom. People move on as well as careers. And Big Voice *was* moving on. Day of the Locust was swelling like a storm cloud on the horizon and he was no longer around the corner. Only in the fields have I seen him running faster than usual more than likely to get away from the police.

'Big Voice, I have been thinking,' I said. 'Do you think one silver bullet will be enough? What if you miss?'

Big Voice averted his eyes from the blue ocean of the screen. Gave a serious look in my direction. 'Do you really think I want to go to prison?'

In movies you kill the werewolf and the story ends. In real life you kill a werewolf and you can also be guilty of killing a man. I'd forgotten about that. In a movie everybody who thought you were mad will in the end thank you and a hero you will be.

I know in the end nobody is going to thank us. There will be no pats on the back and no congratulations. No big handshakes and no big prizes. At least not for me. I wasn't expecting any of that.

THE TRUE MEANING OF REWARD

There is a nameless corner shop at Sheung Shui close to Mad Uncle's. A passing point to the railway and to bigger cities, it has a glass-doored refrigerator inside which there is a pool of cold water chilling at minus twenty odd, filled with great-tasting bottles. A must. I saw Ar-Fun standing next to it. She was staring longingly up at paradise.

I couldn't refuse her.

I gave the old man four cents (equivalent to two bottles of 7UP) and asked for a small tube of Smarties.

'You must love your sister very much.'

I nodded. 'Yes. I do. Thank you.' And walked away.

A reward is not just personal. To see the surprise and elation in someone you love can be a million times more rewarding.

It had become customary for me, after years of humbled financial success, to buy (if Amber was not among us, as her generosity was beyond mine) and open all the team's end-of-the-day drinks – Schweppes's cream soda, Green Spot orange, Welch's purple grape juice. It was there, amidst the heat, the banging trucks and the baking street, the endless kumquats and persimmons and wampees festooned from stall to stall, among the comics of princes and heroes, that Three-Eye first told me about *Great Expectations*.

'In that story,' he intoned, 'a rich girl, out of boredom, befriends a common boy, like you, just to amuse herself. But in reality she doesn't like or think much of him. Better make sure that doesn't happen to you.'

He had been turning through the pages of *Ultra Man*, volume five of 'Battle Against the Astro Beast'.

I assured him I was OK. I was no dreamer. 'She won't break my heart.'

'I wasn't thinking about that. But I guess you'll be OK.'

And maybe I was.

Catching fast lizards is all about reaction time. In the entanglement of ferns, a prized Grass Lizard's tail can look no different from a small poisonous snake's. Once you see a tail, you have to pounce. There is no time to think or judge. The moment you begin to fear being bitten is the moment when you lose the potential to be a great hunter. I have never feared that. But occasionally I did have my doubts – the kind of doubts that had to do with my status. I was a common, coarse boy, like

Big Voice and maybe to a lesser degree, Three-Eye, without title or background. A fact I acknowledged well. A fact *they*, perhaps, at times acknowledged too well. And often, to make myself feel OK, I would turn to Ar-Fun for clues to the map of the emotional heart. When walking past Lane Crawford of Salisbury Road with its Mikimoto pearls, Dior shoes and perfumes it was her preference to link onto Amber and me, her tiny lightweight figure glued in between the two of us as if it was all perfect. The princess and the pauper. It was OK. Status didn't matter.

The streets eternally dressed in Omega, Sony, Sheaffer and pictures of Elaine Sung, winner of Miss Hong Kong 1973, and status didn't matter, just money. Meeting up first at Mad Uncle's then later at the quick noodle bar next to our favourite basketball pitch before making our way into Kowloon and the Street of Singers. Drinking small cans of guava nectar on the train while going 3rd Class. Generally buying anything that came my way.

The question: what to buy a girl who has everything? Pacific pearls? Gold slippers? Time was about all I could give ... and the occasional plastic flower, because sadly the real ones don't stand the test of time, and also I couldn't afford better.

I said I'd take her to Poor Man's Nightclub just off Connaught Road, as mentioned in the 1970 booklet published by the HK and Shangai Bank, but that, of course, wasn't how I actually said it. 'Let me take you to Poor Man's Nightclub!' No. Instead I said, 'Let's go to *Ping Yan Yeah Jung Wui*,' as we say in Cantonese, which I can tell you right now sounded less broke and more ordinary. Not a 'nightclub' as such in the adult sense,

194

with a disco and bright lights etc, but the kind of on-street market place where you could get a whole night's entertainment and food for less than a dollar. Dancing girls and scandalous pretty girls sell chewing-gum for twice the normal selling price while their bare sweet shoulders rub against yours. 'Some sweet-tasting chewing-gum, sir?' 'Got no money.' *'Pah!'* Then they move on, unimpressed.

I remember the first time Big Voice walked me in; it was the dancing and chewing-gum girls that caught my eye, while he got a mouthful after telling them the worst thing you could possibly say, 'I've got no money . . .' There was the old-fashioned music and their birdlike twittering under both moonlight and bulb light. So I guess the 'nightclub' part of the translation wasn't far off. There was constant live music after 8 p.m., and it was thick with people. It was a good place to see how smart city girls hit the evening streets dressed in nothing more than their pyjamas and slippers. Or just get sweet-talked into buying extortionate gum.

By the time I knew Amber, after I had grown a few more inches in height, I found them coming up to me also, or was it Amber they came up to? 'Thank you so much! I hope you enjoy the show, you darlings!' The extortionate chewie (not forgetting), was also the price of admission. But did it taste better than ordinary gum? I think I can safely say 'yes!'

Alternative places to go were Ladder Street and Cat Street where you could rub at the Tang Dynasty versions of the genie in the bottle. 'These are the non-exotic places I hang out,' I'd tell her, as I shouldered her school bag that was always so heavy. Besides her books and pencils, it contained a portable SONY cassette-player weighing a good twenty kilos! So there I'd go, carrying that dainty coloured bag for her, not in anyway up-marketing my status quo – but at least I made it clear I could offer nothing special. Just the simple, costless, priceless things. The wild air, the field that contains just the single bloom of gooseberries, so when you do find the bush after a long thirsty walk, it is like destiny, as if it was meant just for you and nobody else.

'I accept,' Amber smiled, taking my gift with a curtsy and a gentle nod of the head. It was a plastic flower necklace costing a cent from one of the numerous side-street machines at the turn of a handle. 'But of course, as you already know, I prefer things that are living.' This in reference to her ambition to heal, become a doctor. Like Mad Uncle, a man who made a living from healing.

'What? You want to be like me?' he said, eyeing her up and down and gulping tea one hazy summer afternoon. 'Good! When the two of you get it together you can open up a practice. The healer and the herb lover. Perfect! When *are* the two of you getting it together?'

He must have been in good spirits then. And if there's one thing in HK that gets old people going it's matrimonial speculation. They just seem to love it. To this question I routinely replied, 'I don't think her parents would approve.'

'Approve of what?' She turned to me with an inquisitive stare.

As I've already mentioned, I only met her parents once. The conversation, as I recall, was brief – but so was their stay. They were always on business in

196

New York – the reason why Amber, their only child, would probably soon leave the Colony.

'They *will* approve,' said the bearded man who could work miracles, whose ancestry was part-Canadian, part-Scottish, which may explain that bushy European beard he has, talking from his herb alcoves about mankind's balance. 'Where there is the rich there must be the poor. After excessive "rich" food, the tongue must taste the "poor", bad-tasting medicine in order to gain rebalance. The rich and the poor must come together, as the two of you have. Don't you agree?'

And maybe he was right. I should have taken the time to listen. After all, the old-timer had been looking out for me, both body and mind, all my life – so how could he be wrong? Maybe Amber *did* like me more than I'll ever know, the mild-mannered way I helped old ladies across Nathan Road's turbulence, even the ones not so old, always getting a genuine smile. 'You are a good boy, heh?' they'd say, giving me a pat on the head the way I'd pat my dog. 'A good boy.' Maybe even as good as a dog. Why not? It was no big thing to me. I wasn't doing it to impress anyone. I did it because I was taught to do so by Mad Dog.

But like I said, I had no time to listen, or to agree. I gulped down a Yakult (the cheapest drink there was) and made my excuse about preparations, then hurriedly slipped away south through Kee Saw Street.

THE PREPARATION

Just as a ball is vital to a game of football, the basket is vital to our game. Without it you can't store your catch so how can you play? Woven in rattan, 20cm long and 15cm in diameter, with its neck shaped out more like a vase than a basket, it was designed and manufactured for the sole purpose of holding insects. If, say, tomorrow I stopped playing for ever and everybody else along with me, then this object would be phased out altogether. Because who would want such a specific item?

At Ang's, our local rattan hardware shop, I finally obtained two bigger, specially made-to-order baskets, beehive-shaped for maximum carriage. My request was irregular, since their best-selling line was the standard hawking baskets Grandma used for shipping around her vegetables or for carrying new hatchlings.

If this truly was kissing goodbye to a fine lifestyle, then the last thing I wanted was to enter Day of the Locust looking like I was going after red berries. Not when I was up against a Supernatural. But I needn't have worried. I was in good hands. Ang's had done an excellent job, right down to the detail of the bottom tip, just like a beehive. And the saddest part was, there were no more going to be made. Ever.

On leaving the old, arid-smelling premises the elderly rattan man himself wished us, 'the very best of luck.' Near the Ambassador Hotel I got plastic sunglasses, a new pair of plimsolls called 'Sneakers' made by Nike which I'd been saving up months for, but changed my mind about buying a new straw hat. I've this split in my old battered hat, you see. At the brim, just above the left brow. It's a useful split, as I can see through it, aim through it. It is the best hat I've ever had, and I've had it for years. I met Amber when I was wearing this hat. She drew me wearing it. So no way was I about to replace a hat that had had so much history.

Down past Prince Edward Road, Big Voice asked if he could borrow three dollars – it seemed I was always giving him three dollars. He and Three-Eye quickly disappeared round the next turn and I was left with Ar-Fun, once again gazing up at something.

'What is it?' I asked, walking over to see what she was eyeing. It was a set of Rexel coloured pencils. The price was 3 cents. I checked my pockets to ensure I had enough for the fare home, then just as I was about to pay for them, clumsily dropping the coins in the process because of my bad thumb, Amber appeared, the pencils already held in her hand. She passed the gift onto Ar-Fun who even at her tender age will probably remember this for years to come.

'Got what you came for?' she asked me.

'I think so.'

'Ready for the biggest day of your life?'

'I'd better be.'

'Are you sure there's nothing else you need?'

'I'll let you know when I see it.' Staring at her as I said this, till she saw the other meaning to my reply.

On TV there were ads about the villainous 'rubbish monster' and how we all can become like him – a green, spotty T-rex thug. More ads, about what happens if you don't wear a crash helmet on a motorbike: showing you an inter-cut scene with a raw egg breaking with a crunch against a hard rock. Stark realities in a stark world. Yet around the corner at the Royal Cinema was *The Way We Were*, one of three Robert Redford films showing in HK around 12 May 1973. There was *The Sting* at the Majestic, and of course *Butch Cassidy and the*

Sundance Kid at the Princess. I had seen this film about three times, and the more I saw it, the more I felt my nickname was OK; also the more the face of the ace pilot who had said he was my father appeared like Redford.

'A great film,' Amber told me, indicating *The Way We Were*. 'A love story.'

We were walking past it, maybe thinking about seeing it, when Ar-Fun by her own accord stopped by the movie's poster and began an attempt to sketch it.

'You like that?'

Not looking at me, she nodded.

'Five minutes,' I told her. 'Then we must move on. OK?'

And five minutes it was. Yet the finished result was less of a direct copy, more an interpretation. Instead of two people strolling hand-in-hand there were five, and a dog. Not a sandy shore but a Technicolor field.

'Is that supposed to be me?'

There came a positive nod.

'And who is that?' I pointed at the figure standing next to me in the sketch.

'Ahh. That's Amber, I see. She is what? Right. She is holding my hand. I see.'

We smiled.

I stood above Ar-Fun, the way an adult would stand above a small child, looking down onto her two-dimensional world and thinking it should look naive and idealistic, but it wasn't. She tore the picture from her exercise book and handed it to me. I took it. Looked at it for more than a minute. There was a tiny figure of an angel in flight, just above the head of a hunter.

Millions of years back they drew buffalo, deer and mammoths on cave walls, showing what they hunted. In the late twentieth century a young village girl drew locusts and lizards and money, what modern man hunted. In fact, she drew everywhere, on trees as well as caves, finding her canvas as she went which could be anything from a road or a wall or the back cover of my geography book. Her most cynical works were chalked arrows which would point to where she had moved: if you followed them, they would lead you right to her, like a treasure map. Except most people didn't see her that way.

The girl named Ar-Fun came from a small village two miles from Tortoise Spring. She was a mute, communicating through gestures and pictures. I had made up my mind it was my duty to look after her, protect her from this money-hungry climate where few could understand or tolerate a character of her disposition. Perhaps I saw something primordial in her which I felt needed preservation, or even something which reflected myself: someone who came to a place where he or she did not belong yet had somehow made it their home. Though I have to confess, her urge to play rugby with other people's property – melons and cabbages left for collection by the roadside, leaving the melons splattered and cabbages repositioned only later to be discovered by their rightful owners pickled in the local latrines, was something beyond my own power of understanding. That kind of behaviour was part of her own mystery, one very good reason why I felt she needed protection. But of course I can only protect if there is somebody left to protect.

DISAPPEARANCES

At my age, that can happen sometimes. You have no power over personal destiny. No say about the future. One minute you are surrounded and cushioned by a choir of angels, then the next, nothing. Just silent leaves.

When I hadn't seen her for more than a week, I went to her village feeling quite worried. Not knowing the house or her family name, I got no logical reply. 'No such person,' they said. At first I was more confused than angry. 'What do you mean there is no such person?' I showed them three crayoned pictures belonging to her, as evidence of her existence. Three pictures in cinematic order I can never forget. A tortoise. A werewolf, eyes red, sharp teeth dripping with blood. Then in the third picture there was no tortoise, just a green forest.

My desire has always been to be with people. Whether in the village or the city, a field of insects or a field of rice, only by people – and not insects, or my dog, and not by a hundred-dollar note – do I hear my name spoken with clarity.

'*Ay Sundance! What are you doing? Don't want to stay here for ever, do you?*'

In times of tranquillity, such a question would be greeted with a happy: '*Yes, of course I do!*'

However, in times of danger, when there were scents of a tiger or an angry territorial boar, I would hear, '*Don't ask questions. You'd better go now.*' And I listened, and lived.

Those same avuncular voices were now telling me to leave. '*They will get you. No matter what. Where can you hide?*'

But I didn't want to hear all that. I had my ideals. I didn't want to hear there was no Ar-Fun because there was and still is. Couldn't they understand? I believe she will come back. I know she will. I am someone who, as the wise may say, is not yet mortal. I see the world around me as paradise, everlasting. I once saw a mouse come into our rice field to catch insects and small frogs in turn it attracted a snake who'd followed to catch the mouse. We had watched this together with fascination when we should have seen it as a matter of survival. Swimmers and hunters on shallow water moving at frantic speeds. Predators in the blue sky, the grey appearance of hawks and peregrines who arced out from around the lush hills looking for a meal, preferably a chick and striking down at the chosen moment. Sometimes they might catch something while at other times, Echo and I managed to beat them off. I have sat with Ar-Fun, with her innocent round eyes and my exercise book crammed with her drawings. The three of us watching the rice-harvest, the world going by and by.

'What was that you say? Do I love her?'

I remember she held my hand or was it the other way round? It seemed to me I was always holding her small, Barbie-like hand. Her questioning face reminded me of the wind in the trees – wild and unpredictable. Then I placed my locust-scarred palm over her head.

'You can tell me that . . .'

V

Street of Singers

THERE'S A HILL *just south of the village called Peregrine Crest. From this vantage point, I can see my home below. Where I live. How I live. This is the place where I want to take someone, and sitting next to them at the top of the hill, be able to say: 'From here I can show you my world. Look down there.*

'There's the old bicycle man named "Buckets" who is our living, breathing, mobile noodle bar, complete with fish balls, plates, sauces, a built-in paraffin stove and even a stool! He's riding in now, whereas Mad Dog is leaving. The truck is coming to take him home, rolling lazily in through the pulse of banana leaves to collect him, then swinging back out again, heading all the way back through the blue/purple haze towards the city that's now glowing mildly in the distance.

'And it's there . . . In the slow distant glow, just a little further beyond the gaze of a bird's eye, is Mad Uncle's. Ready to close up, I should think. Time also for the tantalising drinks pool of 7UP to close up too, where I can imagine myself yank open a cool drenched bottle against the opener stuck to the fridge's side.

'And beyond this, just a little further in the distance, where my finger can barely pinpoint now, somewhere in between the light and the sea, is the Street of Singers . . .'

HONG LOK STREET, MONG KOK

Whenever I stand on Hong Lok Street round about 6.30 p.m. with all the noise and echo of HK city traffic, it always feels like I am standing among angels. For decades, Hong Lok Street has been that rare place where a man, woman or a child can buy a singing bird from ten dollars to ten thousand, and carry it home almost believing angels can and do exist here on earth, in the form of birds. When you have purchased your desired bird, all you have to do is walk with it, and feed it, preferably on live grasshoppers and, every now and again as a special treat, the odd Grass Lizard – after which your bird will sing a heavenly song for you, so much so that you can believe you're no longer trapped in a tiny flat within an overcrowded, adrenaline-pumped-up city of 3.9 million people but in a much better place. This has prompted the street's (and the Colony's) most famous catch-phrase. If somebody happens to talk too much, a polite alternative to *shut up*, is to say: *'Have you been eating Grass Lizards?'*

Big Voice evidently had eaten lots of Grass Lizards. So much so, in fact, that new phrases had been especially developed for him, like: 'Why don't you have a cup of tea, Big Voice?' or 'I think your mum's on the phone . . .' And to that he always grinned his cheesy grin followed by the slapping of a few arms. The Street of Singers was like a second home to him, just like it was to me and Three-Eye.

Hong Lok Street was the name to remember. I felt good here. I felt wide-awake – 200 per cent. Here were grown men falling in love with birds instead of their wives. Taking walks and going to restaurants with birds instead of people, and thinking this was the coolest *thang* they could do. 'You're so beautiful, you know?' I'd hear them say to their bird, as if it was better than a Rolls or a Rolex – and maybe it was. They even went as far as swearing their bird was more beautiful than beauty pageant winner Miss Hong Kong!

Of course, for any locust hunter, this was *the* place to be; where a freshly caught bag of insects could mean gold. Walk by any musical stand and you would notice grasshoppers and lizards kept in their millions. It was the perfect place to take somebody on a casual day out. Everybody went there, bus drivers, shopowners, farmers, millionaires – all wanting to talk bird. Round another stall and the language could become even more passionate.

'That . . . eye is the best!'

'. . . your mother!'

'You must be . . . blind!'

But it was a bird society, after all. Members met regularly at an outdoor café/club at the end of the street – a club I was part of from 1971 to 1973; I would only have to be within a few paces of its narrow paving for the family connection to be made. People called out my name as I walked past. I was the bird-food hunter. I could get you anything you wanted. Size, colour, season. As long as the advertised price was right. Whereas when Three-Eye walked by, the name of a bird would be called out. And it was he who could get *that*. His association with the place went back much further than mine. It was in his blood. In his thinking.

The quality of a bird can be judged at the time of capture. An infant bird opening its eye for the first time will adapt to what it sees. Caught at the right moment, it will think of humans as parents, turn domestic and consider its world no bigger than a bamboo cage.

Sometime in May, 1972. A tree, somewhere inside Baltimore Forest. After months of tentative stalking, we finally succeed in the harvest of five laughing dove chicks. The doves are a sensitive species which will abandon their eggs once they detect the slightest sign of human interference, even observation. Harvest, naturally, required fresh 'hatchlings' (no more than a week old), and that could only be achieved by patience and observation at a distance.

'Three-Eye,' I said, seeing we were in good spirits, 'do you know that some people think it's cruel to cage birds? They say they should be free in the air. Not caged. Not kept. I was thinking maybe they have a point.'

He stopped walking and turned to me on one of the numerous fields rich with a unique 'hypnotic' herb.

'Act your age,' he muttered.

THE HYPNOTIC HERB

Every place and society has its jokers and poets. And to the Sea of Whispers and the Street of Singers, Three-Eye was a poet, a book person. He always carried one. He steered the course of the fragile evening process into serious exploration. Near a day's end every catch had a name, every slice of grass and light. And with good reason. I believe he was in the process of inventing a potion not a lot of people knew about, not even his mother. It was a concoction of pine gum and *Baeckia* herbs and microscopic buds, and when applied to certain parts of the body, could protect you from bruising physical damage. So far, he had only tested it on his hands, until Big Voice volunteered to try it after again blowing his father's pigeon money or doing some bad deed or other, and went applying it to his nether regions in preparation for pleading guilty.

If you can catch a bird, they call you a 'birdman' or 'bird king'. The common belief was: if you can catch it, you become it. That time I asked Three-Eye if he'd ever considered it cruel to cage birds he told me he couldn't understand why it was so bad. 'I am a man of birds,' he explained, a slur in his voice, always sounding wiser than he looked. 'This is my home. I was born here the way my birds are born inside a cage. We know nothing else. So how can it be cruel?' And I turned, and agreed. America, England, Europe. These meant nothing to us. We were far too attached to whispering fields and singing corridors, just like the birds Three-Eye raised to sell, and once they were sold they were content within their bamboo cage, this home being all they knew.

Neither I nor any of the harvested birds would ever know how to make a living on the outside. And perhaps this kind of thinking reflected HK psychology. We lived in a small space. A coliseum – and we're trapped here, so we'd better make the most of it. And people did. The Bird Master, Mr Twilight, the Council – they made the most of what a small world offered. Back in

211

1952, Hong Lok Street was nothing more than a place with a simple need to survive – you hear stories of hawking goldfish, a buckled-wheel bicycle hanging with birds – until it gradually became what it is today, the Street of Singers – a lifestyle, 365 days a year, 9 a.m. to 8 p.m. where even the New Year is celebrated among the singers from heaven.

'There's no way I can live on the outside,' Three-Eye confessed.

But all the same, our team was disbanding. On 22 May, at 7.50 p.m. from Kai Tak airport, Kowloon, Three-Eye, our angel catcher, vanished into thin air just three weeks before Amber left for New York. His family were emigrating to Holland.

In spite of what he said, he was forced beyond his own will to make it on the outside. You could say he was one of those strange individuals who desire confinement. But I don't think so. To be imprisoned in a place of the heart makes sense. To fall apart the day you realise you can no longer be at the heart, also makes sense.

He kept yelling: 'I don't want to go! Help me, Sundance! I don't want to go!' while his mother, eyes hung with tears also, dragged him screaming through the grit and dust and onto an impatiently waiting truck, herself yelling, 'You have to go, you damned four-eyed kid! You have to go!' pulling at his cheeks, accidentally nudging off the all-important glasses from his crying face as if she hated him, but of course it was the sign of a mother's deep love. I know. I could tell.

'Be good!' she kept reasoning with him. But he wasn't. He was defiant. On the tired and worn road heading out of the village, flanked by the exaggerated gestures of banana trees, he was defiant as ever. And powerless to aid him, I had watched it all. I'd picked up his cracked lenses, finding they had split into two and were completely useless. 'We have to go!' she continued. But he was undeterred. 'No! Leave me alone! I'll go when I am sixteen! You hear me?! *Sixteen!*' His last words. The sporadic fingers reached out. Face wet with rage, sadness, fear. Crushed specs in my hand. All these things. But still, what clever words. '*I'll go when I am sixteen.*' As if he was still bargaining for a locust or a bird. Still a great player, pitching right to the very bitter end. Like saying '*Money is not a problem. . . .*' when I ordered that specially shaped basket at Ang's. He told the old rattan-maker money wasn't a problem as long as '*my pal*' got the exact spec and dimension. Three-Eye could come out with sentences like that. He did it with great style. But there was nothing stylish about him during that chimney-smoked evening. Kicking, screaming, he tried to get away, but without his glasses he was just a blind man groping in a dark alley, stumbling idiotically and going nowhere. He had locked himself in the old wooden lavatory that used burnt ash to cover up the muck and refused to budge. Earlier on he had asked for a personal favour. '*Hide me.*' Such a simple request from a great team player and personal friend who once saved my life, who gifted me with the spectacle of conclusion, the Street of Singers hidden deep in the city jungle. 'No problem,' I said. Thinking it was all part of the evening process. Believing it was just another game. No problem, when I should have really said, 'Goodbye.'

Back here, like me, he was 'somebody'. He had a profession and a trade-name. It all worked beautifully.

213

He was part of a system, a great team, and he had no wish to retire.

Like a magical field in a dream, the sun wanted to set; night was about to fall, but somehow it just hung on. As long as the players hung on, the light would remain. Everything is still possible *as long as you stay*. But if you do tire and leave, walk past this line, tomorrow there will be no game to come back to. No field and no players. This is the nightmare of every player in every game mankind has ever invented. Retire and you die.

'I am the angel catcher.'

'I am the locust hunter.'

In earlier days, our expeditions were rough, unmanaged. More like a race than a hunt. Teams were extempore, nameless. You didn't have to know anything about it or to have passion in order to hunt. You didn't have to know there was a Street of Singers in the city far from Tortoise Spring which fuelled the need to game, without which my life would have been meaningless. However, angel catchers knew all about it. They knew all about the society's geography. 'Take the train and step off at Mong Kok, then hitch the 1314 minibus westward till you see the big 7UP sign,' they told us. So one day back in 1971 Big Voice and I did just that, and eventually we came to a point in the city where it no longer sounded like a city.

At the furthest end of the Street of Singers where it becomes almost labyrinthine, there are performers who have set standards. Move past the crossroad of birdwatchers, north-east, and you find the birds trained like circus acts – tiny wrens that somersault within a minuscule cage. Schoolchildren gather here in numbers.

I once stood there with Amber. I had been showing her mankind's desire to gamble, showing her their fascination for the ferocity of fighting crickets.

Suddenly she said to me, 'Do you think it's possible we can meet back here again in twelve years' time, when we are grown up?' She was looking at me quizzically. I paused.

'That would be nice,' I replied. But of course, I couldn't envisage so far ahead. I was holding her hand, and for me, that was what mattered.

BE OK IF WE ALL LISTENED TO ANGELS. BE OK IF WE DID NOTHING ELSE.

There are only three earthly species any true music-lover needs to know about. First is the Hill Mynah, also known as the 'whirlwind'; its tongue, when surgically 'scraped', is almost human, vocally commanding six words or more. There is the Japanese White Eye, which has infinite sonatas, an explosion of sound, yet is barely visible. And then there is the Hwamei, a thrush, a descendant of Queen Cleopatra or in my opinion, the nearest bloodline to Paradise. All three species live in the present tense, are local and popular, with shimmering qualities unique to their character.

Then there are the other birds that appear like winds, coming and going without warning. They are from all over the world, mostly Africa, Latin America and Australia — bluebirds, sunbirds, hummingbirds with indescribably beautiful expressions.

And then there are the 'birds of rumour' . . . The traders rave about 'extra-terrestrial species' — the Big

Amber species for example, which has to be considered a fable. In 1966, The Big Amber outlawed sparrows; birds there are considered in a different light – they are like mirages and can only be found in books.

I love the evening birds that shouldn't be caught and remain incognito; they remain like air, hanging, calling, telling you about the day's end. A soothing, relaxed sound. A necessity.

'Do you have to go?' I asked.

She was in her cream uniform. Ivory white shirt and an elaborately embroidered school badge.

'When will you be back?'

She twitched her shoulders. Her right hand rose as if to stroke a bird but instead it brushed the fringe from my eyes. 'I honestly don't know,' she said.

Our rendezvous time was usually a Friday, when the city atmosphere bloomed. Her school was only across the harbour, no more than fifteen minutes from the Street of Singers. We used to meet by stall 303, which belonged to the Bird Master, the mild-mannered maker of birdcages. His stall looked about the same as the rest of the street till you came up close and felt its calm, organised veneer. All the time in the world was there. No clock. No flapping of birds. Only old photos in the background of the craftsman himself in younger years, as a trainee, working under the eye of his tutor. When making my way through the fumes of Nathan Road, this is how I would see her, sitting comfortably, knees together, her red bag at one side of her chair. There were three chairs at the stall, three chairs that formed the audience part of his set-up. And each night when the Bird Master closed up, his last act after packing away his craft knives, cleaning his brushes and pulling down the shutters, was to stack away these three very different chairs. One, it seemed, had origins from a high-class restaurant while another was a director's chair. Amber liked the bamboo one. The one more like a throne.

In my mind's eye, I can still see her talking to him. Her hair curled across her forehead, a drink in one hand which later would be in my hand. The Bird Master brushing on varnish to an almost completed cage, his movement mechanical, his eyes now and again staring up at passers-by through the drooped angle of his glasses. On average, from a bamboo pole eight feet long he could create two cages a day. There were seven classic designs. 'When a bird moves house,' he often told me, 'it always prefers the new cage to be identical to the old one. The truth is, if a bird had a choice, no way would it move. Wouldn't you agree?'

But the truth is, he could have been talking about people. And the market was free style, it consisted of all kinds of people, whether an angel or a princess. The Street of Singers has long become used to international riverings. Making my way there, I'd be accompanied by the familiar background shouts. 'Hey, Locust Boy! Looking for your girlfriend? She is over there . . .'

COUNCIL OF THE BIRD PEOPLE

With birds as objects of desire, there is much instant social interaction. People may see somebody with a bird, and desire to hear it sing or talk to the owner of the angel.

Sometime in 1971 I heard about a café where there was all the time in the world, where a man could sit and talk and escape time. The worries of the city were no longer around you, as long as didn't mind the passion of bird talk. From the outside the place looked ordinary enough, chairs and round tables spilling through a communal courtyard, people gathering together after a long day's work. In their dark office suits or a common white vest, depending on profession, they sat down casually with their prized angels and within the small semi-enclosed garden circle blooming with overhung grapevines and honeysuckle just off Reclamation Road, they talked of business, of life, bird baths and tea.

'Name?'
  'Sundance.'
  'How old are you?'
  'Nine.'
  'Have you ever seen a ghost?'
  'No.'
  'Would you be scared?'
  'Don't think so.'

My appointment was at 7.30 p.m., a few minutes before summertime dusk when the rain of traffic seemed almost dampened. Most of the city at this hour was going home. I arrived too early so Amber and I went to the Kwok Wah Wonton Bar, corner of Portland Street, where noodles cost a dollar a bowl. We left five minutes later and made our way into a courtyard cocooned within murky-coloured buildings. In the middle of this courtyard, below a banyan dangling with aerial roots which bestowed upon the tree the Sadhu appearance of long matted hair, seven men were sat around a table. Their birds hung above them. We greeted each of the uncles respectively and they affirmed our presence with a simple tea-drinking nod. I did not know all of them personally, but they seemed to know who I was. They began by asking me my name, and what my intentions were at Day of the Locust. I told them it was quite simply 'to win', but of course winning was never that simple. Almost immediately, like a pebble dropped into a well, they fell silent to my answer, a grave silence.

It is true that cockiness never goes down well in a cocky place. Over-ambitiousness at my age did not ring church bells. I could tell that that was the lesson of the day. I was dismissed soon after. 'You can go now,' they gestured. The birds started to sing again. In orderly fashion we left the fine assembly of shop-fitters and civil servants and bee-keepers and teachers to continue their debate, their voices growing fainter the further away we walked.

'*How much older is the werewolf?*'
'*Older. Much older.*'
'*And the hunter is younger?*'
'*Much younger.*'
'*Sounds bad . . .*'
'*And the werewolf is skilled in martial arts.*'
'*I know.*'
'*So?*'
'*It's still possible. The hunter might win.*'
'*How? Explain.*'
'*Because this is a rare profession where youth has the upper hand. Nine is a prime age. He's at the peak of his profession. There's no way you can get better . . .*'

It was true: at my age pain was not a problem, just a hindrance. I never complained. I could go barefoot and not worry about splinters. I could tolerate heat, sun-burn, dehydration, kickbacks from the sharp, serrated hind legs of a big locust and even Grandma's tongue-lashings afterwards as long as there was the chance to earn and play.

But you had to be more than a bird-owner to have such knowledge and insight into youth. You had to be someone special.

I turned around. And was right. There he was, dark against the goodbye light and polite as usual. The Locustman.

The bird society is in decline. The reason for this is environmental. In order to keep a bird you have to have a balcony, a view. Caged birds must communicate: singing, whether to oneself or across the balcony to another bird is their exercise and only on balconies can they do this. This is a major psychological factor that has kept them alive.

Soon there will be no more balconies. Buildings are growing higher, so high that it has become impractical to feature balconies. Also the dangers of falling plant pots et cetera marked the end of the balcony and bird era.

The Locustman was the first person to foresee this. He foresaw most things – the birth of a child, the makings of a great hunter and the happiness because of good company. For this he used no tricks and no sorcery but logic. 'A village must crumble when there is nobody left to live there.'

He could say those things in a casual way, as if it was destiny.

'Treasure this. The two of you can't be together for ever . . .'

He could say those things.

Sweet as sweet. Your lips are sweet as sweet.
Like a flower against whistling winds.
Like eternal spring . . .

I see her still. Standing there, not too close to the swing
which is rocked by occasional winds. She waits for me,
not stepping on until my arrival as if in some polite
before-dinner gesture or the start of a great journey.
Hands behind her back. Skirt arced outward from her
knees, layered, like wings.

We stand facing each other on the Sacred Swing. As
she pushes down, thrusting me backwards, her head
going below my belly, I look down and can see the
nametag on the back of her dress. It reads *Laura Ashley.*

Our swinging was all part of the same movement: I
would move by truck, a journey of about twenty-five
minutes, to Sheung Shui. Then continue another ninety
minutes by train, across seven sub-tropical towns,
Fanling, Tai Po, a town of noodles and diasporas, to the
white sand beaches of University. Then Shatin, and
finally Mong Kok and the 1314 minibus that dropped
me off by the large 7UP sign. All this was part of the
same rhythm, the same ongoing swinging movement.
All this, even during a typhoon when the whole of
Hong Kong was at a standstill, the streets empty and
the 7UP sign being blown to pieces, part of a personal
need to move towards a divine hand in one single, uni-
fied stroke.

In the Closed Area I was somebody. I could guide you,
make a path for you even when there was no path.

Show you what it's like to stay a night by the river, catch prawns there. Toast them through fire and straw. Watch kingfishers skim above water. I could do those things. Provide antidotes if you touched the wrong plant. Learn wisdom through a tortoise. Produce a radar named Echo, or a trick to divert danger. I had these skills, you understand. They came naturally to me.

But that was only in the village and its calm surroundings. Once in the city, it was a different story.

One day, Amber told me about this amazing new experience.

'What is it?'

She wouldn't say. 'It's something special.'

We eventually sat down to it by Victoria Harbour, between a line of eucalyptus trees and the railway. All light and the silver pulse of the ferry bouncing neatly across the leaves.

'Amazing!'

'You think so?'

'You bet!'

Our opinion of the newly arrived taste, Kentucky Fried Chicken in the summer of 1972.

I think anyone who has been a child can picture it: Amber and me walking the sign-plastered streets hand-in-hand. A boy. A girl. Young. Both different, yet it worked. But it was no big thing, holding a girl's hand. It was natural to me. Belonged in that time and place. Everybody held hands. I can remember Big Voice holding my hand before I knew how to cross a roaring city street of traffic. He was a brother to me, and ever since, hands had always been of special significance.

So holding Amber's delicate palm was the coolest thing to do. And I took the opportunity as often as I could.

Robinson Crusoe, The Secret Garden, The Jungle Book. There was a series of old classics kept at the back of the classroom on high shelves close to where Mad Dog drank tea. These were books he read to us during sleepy Friday afternoons. Books which, thankfully, kept him off the 'swatting of flies'. Making my way to Amber on a Friday evening, my mind could be fresh with anything from *The Lion, the Witch and the Wardrobe* to *Great Expectations*.

And the story of *The Last of the Mohicans*.

We could identify with these stories. We had decided that Big Voice was Chingachook, and Three-Eye was Uncas, his son. I, fittingly, was Hawk-Eye, the adopted son, who knew no mother or father. The basketry that hung diagonally, the V-necked vest helped: we dressed as if we were Mohican Indians. It was important to look the part. Sergeant Peter Beaumont up at the Robin's Nest hill station was so impressed by our manoeuvre, reaching 2500 feet above sea level, which was where the station was perched to patrol border activity, he welcomed us with open arms and a large jug of iced water.

Our thinking was, if we cancelled all thoughts of exhaustion, nothing was impossible; an angel or even a car could be caught (by hand), which was almost true until one evening a TR6 made its way through the checkpoint with Lord Baltimore, only to rapidly disappear into the city lights. That time our determination wasn't enough. And the Locustman was right. We were a vanishing people.

Three-Eye, 22 May. Amber, 12 June. And Chingachook, mid-June or perhaps before? I don't know. What did happen to him? He wasn't supposed to go anywhere – he said that himself. We even took an early haircut in preparation for Day of the Locust, when the electric trimmer actually short-circuited and blew up right beside his left ear and charcoaled half his face which, if you were superstitious, might have spelled a bad omen. But he got this motorbike one day and two nights later rode off into the sunset and was never seen again. It turned out, much later, he had had some kind of accident.

If Big Voice ever had anything to hide (and Lord, he had a lot to hide) then it was his English name. You know in HK a lot of people have English names. It's a cool thing to have and for once, it's free. Big Voice chose the name Steve. Not Bruce, but Steve. And I reckon he was as much a Steve as a Bruce. Definitely cool, clever, not at all a village bumpkin or slow, especially with that old black smoking Triumph Tiger. I was 200 per cent sure he could jump any border as well as Steve McQueen and on a nice day might even make it.

To Big Voice I had said I was courting a bird. And in a way that was true, as to me Amber was almost an angel. 'You're taking a long time making your mind up,' he said to me. Did he know I had been after the impossible? It was very hard to deceive him. He said, 'Winners and losers don't mix,' just as princesses and paupers don't mix. He knew every thought and move we made on and off the field. He even knew about Three-Eye's sad departure before Three-Eye knew of it himself. As for his own sudden departure . . . I wonder, did he know his own destiny in advance?

*   *   *

When he kicked the engine into life that evening,
everything seemed fine. There was the usual call of
laughing doves. He was his regular self. He even used
the old farewell, 'Give me some water,' meaning: Give
me money.

Big Voice never wrote a word. Never read a book.
Perhaps he thought time was too precious for words.
His midnight disappearances and morning reappear-
ances had always made him hard to locate. During
those last days he asked if I'd made up my mind about
which bird I preferred. He was about to ride away. I
was standing still. 'The rich go only with the rich. That
is the law of nature,' he said, stepping onto the
machine, knowing I had a tendency to fantasize, but
knowing also I never much believed it.

I remember he slipped on his white crash helmet,
grinning. And I grinned too. 'Be right behind you,' he
said, confident it was going to stay that way. And there
might have been a sadness in his eyes he didn't want to
reveal, trying to live it out like a Sam song. Lost something you love? Don't worry. You'll survive. You'll
smile. You'll move on. Maybe that was how he got over
Three-Eye. By singing. But I think it was actually a Ben
E. King number he was singing: 'Stand By Me'. Then
with one firm stroke, both of us gave right-armed salutes
at the Union Jack flying 500 yards north of the border.

The road ahead of him was good. The day had been
light with no rain, though there were forecasts of thunder for the next day. He sped down the road and the
world was suddenly warped around him. Noise was
everywhere as he roared past bends, people, small
bridges, pools of light. His chest was low, almost

225

touching the petrol tank, and taking the next turn, he almost hit an oncoming truck. He headed west, then south. He stopped for nothing and nobody – though it was clear from the moment he sped away that he would stop for somebody who was legally a nobody.

It was not yet dark. The pick-up point was the spooky bamboo grove half a mile west of Tak Wuling. It took him about ten minutes to get there. There was the usual change of clothes, and exchange of agreement before the next move, which was 'freedom'. At the checkpoint they dawdled behind a minibus. When his turn came, he held out two ID cards, one with his name clearly printed on it and the other, his brother's. The policeman began the usual questions and Big Voice gave the usual answers. It seemed they were about to be allowed through. The bike engine was still running, the city only a matter of three miles away and visible. Yet five seconds later the bike smashed through the barrier, and he was on the run. Down the highway he sped at maximum throttle, each time looking back to see police vehicles in pursuit, closing in. He pulled up more throttle. The bike shot up, strangely with a wobble. He decided to leave the highway that cuts past Tolo Harbour and swerved into a sharp bend. The bend was not deadly but he lost control all the same. The speeding bike skidded from side to side as he struggled to keep it straight.

After a seventeen-minute pursuit the motorbike and its two passengers, according to the police report, smashed head-on into a side barrier at 60 m.p.h. A problem with the balance, was the official verdict. But the real problem was not the balance. It was both funny and sad, like a Charlie Chaplin movie. The real problem was the passenger. Coming from a land of zero technology, he had never seen a motorbike and never been on one. Never learned you had to lean with the rider during a bend so there is equilibrium. Never even travelled through a landscape so fast, I guess. So they crashed.

But wait. That wasn't supposed to happen. Chingachook wasn't supposed to end that way, was he? In the book his character was immune. Uncas had an excuse because in *The Last of the Mohicans* he did die.

How could this be? Everything was falling apart. We were a team. A team because of a game. And when there is no team, there is no game. Day of the Locust was only a matter of days away and there should have been three of us. Big Voice, Three-Eye and me. There should have been a team. What was happening?

Maybe it was all those fast evenings, made us desire the city and her stars. Looking ahead from our darkness, imagining the experience of being there, people still awake and walking through streets of culinary aroma while silence layered our village. Or maybe the game spoiled Big Voice. All those moments when we had nothing to do with the real world. Not caring about anything. Just us and the flowers and the musical circus. Yes. Maybe Big Voice the Ghost was tempted by reality. The need to move on, move ahead. And one evening with the help of a flying carpet called a motorbike, he did just that.

I loved his overshadowing of all things. His sad apologies to each sold pigeon. The birds were a family to him. I would be asked a question and, true to his character, he would answer on my behalf, shielding me from problems that came my way and in return, be told to mind his own business! He was a communal man.

He taught me how to bury and cook sweet potatoes around a campfire. He kept us close by in the fields almost like flocks in the sky. Still, he was not the kind of person to believe in angels. And I was the kind of character who could walk towards a swing and see it.

'For a meal or two, you would do any kind of work, old king,' he used to sing. 'In the desert once you find water (money) there will be no more pain . . .'

The times I've rescued Amber from snakebites and fires, carrying her from danger with my bare arms, her entire body slung over my shoulders. Bragging afterwards, 'I saved a millionaire's daughter!' But always discreetly, and always to a discerning friend.

'And what was your reward?' he would ask, half grinning.

'What reward?'

'You know, something like money or a kiss.'

'This is reality, Big Voice. Those things don't happen.'

I am the herd boy. I am sentimental – I can't help it. I was used to showing the way to new pastures, fresh fields, navigating dangers so the journey was made safe. I have always carried a responsibility for others. That splinter I took out from under her sole the time we swam half-naked. 'Don't look at the knife,' I said, telling her instead to look at the silver birches. 'Can you see the blue lightning? Can you see the kingfisher? Got it!' Raising my left hand, I showed her the cruel thorn I had extracted.

And maybe she was simply cold, her white marble skin wanting to be close to my body for warmth. Was that what they called a kiss? Face to face as her lips touched me, as my heart missed a beat (but not fully understanding why it did so).

There was the Temple of Ten Thousand Buddhas – 10,000 gold Buddhas stretched in one long endless wall from top to bottom, east to west. It was our last day together and Amber had planned our itinerary. Our first call was the hilltop Temple at Shatin. I already knew of it from Grandma because it was one of Grandad's main hang-outs. And I could understand why. The name *was* awe-inspiring: you went there thinking you were going to be blessed and swallowed by the holiest place on earth. But in actual fact, 98 per cent of the Buddhas were no bigger than a glass of water! But I guess the lure was: if one Buddha wouldn't listen to your prayers then maybe the next one would, or the one after that. Among more than ten thousand, it must surely be possible to find one that would listen. Maybe Amber felt I personally could do with some blessing? Especially one that worked.

We began the climb at two o'clock in the afternoon. I had bunked off school early, or what was left of school, and met her at Shatin station. From there the walk was supposed to be thirty minutes uphill but we didn't arrive until well after three, partly because we made two stops for refreshment. I was dressed in my best today. Not simply an ironed shirt but a brand new one. I had spent the night before polishing my shoes till they shone like diamonds, and the creases Grandma had ironed in my navy-blue shorts were sharp enough to slice through meat.

Amber as usual looked on top of the world. She was in a pink dress, but up close it was more like Champagne. We held hands most of the way and because it was a Monday and fewer people were around, nobody came staring at us with the usual 'Awww, aren't they sweet?' She had hold of my left hand, telling me in her soft Americanised accent that she preferred this hand as it wasn't so scarred by locusts. As I said, we stopped twice. Once for a fruit juice, while the next, higher up, was for tofu dessert. The man bragged that his stuff was made with fresh 'local mountain water'.

'What do you think?' she asked.

'Amazing!' I replied, mouth filled, almost drinking it down.

It seemed the higher we went, the higher the prices of goods escalated and who could blame them? I could see the stallholders waiting for us at certain vantage-points, offering tea, pop and even kites. They sat under a rough shack or a parasol just to make those extra few cents. There were no lifts, roads, cars, so everything had to be hauled up by hand. Carried and piggy-backed all the way up the stone steps which tumbled back into a few hundred feet of glassy-looking rice fields; it was difficult to imagine amidst all that silence that down there lived near enough half a million people. By the time we reached the top, I found myself mildly sweating. The new shirt was sticking to my back, but luckily there was a blessedly cool breeze. I watched Amber remove her 'Hepburn' hat, as she called it, in enjoyment of this breeze, and saw how it made her dress flow and ripple like the village Union Jack.

As we went through the central courtyard in order to reach the main prayer hall I heard something strange and for me, oddly compelling. It was sounding off around us like beehives, like the most comforting rhythm in the world. As if it knew the answer to everything. This glorious sound, like the music of a thousand waves crashing ashore consisted of the monks' mantras, echoing from another part of the temple complex.

At this point, in a shock of recognition I understood immediately why Grandma took my becoming a monk joke so seriously. She knew me well, knew that I was the kind of soul who, if a perfect stranger told me a sad story and asked for a dollar, I'd give it to him. This was something Big Voice would never do because he knew better. So maybe my pacifist mannerisms were frighteningly in tune with the monastic ideals. A shaven-headed Sundance? *No chance.* Grandma was going to have me married off fast and that was that. Maybe, if I hadn't come across Amber then yes, that's how it would have been; me shying away from women and humming as a monk. But at that moment, I was far from shying away from anybody.

Before entering the prayer hall we purchased some incense costing less than a cent a pack, lit them and planted three each at the courtyard's central cauldron.

Once inside, the visual repetition no matter how laughably small, still hit me like an unexpected wave. There was a panorama of golden Buddhas gleaming softly against us through the late afternoon sunlight. I saw maybe six or seven people deep in prayer and could hear snippets of them. One went something like: 'Dear Buddha, This is the number of the horse I am betting on tomorrow . . . 198. Do you hear? 198. If it turns out a winner I will bring you a roast piglet.' Then another: 'I know my wife is seeing somebody. Tell me what to do. Have I been working too much and not paying her

231

enough attention? Or does she know I am seeing some-body else myself?'

I turned away, unimpressed. Then took my turn, wondering would I be any less impressive? We both said our own prayers. Mine, obviously, consisted of: 'I just hope we can make it through Thursday the twenty-first', the 'we' meaning Big Voice and me. For we would be the only ones left that day. I didn't know at the time that he too would soon disappear.

Meanwhile, Amber, her eyes closed yet aimed at heaven, said something ending with, '. . . in twelve years' time.' And that was all I heard. But I was certain that at least one of the ten thousand Buddhas must have been paying attention.

After prayer we descended quickly and I remember counting more than four hundred steps. Back in town we came across Lung Wah, the roast pigeon specialist where Big Voice had made several unsuccessful attempts at finding a client, but of course his pigeons weren't twenty-five days young, which is the standard require-ment of an establishment famed throughout HK, so famed that Rolls-Royces parked there on a daily basis. Out of the two thousand pigeons roasted daily you had the choice of oyster sauce, lemon sauce, wine sauce, soya sauce and baked in salt, but we chose the old classic, roasted. Though at ten dollars a shot, it was no bargain.

Amber said, 'This evening is courtesy of me.' And wasn't it always?

Because I was broke, it was always her treat, always her paying the bill for food, for drinks, and me saying, 'Thanks,' and her replying, 'Avec plaisir.'

Today, more than ever it was 'on her' because it was our last day together, perhaps for ever. At my age, when

232

you wave goodbye to someone, your future is in the hands of uncertainty. Growing up moves you on and you go with the flow. So many things are lost. Memories, things said, addresses and promises. Her future was bright – and mine? I just couldn't tell. I was learning to live for the moment. As now. Having fun, enjoying each other's chemistry not knowing it was chemistry. Not knowing that the day after I would miss her like a warm jumper in winter. Not yet, though. Not now. Not while we were having such a smashing time.

THE ALL-INTERNATIONAL SMILE

We were in Ladies Street, north of Fa Yeun Street, the most colourful street I have ever seen. It was the place of international flowers. The orchid named Michelia we had plenty of for free back at the village, yet here the asking price was one cent. But fair's fair, the blossoms were neatly wrapped in between two leaves and were way better for your health and pocket than Chanel No.5. Amber was taking me through these places, hotel rooms she had stayed in at $132 a night, guiding me the way I guided a herd or the way Echo would guide me home through darkness. Coming up to me by the silk dressmaker with a Dairy Farm ice lolly. Then ten minutes later, another Dairy Farm ice lolly, as if from out of thin air. She seemed a different person then, no longer dependent on the herd boy. In fact, the herd boy was powerless. Instead of him leading the way it was now her.

She led. And ordinary things, bland city events that I wouldn't normally have noticed or had the time to notice, because of her were given meaning, tasted sweeter, looked affordable. A soya dessert plucked at the run-down Chungking Mansions was free of the usual ubiquitous germs. A street cafeteria serving guava juice seemed cosy. A simple Star Ferry boat-ride sparkled. Things crystallised. Time was erased. She could do these miraculous things – sterilise a spoon or a chopstick before we ate. In the city that's how it was with Amber. There was real, ultra-refined 'Madonna' courtesy.

The all-international smile.

'I would like you to meet Aunty Do Do and Uncle Sammo.' An old couple she knew. And she knew many. She was quite proud to tell them who I was. 'A locust hunter.' To that, there was usually a smile, a pat across the back as we watched their myna bird hung in its bamboo cage above low sunlight near the shop-front. The soft evening hum of street and traffic was around us. For a time I was something of a celebrity. This was the only city in the world where you can catch grass-hoppers and be considered a hero.

She said her flight was the next morning at 7.50 p.m.

I tried to smile.

How often through the history of exploration can you claim the right to a discovery? Ownership, I mean. Of a new species. A new name. A new smile. How does a smile become a smile? Or a smile become a lullaby? I don't know. 'You just have to come tomorrow,' I kept saying, as if it was a matter of life and death. And yes, most of the time she did come. And if she didn't show up, I would make some excuse for her. Amber was an angel, and as an angel she needed to fly, occasionally. It was in her nature. If you truly love someone you have to set them free – a gesture Three-Eye could never understand, or simply didn't want to. His love was possessive, based upon dependency – the reason why I never caged birds.

'Angels fly away, but they come back.'

But she wasn't coming back. And I wasn't staying. After 21 June, I might not even have a future. In twelve years' time we'd meet again, she had said, and reassured me with her haloed look some thirty storeys high on the roof of the Mandarin Hotel, above all the other illuminated halos of Hong Kong and its midnight harbour. Her bright-eyed haloed look after all we'd been through – twelve months and thirteen days, including today, the memory of a perfect day. The temple, the streets, the dinner at eight where she almost told me everything about herself, and where I finally understood why she had been crying over me that day on Temple Street when I was fresh with bruises.

Like most parents of an only child, Amber's mother and father wanted to protect her, to shield their child from terror. But in reality, this often does them more harm than good. I know. If it wasn't for something that happened to Amber, I reckon she'd be just another spoiled little rich girl.

In an attempt to cheer me up she had told me we were going to have abalone that evening. 'At the Mandarin Hotel.'

'What?' I exclaimed, mouth open. 'You mean *the* Mandarin Hotel? The famous Mandarin where Bruce had lunch?'

She had whispered this name into my ear, her breath

against my neck. A name which, if anybody else had said it, would surely have given me the shakes. *The Mandarin Hotel is a hotel in the top class. Its general aura of restrained luxury and good taste is present in every part of the building, not least in its restaurants.* And not least in its prices. A single room cost between 78 to 132 dollars, which is a whole month's wage for most people. In other words, the Mandarin is a place you don't want to bother with unless you have a fat wallet. You could tell it was a fancy place because the waiters and waitresses daren't look at you. So at 8 p.m., in the Mandarin Hotel, on the twenty-fifth floor at the Harbour View Restaurant, the abalones came steamed, dressed simply in soya sauce and spring onions.

'*Mmmm,*' she sighed, taking the first bite. Then asking me, 'Have you ever had abalone before?' Asking this while sat across from me on what looked like a football pitch of a table.

'Only dried or in tins,' I replied, and politely sniggered, looking around myself at all the other well-dressed people while straightening my own collar. If a fortune-teller had predicted I'd be sat eating expensive abalone courtesy of a millionaire's daughter twelve months ago, I'd have told him where to go. And expensive it was – $30 a piece.

'WAH!' I cried, shocked at the price, almost jumping out of my chair and causing everybody around the room to turn in my direction, the waiters with their bow ties and the waitresses in cheongsams, the whole harbour view in sunset, in fact. All except Amber, who wore this bemused look. 'If Big Voice was here he'd hit the roof!' I whispered, now leaning forward. And I didn't mean with his fist or a flying kick. But it was our last night, after all, so what was wrong with a little self-indulgence?

Amber may have been a princess and me a pauper, but we did have something in common. I told you about her upbringing in India, but I never told you where she lived. It was a village called Nataka, five miles outside Pondicherry. A small village painted in cows and hills and birds not unlike Tortoise Spring. There was even a photo she had, showing her with a dog, quite like my dog except it was smaller and white. She was kneeling a foot or two higher than the squatted pooch. Smiling a bright smile even then.

Was this the reason why she preferred coming to a place like Tortoise Spring? It certainly gave me food for thought.

At 10 p.m. with the piano playing and a dessert called *zabaglione al marsala* she announced, 'My dog died to save my life.'

'Yes?' I leaned back, looking surprised, wanting to hear more.

She eventually told me the whole story on the roof of the hotel, below its famously gargantuan neon sign *The Mandarin*, so bright behind us it was like the glow of eleven moons. We had sneaked up to where she told me there used to be a swimming pool, but now it was a landing pad for helicopters. In the occasional breeze drifting in from the night harbour, it was coming up close to twelve midnight and all there was between us and what definitely has to be a massive yet mesmerising drop was this four-foot metal railing. We dared not look down.

'I had been asleep for about half an hour,' she began, her voice descending to a near whisper. Telling me in great detail, right down to what she had eaten that evening, what she had said during a long-distance phone call with her parents who were as usual, away. What books she'd been reading before going to bed and what gods (Ganesh and Hanuman) lay at her bedside table. Even what the room temperature was – a comfortable air-conditioned 21 degrees Celsius. She remembers all this clearly before it happened.

'The barking began sometime past eleven . . .'

At first, she didn't think it could be her dog because he was so well-behaved. But then she recognised the pitch – it came from a small dog, and there weren't that many small dogs around these parts that sounded like that. That was when she got out of bed and came downstairs into the main living room, into the presence of two strangers she had never seen before and no doubt will never forget. 'I remember the one with the damask hood,' she slowly said, her eyes miles away in the distance. 'I remember him the most because he was the one who scared me and tried to put me in a sack. Yes, he did. This was the man my dog seized and would not let go.'

Her little white dog had chewed through his own rope which restrained him and dutifully made his way back into the house to face the intruders, who turned out to be, in actual fact, kidnappers.

'The police reckoned their intention was ransom. A lot of people knew who my father was. They thought by kidnapping me they could get money.'

'But how did they get in?' I asked. 'Didn't you have security?'

'Yes. We had security.' And she described that in detail also.

I used to think the HK rich had good security, but in India, they went one step better. Walls were higher, barbed wire was sharper, there were more guard dogs and electrical voltages were trebled. Yet these men had poisoned the three main guard dogs and just strolled in. There was apparently an insider at work who let them in – somebody the family had recently employed. Amber's pet dog was spared, possibly because they figured it was too small to be a threat or maybe the dog was too clever to eat their fetid meat. In the end though, all three members of the gang were caught and punished for attempted kidnap and murder.

'I don't hate them,' she kept saying, but maybe she did. I've heard people say they're not this or that, but in truth they are. Yet somehow, the tremble in her voice convinced me she was telling the truth.

'My father told me the dog was special. Bred during the time of Buddha to safeguard the royal family and particularly good with children, but also loyal unto death . . .' She paused. And this was the part of the story she found difficult to tell. Found it difficult to breathe and talk at the same time. Her head within the halo of blue light, she turned to me and looked directly into my eyes.

'He was a very brave dog, Sundance. You would have liked him. Really, you would have. He thought I was his. He was proud I was his. He thought that man was about to harm me so he sank his jaws deep into the back of his leg. I've never seen a dog do that before, have you?' Yes, I had. Many times. Got the scars to prove it. 'A grown man scream with such terror?' No, not yet. 'But the thief got hold of this object.' She didn't describe what the object was. All I know is that it was

239

heavy, and blunt. 'How many times was he hit? Maybe twenty, maybe more. I don't know. I couldn't bear to watch. Blood was everywhere, over his eyes, nose, yet he still held on. No one came to our aid. But my dog held on . . .'

By now I could see the tears come like petals, one after the other, and no longer did I care whether they tasted sweet or smelled like perfume. These were genuine tears, and they just kept coming. It was the third and final time I would see Amber cry.

'In the end when the police came they had to pry open my dog's jaws from the thief. I could only watch as he lay on his right side, dying. The left eye was unrecognisable. Only the right eye moved. He even managed to wag his tail, but only slightly, knowing it was me . . .' She stopped talking for a full minute after this, her face wet and gleaming like a mirror, the whole of Victoria Harbour seeming to flow off her apple-shaped cheeks. At this point I wasn't too bothered any more about hearing the rest of the story, unsure whether I should console her or whether I should even try. Pets are a touchy subject-matter and in some cases people tend to keep it to themselves and prefer it that way. But she came round again, as I knew she would. She was a tough cookie.

'I watched him die, Sundance, his once lovely white body now stained in dried blood. He was suffering with every breath and about to die all because of me. I don't think I've ever felt more sad in my entire life. I crouched down next to him, touched him and after an hour, felt his final breath slowly fade away. He died peacefully at my father's house on January the seventeenth, at precisely twelve midnight. And you know what the saddest thing is? We never even had a name for him . . . Isn't that terrible?'

Her head was against my shoulder now. I held onto her, my shirt once again soaked with her tears. 'Yes.' I nodded, knowing she was right. No pet should die without a name. Not unless they didn't mean anything to you. And they almost always do.

I know in India they cremate elephants and monkeys like they would cremate a human because they believe they are the living embodiments of the gods Ganesha and Hanuman, bestowing on them the honour worthy of a living god. And through Amber's insistence, her dog received the same honour. On the actual day of cremation she told me she honestly saw cows cry. As the strange floral cortège moved through the village in the direction of the river she saw white sacred Hindu cows with wet shiny eyes.

'I swear to God that's what I saw.'

I said I believed her. I always did.

Our heads were together; we were leaning against one another like two converged classical Greek stone columns. Not far off from a good romantic movie poster or a novel, I guess. But at that moment it didn't occur to me that we were in any way looking romantic.

I wanted to say, 'He died so you could live.' To say, 'I'd do the same.' Say her name given at birth. A name meaning 'Majestic Cloud'. But I couldn't. It would sound too corny.

An hour later at Fragrant Garden Boulevard gateway, with the stone-faced gateman about to open up, we finally said goodbye.

'So, *will* you?' And to this I said OK. 'Sure.' Adding

that I'd prefer to meet back in the village, if that was in any way possible. Back at the Sacred Swing where things made sense. In twelve years' time. In the place where a hunter's life can remain fossilised.

'Then I guess this is it.'

'That's right.'

She came up, placed both hands on my shoulders and awarded me a kiss on the left cheek. 'You're going to be OK.'

'I will be OK.'

Then she pulled away, but not before unravelling something from her tiny dress pocket.

'Here,' she said, and gave it to me. It was a watch.

'For me?'

'Yes. I think you'll find it useful.'

It was a Mickey Mouse analogue watch. It was beautiful. I didn't know what to say.

'Take care, Sundance.'

'You too, Amber.'

She turned to face the dry night and was about to walk away.

'Amber,' I said, one last time, awkwardly moving forward, placing something into her small hand. A flower. A gift. A Michelia orchid. 'So you won't forget . . .'

How was this possible? To separate, say goodbye. The end. How could it make sense? We were together, holding hands and crossing the crystal stream at the back of the school, rich with sand clams and prawns. Prawns that could easily be caught, once you understood they can only swim in reverse. I had taken her on my bicycle through the menacing spectacle of the Locust Hall of

242

Fame, and to places whose names I don't know and on mountains I don't remember, where the only thing I did recognise was the deep-valley howls of the Koel bird. I even took her through that notoriously spooky detour past the tree and rock deity guarded sometimes by the slouched presence of a giant python who fears no human and no firecrackers, where she anxiously pulled me back, asked if I believed in the old legend and I said, 'There is no way a big snake can be the reincarnation of a saint.'

You fall in love because of history. I had known her. Swung with her. Danced with her. There was a past. A book written somewhere.

It is only human to become attached, whether to something inanimate or animate. One gets used to collecting both flowers and people. As a herd boy/locust hunter, I had the perfect excuse. It's what I do. After a successful game, we used to celebrate, Big Voice, out of financial joy, giving me the thumbs-up and encouraging me with words like: 'Good boy! You're doing good! The best!' Words which mattered to a boy like me. Shaking hands with the cynical Locustman. Three-Eye's talking, laughing mynah bird. The cheers that erupted around me. A tremendous prize because of five lizards. We were always together in celebrating these successes. We were a team. Could life go on without this? Would the world still turn?

It shouldn't have ended this way.

But it did.

AT 7.27 pm. LAST-MINUTE DASH.

I found myself doing hurdles past traffic and minibuses to arrive at the great open coliseum that airports are, past the Kentucky Fried Chicken stall and the wall of magazines, in my newly pressed shorts and shirt. But no matter where I looked I couldn't see her. I edged my way past hips and arms to the far end and asked someone at one of the desks, only to be told that the 19.50 flight to New York was in the process of departing.

'Are you a relative of the passenger? What is your name? Is it urgent? I can contact the plane if it is urgent.'

Did she? Did the well-dressed lady at the kiosk call the plane? Did I give her the right answer? Did Amber wave from the window of the Pan Am? Was that her marble-white hand? The guardian angel who flew away. The soothing fabric that fell across me when the swing swung forward.

I still don't know. Don't know if that did happen or not.

For a long time I've done nothing but sit here, staring at my Mickey Mouse watch or at the ghostly cream windows or up at the old classroom fans no longer spinning shakily above me. It feels like days, months, that I have sat here, months since my dog has sat, Sphinx-like, patiently waiting for me just beyond the green school gate. Perhaps he has been guarding me, protecting me from any more thumb-breaking assaults while he snaps at a few flies. Yes, it is a pretty stupid place to be after all that's happened. But I don't care. I am too numb to be afraid. The desks gleam like

244

beetle-shells now and again in the soft thumb-print visitation of sunlight. I am sitting here all by myself and writing what you are now reading, which I hope hasn't wasted too much of your time. I hope that it has somehow made sense. I have tried to tell you something about myself and how birds made a real difference to my life.

A few seconds ago, a thought drifted by like a sweet-wrapper down noisy rapids, a thought I know Big Voice would object to 100 per cent because it would insult his intelligence as well as our brotherhood. The thought was: what if we had never challenged the Supernaturals? What if we had just ignored the terrible theft of Lord Baltimore and continued along the path of our childhood? Would we all still be the same? Just like before, as we had been in the field? Three-Eye's hand on my left shoulder, leaning in to admire that king of a Bombay locust I just caught, a locust so humongous it flew like a bird. Or to a lesser extent, would Amber and I still have strolled hand-in-hand through the Street of Singers, prompting onlookers to smile and make remarks like, 'You two were made for each other!' Or to an even lesser extent, would she sit, skirt over her tanned knees, in the shade and petals, listening to my futile story about searching for a father, me telling it whimsically, expecting her to at least find it funny – but she found it nothing of the sort. Instead she leaned forward, placed her hand on top of mine and looked up at me, then said, 'You are so, so sweet!'

Did Supernaturals end all that with their paws at the throat of our destiny? Did Three-Eye have to emigrate like that? Screaming and totally out of his fine character? The rice business wasn't doing all that badly, it was making money, or was it because his father was seeking treatment abroad for his blindness? Amber didn't need to go to the US either. She could have studied here in Hong Kong like the thousands of others. She didn't have to leave before 21 June, and with the money her folks had, she could have easily returned anytime, so why go now? Why were none of my team around me any more? Why couldn't Big Voice do a Steve McQueen? Was going against the Supernaturals that total? That fatal? Could they have the power to do all this because we had defied them? So many questions, but no answers. Not a single one.

The school has been closed for more than two weeks now. The clock dead ahead on the wall, the one that was always on time, has finally stopped working. At 10.43 a.m. the smooth almost inaudible click just came to a halt, the seconds hand forever pointing at twenty-two. At 10.43 a.m. and 22 seconds, power was cut to Tortoise Spring school for ever. And ever. So now, as Amber had predicted, I am relying purely on her Mickey Mouse watch. It has become 'useful' after all.

I began my memoir in pieces. I began writing in bandages, slowly and painfully, not chronologically because I had not planned on writing anything at all. But everyone's gone, and that includes Mad Uncle. Suddenly he just wasn't there any more; he was no longer sat at the shop sipping his tea and mumbling in his chuckling, pipe-smoker's voice. The biggest day in my life is marching closer, and I don't mean my wedding day; it is just a few hours away, in fact too close for comfort and I need to talk to somebody badly but there is nobody around. *Nobody*.

The time now is 3.54 p.m. I am three hours and

thirty-six minutes away from the starting line of Day of the Locust. And what am I doing? I am falling to pieces. That is my problem. I feel I've been tricked into a bad set-up; even if that isn't so, the truth of the matter still stands: I *am* the only one left and I have to decide whether or not to cross the old wreck of a bridge knowing very well that halfway over, it's all going to crumble and fall away right under me.

So what am I going to do? What *can* I do? Besides kneeling down to pray by the Sacred Swing.

In the old days when I got scared or was in pain I used to cuddle up to Big Voice or Grandma for comfort. No matter who you are, as a human being you need comforting. I still felt like cuddling up to Grandma, who could quite possibly take on any werewolf and win. But that, of course, would be too easy. One WALLOP from her mighty right hand would be enough to smack down the Great Wall of China, let alone a Supernatural.

Yes, I felt like cuddling up to Grandma, and longed for Big Voice's support, but now as I am, at my age, it would be the laugh of the entire village.

It would not make Big Voice the Ghost proud.

I am running at full speed, my arms and legs moving in a dazzling display of co-ordination and agility. I am running with Big Voice. We are trying to outrun the oncoming storm, the dark monsoon rain that's about to catch us up. We can see it behind us in the distance falling like arrows, blanketing the mountains like a huge bat as it pursues us. We are five miles from our point of destination when this dark bat swamps us. Lead-weight rain and beastly heart-jabbing thunder and lightning explode like a billion stereos going off around us all at once. Shockwave after shockwave. Now suddenly, the road we're running on has turned into a river of bright yellow mud; and water is bursting down the slopes, washing away anything in its path. I am drenched. All the weight of water in my hair and clothes and skin is making it impossible to move. I don't feel I am getting anywhere at all. Thunder is in our path, its explosion much louder now, penetrating right down through my bowels and down to my hurting naked feet. My heart is thumping like never before. This stops me. I am tired. I start to cry. I see Big Voice's running body leave me behind. I shout out to him, 'I am scared, Big Voice!' Standing under a huddle of blistering wet banana leaves I am calling out to him like a bird in its nest. My entire body is shaking, my shoulders are hunched. 'I can't go on . . .' I want to stay, I tell him, and wait for the storm to pass. This feeble explanation, of course, clearly disgusts the Bruce Lee fan. 'Come on!' he shouts, his right hand beckoning, coming back for me through the eddy. As he grabs me, another fork of lightning smacks down less than twenty feet away. We both duck. It was too close for comfort. 'Sundance!' He tugs at me, annoyed, water pouring from his sharp face like a jug. 'Listen to me! Stop now and the lightning will get you – understand? You can't stay here! The monster will get you! Come on!'

I look at him hard. I look at him like he is going to kill me.

After that I flick up like a steel ball and bolt right out of it. Don't know where the extra energy comes from, but come it does and I run all five remaining Olympian miles non-stop till I finally I am home.

To this day, I have no idea how I gathered the strength to complete that run, to keep up with Big Voice's absurd but totally appropriate version of 'Singin' in the rain', screaming it to the point where there was actual steam sizzling out of my body. Every millimetre of my muscles felt used, streamlined, a Rolls-Royce Merlin engine performing at 100 per cent. It was one of the most awesome and unbelievably exhilarating runs I've ever had in my life.

I know I can still do that. I know I can still pull it off. Even without Big Voice I know I can.

In the next five minutes, this is what I think I am going to do.

I am going to leave school. Grab a quick bite of instant noodles and maybe a banana. Give Grandma a hand with the chores. Then I am going to get washed, get changed, keep my concentration, not think about anything else, just PRAY, then leave the house at seven and bike it calmly past the eerie Locust Hall of Fame at 7.15, and not a minute early or a minute late. I'll see today through a hallway of stone or see blinding stars. I'll see today through a hallway of people or no people. I'll see it all or be dwarfed by it all. The thousands upon thousands of hips and thighs will dwarf a pint-sized me and I'll be dwarfed even further still by (who else?) werewolves. At the end of this human hallway there will be judges and werewolves – big bad ones, so bad I can't tell you, but they make me tremble. And today, more than any other day I am trembling, as if to a Dracula movie, because today will probably be theirs (whether this dancing boy turns up or not). The man of the hour, king of territoriality, born-to-win, stone-eyed 'Millions/Brilliant' will probably keep up the family honour and turn out the winning horse. Because it's *his* year, right? 1973, Year of the Ox. This is *his* year and anything less would be downright blasphemous, against the laws of astrology.

Yet still . . . I will be there. I *will*. Why? Because I do not wish my neighbours to spread any more unruly rumours about me. '*How incompetent!*' I can already hear them jeer. '*When he was a baby and had all the chance in the world to crawl away on all fours from an impending house fire, he didn't. Now, almost a man, what does he do? He crawls away from an oncoming fight like a petrified animal, when he should be standing like a man!*'

I am not about to put up with another undeserving description of my 'Upright' self. Let alone, further drag Grandma's divine reputation down the drain.

At the chalked starting line of Day of the Locust, *this* is what I must remember.

1. Stand firm. So rock-solid firm I cannot tell you how much. Horse's rear end firm. Grandma's spring melons firm. At least firm enough to stare down at the field that's at least two thousand yards in length – nearly two miles long before it hits a noisy river.

2. Look calm, stay calm, and never be chicken, not phased by all the festive noise and the multi-coloured wind-blown banners and people chewing on giblets and cheap snacks. Remember, nobody will give a peanut or pay any attention to a shrimp walking in, walking up. I will stand upright at my mark. I have ripped baggy shorts and skinny arms, but this is not a fashion show, nor is it Mr Universe. So do not worry. Be calm.

3. Be cool, dowse my entire body with water. For the field, a field thick with tall herbs, both beneficial

and poisonous, will soon burn. Once this happens, the air will be hallucinogenic, and the chances of my head becoming hippie 'high' will be great. There is the chance too of crying eyes due to acid-stinging smoke. The herbs are tinder dry and they *will* burn, like hell, as according to the rules and conditions of the day. The field of incense will burn and billow angrily right behind me and the other forty or so participants at precisely 7.30 p.m. and only water (and Bruce's thinking), will stop *me* from burning.

4. Do not flap feathers. Repeat, do not! Not this time, and imperatively not in the face of 'Millions/ Brilliant'. By showing fear, you will have fallen into his tyrannical grasp all too easily. Do not be perturbed by his sharky 172cm high physique glaring down at you. You are not a tadpole.

5. 'You should not consider your enemy,' as Big Voice will no doubt advise. 'Do not consider his exist-ence. All focus must be on your optimum athletic performance,' which is:

6. To catch as many grasshoppers as humanly pos-sible. For they will be pouring out of my shorts. I will have a cloak made of them. A hat that appears alive. Think of the buckets, truckloads you will have, and never think peanuts.

7. Remember stealth, technique. Use both hands. Double swipes, double slings, slams, dunks. My arms must be, will be, like a water-wheel scooping

up grasshoppers and lizards with so many revolu-tions-per-minute fury that afterwards, the whole field will have the appearance of a freshly lawn-mowered English garden.

8. Keep in mind Mad Uncle's wisdom: 'We can be cretins. We can be pigs, dogs, dumb and watered down-and-out-beggars. Me. You. We can be that. But not *him*, not "Millions/Brilliant". You can turn up, if you don't win, nothing happens. But at least you would be remembered as a MAN and not a worm. At least you WALKED. At least you showed your face.'

9. At least show my face. *Right*. At least let the world know. *Yes*. I have to at least turn up so I can stand at the grassy starting line looking fine and com-posed. In other words my mind and body needs to be tuned into myth, so inhumanly tuned to crys-tal-clear waters so as to concentrate on nothing else but the Sea of Whispers. Give it my best shot when the gun shouts *bang!* at 7.30.

10. I will be late for tea tonight. Remember to tell Grandma.

Anyhow, that's my list. This is what I am going to do: I shall keep believing I am still in that storm. Still run-ning with Big Voice. Still unstoppable. I can do that, I know I can, even though my knees and hands are start-ing to wobble. It is not fear – not the fear that I could die, get slain like a wild animal – it's just nerves. I'll be fine once I get into the swing of things. I have this promise to keep, you see. I gave my word. And I have to prove once and for all that my 'Uprightness' was an evolutionary act of intellect and not bull-stubbornness. The odds are massive against me, I know. The Day of the Locust mythology is too big to even think about. And HK is no fairytale place. It is harsh, hot, punishing, with beggars everywhere. How many fairytale endings have you heard from this place or have I?

My plan had been to show this memoir to Mad Dog once I got it finished – that is of course, with due respect to my teacher, after I had omitted 'Mad Dog' and replaced it with 'Mr Wong' in all the right places, in the hope that he might go over it for me, edit it, so to speak. So he could understand how my mind worked, see that I was more than just an insect catcher/cow herder. So that he would remember what I was all about before I got *hammered*. And for that reason alone, I have omitted all forms of swearing and violence in this story, knowing well that he would object and probably wouldn't even look at it.

I've been telling it straight, how it happened. It's my autobiography. My life, so far . . . and I'd never thought I could have written it down so fast, three full exercise books and four worn-down pencils with equally worn-down erasers. Impressive or what?! All written at this desk, in this classroom. In the gradual oncoming of darkness. Thinking, remembering, trying to relive my story on paper. And the more I tell it, the more I think maybe Big Voice was right. I am a village boy, not a city boy. I am simply too into the minor, intimate, irrelevant things. What her last words were, for example. An enchanting, delicate birdsong: '*I wonder*

. . . when will I see you again?' Continually thinking about its fragility. About my awkward answer, *'Soon.'* As if I did know, which I did not. As if that moment could suddenly break and collapse, like gossamer. As if a rich girl could fall in love with a cow herder and not a rich man.

As if.

The light is disappearing quickly now. There's not a sound or a whisper. Nothing, not even the sigh of a clock barely ticking away high up on the wall. And barely am I able to see this.

VI

Day of the Locust

Runner's-up medal, 3rd place, 1933

DANCING FOR LOCUSTS. Brushing for locusts. Sweeping for locusts. I was dancing for locusts. And always they came like fountains, like controlled explosions.

1223, Broadway, New York, USA

Dear Amber,

By the time you receive this letter, Day of the Locust will have been over for five days, the time it takes a letter to reach America. I hope you got my last one. Here, this moment in Tortoise Spring, it is almost dark. 8.05 p.m. on 21 June.

I promised to tell you what happened. You said it didn't matter if I lost, but Hong Kong is not a good place for losers. Losers don't get the money. Don't get the girl. And you are not with me, are you?

This morning the sun rose at 6.40 a.m. I heard Grandma downstairs thirty minutes before light, then the usual Gurkha patrol followed by the unnerving sounds of the ocean. Sounds which, as you know, make each day special here. At school, in the hush again, I watched Mad Dog and his wife packing up medals and books, the glass cabinets slowly being emptied. Today was his last day as our

257

village schoolteacher. He was about to leave, a good thirteen years of life.

I was about to leave before him, for Day of the Locust. Till I heard the gunshot, loud and clear, like thunder.

Some people can write as if they are gliding on thermals – people like you and Three-Eye. I am no author, and at this moment in time I cannot write another word without first referring to the meaning of life. Why it can't last. Why you. Why me. Why we can't keep on playing games. Why it was important to have company. The original plan was for three of us to unite against a werewolf. I thought I could still go through with it, just me and my dog. I hadn't planned on going it alone.

I know you liked him. I know in some ways he reminded you of your dog. And yes, at least he had a name. That he did have, because he earned and deserved it. Because he was one of the few dogs who knew courtesy, kept his paws to himself. Kept his enthusiasm off people's clothes and dresses. A simple wag of his tail was enough. A simple smile. A simple bullet.

Don't you agree it's sad, Amber? Echo was the one good thing I had left and I thought, since school was over, after Day of the Locust, he and I could go cat fishing or explore that old ruined monastery. We could even joke at his 'digging' antics, his nature's calling. Shouting, 'You won't find any treasure there!'

Whatever happens, I had thought, win or lose, at least there would still be somebody loyal by my side.

We said goodbye, you and I. At least we had that

chance. But with Echo there was nothing. Words couldn't come fast enough. The Colonel's bullet was faster.

As the dog hunter, he was once kind enough to save a dog. I am sure, if he could, he would have spared Echo. I am sure.

My pace still calm and controlled, I walked through the dispersal of gunsmoke to where Echo lay, and slowly knelt beside him. His siennese-coloured body had turned into the colour of blood. I called to him, clapped my hands twice, but he did not respond. Finally I whispered into his still ears, telling him, 'It's OK. You can sleep now. You don't have to worry about me. Everything's fine. Everything's going to be OK.'

Was it because of the werewolves? I am not sure. But then again, that has been the constant theme of this story. How *can* you be entirely sure of the fantastic, of the Supernatural? I heard the slam of a car door. I saw a car being quickly driven away leaving behind a blanket of dust and loose gravel. It could have been a TR6. Could have been retaliation of the beast. There was an empty bowl by the road-side but what was it doing there? It was the kind of cracked bowl often left by vengeful farmers who poison dogs they blame for damaging their crops.

The Colonel uncocked his rifle and out fell two empty shells. 'Sorry, son,' he said. 'Had to be done. He had rabies.'

Did that bowl left by the TR6 bring on Echo's death? His mouth dribbling with saliva. According to the Colonel, the first sign of rabies is frothing at the mouth.

But what is wonderful is, even as Echo lay there, completely red, he was still smiling.

Everything is a gift to me. A pebble or a barley-sugar sweet carried in on a bicycle. Discovering and catching supposedly new insects. Singing 'Raindrops Keep Falling' with Big Voice and Three-Eye. The unusual appearance of the city girl named Amber. The night I carried her on wheels, her arms worn around my neck like rescuing wings. Her dress so bright as I look back during the hunt to establish my position in the swirling field. All these priceless things. For I am a searcher of angels. It was no big secret. And throughout these treasure hunts, Echo would accompany me. On the way back from the city, I recall his jubilation. On the way through deranged dogs, his protection of me – despite being greatly outnumbered. I recall the time the boar tusk entered his body, leaving a cavity which later became infected by maggots. Grandma had to pour paraffin into the wound, and it was so painful, poor Echo ran away howling. Nobody believed that story, except you, Amber. Because he was with us on the night we first met. It wasn't me who guided you home. I was just the translator, his disciple. And only he could have discreetly aided Big Voice in identifying the presence of Snakes, often making him admit: 'This lucky dog made me rich!'

That peculiar dog habit of his, the pursuit of departing trucks, which to us humans appeared so comic and futile – perhaps it was his dog's way of saying goodbye, you suggested. His polite manners. Or was it part of his animal curiosity? 'No,' you said. 'It's because he loves you.'

There are droplets of rain running down my cheeks as I write. I look up, but the sky is clear.

THE NERVE-POINT

Before a big event, it is always important to stroke something for luck and inspiration, be it skin, feather or fur. Captured crickets are often stroked behind their forewing, a nerve-point which brings forth their aggressiveness, so they will fight to the death. Humans also have a similar nerve-point, and quite often when that is disturbed it will bring forth the same effect.

I returned to the falls, pulled up the weapon that was buried underwater. I uncocked the barrel, checking there was still a silver bullet.

THE SURVIVAL GUIDE

If you are a well-prepared hunter, you should have the following item: a branch or a baton, ready when the moment comes to smash your way out of the field of fire. If you want to survive, you should also have a silver bullet. On the other hand, if *winning* is what you desire, then you'd better be Supernatural yourself, for there's no chance you can compete on an equal level.

There are voices who will tell you that Day of the Locust was a festival of fire. The attraction of fire for rural people is like the attraction of money to city people. Fiery giants moulded out of straw, twenty-five feet in height, are supposed to symbolise the dominance of Man over Nature. Their shadows tower over the landscape. Yet in the end they too are destined to burn.

I didn't need a branch. Nor did the werewolf. When I got there and parted through the sea of people, he was standing three places from me looking almost surprised that I'd turned up. Looking, in all honesty, almost human.

THE OPPONENT

Why? Because he has yet to learn the sacredness of life. Money is nothing. Power is nothing. Life is everything. His date of birth: 1961, Year of the Ox – meant nothing. Height: 170 cm, with eyebrows that met at the centre – meant nothing. An official member of The Central School of Kung Fu, an exponent of the 'touch of death' – still meant nothing. But the victims: 152 dogs, 90 civets, various pangolins, owls, 253 snakes, not including numerous rare snakes and lizards and the odd tortoise on the endangered species list who did nobody any harm, all these were *something*.

I don't know what true evil is, but this came close – killing and believing you can absorb the power of what you kill. Did martial arts develop in that way? Maybe, like religion, martial arts too can be twisted to suit a warped individual's ambition.

You have to trust me, Amber, when I tell you this, for there is a good story here somewhere. Maybe a shimmering light. A Sacred Swing. Maybe an answer to the old fortune-teller's question: 'What are the chances of winning against the Supernatural?'

THE QUALIFIER

I told you about Big Voice, but I knew that you never quite understood him. How could you? To Big Voice, we were second-class citizens compared to you. In the city, we country-dwellers are often treated like untrained animals in comparison to people there. This was the kind of imbalance he felt the Triad society could possibly redress. I told you about his both funny and sad goodbye. I remember telling you that.

You once asked if I believed in ghosts and I said I have often been in the company of one. The Ghost who used to live around the corner.

I was nicknamed Sundance after I danced on fire. As it happens, when there is fire, the insects will dance in their thousands, and like stars will fill the heavens. The only time during the game when we didn't have to 'tap dance' was when we set the field alight.

Big Voice the Ghost was named after his fabulous vocal ability. That made sense. But the Ghost part of his nickname didn't always speak for itself. The Ghost was the silent, enigmatic side of him. I thought it was because in darkness he moved like a ghost. I used to think like that – in a folksy, lyrical kind of way. But after he crashed, after the accident, they said he was finished. 'As good as dead.'

I was dejected for days. I was broken. But a crash – what was that to a ghost? How can you kill a ghost? They don't die. Nor do they write. Ghosts like to

263

haunt the living. And that was what he was doing today: Big Voice was haunting me. You cannot imagine how relieved I was to see him! I was amazed. I couldn't believe what I was seeing. Among all the strange faces, his familiar hand was suddenly at my shoulder. I watched him loom up next to me, as he used to do, sweaty and licking his lips at the possibility of a sun-kissed drink, except this time he was limping. And for the first time I realised how true it all was. He couldn't die and hadn't. He was a true ghost. He came to Stand By Me, as promised. Stand by me. A real free spirit. I should have known: no way was a simple motorbike crash going to give *him* the blues. Not when he wore the lifesaving crash helmet so his brains didn't spill out like egg yolk after a collision. I watched him wide-eyed as he put his warm hand on my left shoulder in the way only he knew how, saying: 'Told you I'd be right behind you.' He winked once at me and I winked back.

And suddenly it all seemed to me to be so perfect: one Supernatural against another. Or maybe I was seeing things. I must have been semi-delirious. So many people were tapping me on the shoulder. 'Are you a locust hunter? You'd better get in line!' But I wasn't going to let them get the better of me, the judges, the committees, the line of paraffin that was being poured directly behind our legs, the twenty-minute twin water tower timer which worked much like an hour glass, the makeshift tin pagodas erected especially for this one day with the all-important werewolf family members and VIPs watching the twirl of dragons and fabulous flags, wave after wave of people against the sound of jungle drums.

264

I turned away. I stared at the beast, I stared at the Ghost, at the magnificent field sparking up in front of me. Was that you, Amber, in among the judges and committee people, those familiar faces as if from the Street of Singers? At the blink of an eye I saw brightness and wings and thought it was you, among hunters wearing frowns, beards and fire blankets, girl hunters with face paint, ankle bells and talismans against bad luck. Wave after wave of cloth and colour. At the parting of an eye, I thought it was you. Thought that you had not left me, after all.

I watched Big Voice the Ghost with his limp, caused perhaps by his accident. His eyes were pinned on the wolf, the beast. Eyes that were more like steel, so intense I felt he could have gone against anything, even a wild boar, and won in a fight. I watched him looking all fired-up, pumping, fuming, getting all personal, for it's no big secret he loved my dog more than he loved Lord Baltimore. He wore that piercing die-hard look of a tiger. As if he really had a third eye and could see, scene by scene, how my dog, my brave, kind, strong dog, had died in full agony from strychnine poisoning and two bullets. It is only natural that an Echo should come after a Big Voice. And Big Voice came with Echo. The two cannot exist without the other. He understood this and so did Grandma: a man's best friend will follow you to the ends of the waterless earth, and if for some reason he can't go with you, he'll wait for your return at the exact time and place. And magically 'know' it is you and nobody else. I recall the time we returned from the city, all of us in different coloured shirts from the ones we'd been wearing when we'd left the village, yet he still pounced upon us and surprised us from out of a bush, completely bowling us over with his fantastic sense of humour. Oh yes, both Big Voice and Grandma – she who shed tears for nobody and knew Echo only as 'Dog!' – they surely would have cried louder with the remorse of loss than I ever would have.

My head was lost within the watery bubbles of the crowd's drowning chaos. I felt unable to move. Then I heard Big Voice mutter to me, 'You stay away.' I heard him shout it again as the game, like a motor-bike, kicked into life. 'Stay away from him, you hear? The scum is mine!'

At 7.30 p.m. the day began. At 7.50 p.m. the day ended. At 8.05 p.m. I am writing to you.

I ran like . . . I looked like . . . I was going like . . .

I don't think there is a word I can use to describe my performance. It was like the extraction of a tooth. Like watching a stone, thrown deep down into vertigo valley. Like a fishing hook being dragged from human flesh. I could dance or I could fight or I could disappear. The choice was simple. I decided to dance. Given the circumstance, in the swell of winds and fire and locusts, there was nothing else I could do. After all, it's what I do best.

When the moment came, the signal was given, a loud bang – probably a gun – I ran as if I was dancing barefoot on fire. I felt as if my legs no longer needed the ground to make my strides. Taut and tense, a leopard, I left the human landscape. Left the hunters whose names I didn't know, the smoke, the fires already spreading, induced by paraffin, the dis-

266

rupted trajectory of insects. I left Big Voice the Ghost who was looking less like a ghost as he limped along. It seemed, as I ran, that I was leaving Day of the Locust altogether. There were no more howls of a werewolf. I could hear nothing of the ritual drums. The world became distant as I once again found myself among herbs that can make all problems of the world disappear.

It is a tricky matter writing a letter, as you know. When I write to you, Amber, I can distort things to make them sound the way I want them to sound. I could say I shot a werewolf, or I could say, more realistically, that I didn't even get a chance to point the gun. The silver bullet never got a chance to reach the monster. The animal was too fast. I was too human. That would somehow sound more believable than any traditional hero stuff.

I could also say that for the first ten minutes it was just like old times. Which it was. I didn't think about anything else but grasshoppers. The Sea of Whispers whirled musically around me, but more desperate than usual, because the insects were trying to get away from one of the biggest fires of the year. So big, they would fly and get caught by the flames in mid-air and vanish as burning stars, organic fireworks with a diffused *thudzz*. Looking so beautiful, until you remembered they were actually dying. Charred grass twirled in the air, pirouetting like blistering ballerinas. Smoke stung my eyes as I moved further away from the fires and people. I must have been a good five minutes ahead, the flames burning behind me slowly, although in parts there was a conflagration, fuelled by tinder-dry thickets, some at least a metre high, almost as tall as I was. Cases of hunters suffering from first- and second-degree burns are well-documented. Children coming out with no eyelashes, all the hairs on their arms and legs gone, and even the odd one falling into semi-spiked ditches left for ambushing wild boars. All I had on was a vest, shorts and a pair of white American sneakers that were now not so white. In a more developed part of the world they would say this sport was inhumane and it would surely be banned, but this is a cut-throat society and risk comes as standard no matter what your age.

All my focus had lain in the field's water-like deepness, my hands tearing and swiping through the dry ferns in a performance that was at first crude, with most of the grasshoppers I caught frothing a green pus at the mouth due to my heavy-handed handling of them. But gradually, I calmed. And sure enough, my hands found their nimbleness again. With each tear, each grasp, I felt life kicking in my hand. A feeling that was always miraculous and unexplainable. Everything, from insects to mammals, was fighting to stay alive around me. Inevitably, it was the Force of Nature that inspired me to keep going right to the very end.

I remember spinning round a couple of times thinking someone or something was about to come up from behind, but there was nothing. It could have been my hat on fire. Could have been paranoia. Could have been just my mind trying to deal with the inferno and the heat, and the shocking fact that Echo was dead.

I was heading for the river at the end of the field

(I remember taking you to it once). It runs down from a mountain called Robin's Nest and I was making this two-thousand-yard dash to get there because I needed to stay out and ahead of the burning as long as possible to bag as much as possible, and I knew by instinct that the monster would be at that spot also, at some point. The showdown would take place there. I mean, realistically, even as a Supernatural, you need somewhere to cool off. And for once in my life I knew that was the first and perhaps the last answer I was ever going to get right.

When I arrived at the place of moisture, it was exactly as I imagined. He wore black Kung Fu pants, a muscle-bound vest, and had at least three baskets slung around his waist. My immediate reaction to this was of course, maximum fear. He had been waiting for me, wearing his shades and sporting the coldest grin I have ever seen. I did not dare speak, and he was not moving from his stance. And even if he did bother to speak, too much water was gushing noisily down the rocks and I wouldn't hear him anyhow. Also, the time for verbal warnings was over. It was time, to put it simply, for a world of hurt.

When Bruce fought in his movies, most of the time he did get hurt and so did those involved. Apparently he was kicked in the head so many times his vision wasn't that good any more.

I am no killer, you understand. I never have been. I could never hold a knife, not to mention pull a trigger. To be honest I don't think I can even shoot straight. You know the kind of tricky question the Army sometimes asks when you enrol: 'Would you pull the trigger on somebody?' The answer is, no. You

269

know that. Big Voice knew that. I couldn't have done it, even though the weapon was just below my waist, tied against my right thigh by two pieces of string and quite well-concealed behind my baggy shorts. There was no way I could unstrap it and raise it up in time to aim and pull the trigger. Shoot straight. The kickback would probably do me more harm. Besides, it was not how Mad Uncle would have wished it to end. It would not be noble and not make the world a better place. All the monster had to do was leap forward, spin out a kick and the gun would be out of my hands in no time, which he did. In fact, it felt more as if a bullet had taken it out of my hand. However the second kick was even faster. And deeper. I flew backwards, surely as Big Voice flew when the peeved-off bull horned him up the backside.

I am no Kung Fu man, you understand. I can say that only so many times before I start to sound spineless, just like the people of Tortoise Spring who couldn't and wouldn't stand up for human dignity or for HK as a nation, and in the end it was us – yes, us, the outsiders, the undesired, the ragged underdogs – who cared about what was none of our business in the first place and nothing to do with our heritage. But we didn't care that nobody cared. We didn't care that we were losers, that it was all a lost cause and we stood to gain nothing and nobody would remember what we stood up for. We cared about Lord Baltimore, cared about life in general. We cared especially about memories. Yes. That, we did. I mean: what else is there to live for? I had no name, no parents and Big Voice was clanless and went around asking, 'Do you like smelling shit?' So what future

270

was there? When you have nothing, you learn to flow with the moment. Take what is given. Run as if there is no tomorrow.

This side of the story belongs to Big Voice. Through circumstance, I also became part of that story, just as you did, but this story really belongs to him. He was the real hero – the loser's hero. I knew the story couldn't finish without him. I knew *I* was not the Chosen One. I could never compete on the same level. I was just a herd boy. I was not used to having any blood on my hands except my own.

If I said that by the river at the end of the burning fields I saw a swerve of kingfishers, would that be *more* believable? If I said I saw the werewolf and the gun was kicked out of my hands, would that sound *less* believable? How about if I said Big Voice suddenly turned up and pushed me away and my story ended there, at the river's edge, with him in his Kung Fu pants, his sweaty vest, face to face with the monster for the final confrontation? I was pushed away. 'Go,' he said. 'Leave now!' Would that sound better? A better story?

With the three complementary elements – earth, fire and water – the Werewolf's transformation was complete. His hands could kill in one single stroke. He had an aura of power and mystery. He stood there, by the throttle of water, a first-class semi-human being poised against us, the second-class humans. Contemplating, perhaps, who would make the first move.

–Keep in touch, OK?
–You too.
A pat across the back. A nod.

–Catch you later . . .
–You bet.

Then another nod, another pat across the back. In a dream that's how we said goodbye, Big Voice and I. In a perfect dream that's how we left it. An open goodbye. A hero's goodbye.

We become heroes because we believe that tomorrow there will be brightness. We journey from dark recesses to reach brightness and when we make it over the hill and discover that the myth is true, our desire is to remain forever bright.

Because of Big Voice, this letter can be written. A small story can be told. My little body was only beaten and bruised and not murdered. Because of Big Voice there was hope. For far too often he has been remembered for bad things – his loud mouth, his possession of a sharp knife, his dehumanising occupation as a Snake Head, but when I was advised by him to back away, that was a good thing. A heroic thing. Because my fight was over. My story ended.

I would have liked to have thanked him. *Bravo, cheers, I owe you. I want to stand by you* – that sort of thing. But there was no time. I was leaving. I didn't want him to have to say it twice. I straightened my collar, wiped off the sweat, the ashes, the burned wings. Then I made my way back through the fire, leaving him to what he did best – waiting for the first move, because you always let the opponent (or insect) make the first move: then, and only then, can you strike out. But when I glanced back what I saw was a pair of stone lions. Still standing face to face. Still contemplating with the blossoms of fire around them, who would make the first move.

As the herd boy, the guide, I've always tried to steer you away from the faces of evil when I should have known better. You, who can navigate coarse people like clear riverwater. You, who can select the good, the bad, the average. Places that poured tea into long glasses, the hazardous places, you said, 'Don't eat there.' You can say those things because you know how the world evolves. The workings of a working-class society. You know better than any of us, the tricks of the trade, the tricks of observing someone's wrist, the secret of turning out a winner.

And if I told you I was the winner at Day of the Locust, would you believe me?

I imagined Big Voice the Ghost picking up the revolver.

I imagined him firing the expensive bullet made of silver.

I imagined he destroyed the monster and became a free man.

I imagined him protesting, 'Bruce wouldn't train a scumbag like you!'

I imagined . . . in the future this is how I will remember it.

As he kneels down to tie up his shoelace, a position in which he is vulnerable (and he knows it), the monster will seize the opening (as is the creature's entrepreneurial character) and strike, at which point Big Voice will be like Bruce: in less than a white-hot second, he'll be ready to intercept. Blocking the low kick slicing towards his left eye and somehow getting the upper hand and not another bruised left eye.

Nobody makes the same mistake twice. Not in Hong Kong, not Big Voice. That's one detail I won't have to imagine.

Years from now somebody will dive into that river and find a gun – the nickel-plated Colt 45 Peacemaker kicked out of my hand, then kicked further into the river by Big Voice, who was in my opinion the most sensible person who ever lived. And within the barrel of that gun there may still be a silver bullet.

I could tell you that the werewolves of this world were destroyed and both Lord Baltimore and Echo received resurrection, but that would be a lie. I could tell you that Big Voice fought the monster thinking he was inside Rome's Coliseum as in *The Way of the Dragon*, except the Coliseum didn't have columns of flames and insects. I could tell you also with my sincerest heartfelt thanks, that the Mickey Mouse watch you gave me came in very handy. Mickey smiling to me amidst all the fire and tension as if to say, 'It's OK. You're going to make it back in time,' which I amazingly did. He was telling me that the twenty minutes was up and he couldn't have been more right, because fireworks were exploding high in the sky to signal the end of the contest. Either that or he was laughing in my blackened face, but I don't think that was the case.

However, I could say, and prefer to say: 'Let's meet again in twelve years' time so I can show you this gold medal. The medal of 1973.'

You know, Supernaturals never interested me. As a hunter, as a herd boy, as an explorer I didn't believe in them. Yet I could still stand in front of them; be in their shadow. The long table of judges counting and weighing, asking for my name and number as they continued double-checking again and again as if something was wrong or was too-good-to-be-true in front of an audience of five and half thousand, most of whom were either ruled or cowed by the presence of werewolves, and who already knew, having been told by their fathers and forefathers before them, that only a werewolf can emerge victorious.

And I, the dancing boy, had stood with this ultimate player, a territorial beast, Millions/Brilliant of the Werewolf clan, or Locust clan, whatever. Along with his panache and sheen and status and spiteful attitude, like there was no way I could ever get up to his level. Not in a million years, no matter how many times I scrubbed the toilets. But I ask you – who would want to? What's wrong with just being human? Or even a donkey in a happy field. Just being gentle and peace-loving. What is so wrong with that? Maybe as a Supernatural you can be good at a lot of things – the intercepting fist, the fast car, the clean-cut grades, the business empire ... but you can't be good at everything, right? You can't do everything. Can't be in two places at once, not even if you're a Supernatural. I may not be ace hot at snipping out the gall-bladder of a snake or bashing in a dog's sorry-looking skull or skinning a cat in less than fifteen seconds flat (thank goodness), but there is one thing I *am* good at because I practised it every day, like a violin virtuoso. I can *catch*.

That's a fact.

He came in with a staggering thirty-seven locusts and eight lizards, weighing in at nineteen ounces.

And everyone gasped, the judges included. The entire crowd swayed in admiration ... but all the same, he was going down.

Why?

Good question. Why? *Because that's the way it had to be.* You cannot win for ever, nor can you lose for ever. That's another fact.

Twenty minutes is not a long time to bag something as evasive as a locust. I should know. When I first started out in the game it took me a whole day just to fill one basket, and that with small fry only. In twenty minutes it is a tall order, amounting almost to a joke. Only a real professional can perform at that speed, someone who doesn't care about stings or splinters or about a dozen or so lice biting at his private parts. Someone who can grab a three-inch live bullet, for that's what a locust is – alive, hot, serrated, 'an explosion of red'. Only someone who can dive for an insect like there is no tomorrow and not cry about it till an hour later because he was too numb to cry during the hunt, and who naively thinks that by winning such a contest he can win back everything else, even those gone before, those dead and no longer with us.

A man once said to me, 'If I didn't believe I could do it, if I didn't believe I could swim this far, didn't believe I could swim faster than a shark, or believe that I still had a leg to swim fast, there's no way I'd be standing here in HK, talking to you at this minute. I was willing to put my neck on the line for what I believed. Would you?'

I was willing to put my neck on the line ...

What great words. What jazz. What truth. What I

276

reckon to be the words of a true winner. But of course we knew him as Mr Twilight. The charismatic, ordinary millionaire.

I think I understand what he meant now. And I think I can answer his question. I didn't understand then but now, after Echo, I do. And so, I think, did everyone else – the crowds, the judges, the werewolves included.

Normally you'd have to 'look' for locusts higher and farther away, but in a field that's privately owned, fenced off to all (the Brits included), wild and rich with expensive herbs from physiotherapeutic ones to cancer curing ones, there was no need to look. They exploded around you, as if the place had been condensed and kept just for this event. Once every ten years. Waiting for 'that' name to be announced. And 'that' name was . . .?

'What? You have an English name?'

There was a huge silence. Everyone held their breath. Especially me. I'd laid down my baskets, had written out my chicken-scrawl name and number for that bag-eyed judge. A group of old frocked men sat among some suit-and-tie men from the local government. I even wrote it out in capital letters. My hat firmly in place: taking it off for nobody. Like a character from out of a Paul Newman and Robert Redford film.

'An *English* name?'

The judge stared up at me from his seat under the awning. The locusts were being weighed next to him in plastic bags punctured with holes made by toothpicks so the insects could breathe, and I beamed back with that look which said: 'And why not?'

In the past, all the names at the Locust Hall of Fame were written in Chinese. I think it's about time that changed, got modernised. Time for a new name.

Big Voice had clambered out of the ashes after his near-fatal encounter and found 'his' prize was the Colonel waiting for him (and wanting his gun back). We were the last players to emerge . . . into a crowd of many thousand dusky faces with hats and ploughs and jade bracelets all here to witness the spectacle and a conclusion. There was a long table of bagged insects. There was an evil son of a wolf hovering six yards from me waiting to be beaten, but there was also my undying memory of Lord Baltimore. The undying memory of my dog.

I don't think you believe me, Amber. I can't see your expression but I know you don't believe me when I say I was among the religion of power. A family of the Masonic tradition. A secret people, secret history, secret killings. You probably won't believe me when I tell you of the sweat dripping down across the medal on my bare chest. It was my last hunt. And when you know it's your last, you give it your heart. I caught twelve lizards, all with their body parts intact. Forty-seven locusts – was it? I have lost count now. I know that my baskets were brimming over so I had to use an extra bag. But you don't have to believe me. A werewolf can be destroyed in the same way that a building can be destroyed. You don't have to believe that either. So for this once I am going to brag. On the Day of the Locust 1973 I have proved myself to be the greatest hunter this country of Her Majesty has ever seen or is ever likely to see. And now, the game is over. The bird society is over. After school, children will go to hunt no more. Money will never be made the same way again, with passion. The Day of the Locust is history.

I am Sundance and I have always feared that if I did anything other than that, I would be given another more ominous nickname. After all, I gamed for a living. I wasn't playing around. When your main motive is to survive, the game turns into something serious. It became a natural instinct with me. I could walk towards someone and at the same time catch something in the air. I had an addiction to it, like heroin. The locust junkie. So you can understand where my formidable powers came from.

You're a clever person, Amber. So I won't burden you with the outcomes and reactions of this day, when a proud tradition was broken. The look of disbelief, the change of history, the sudden vanishing of Millions/Brilliant when he finally realised in this game, age *does* matter. Passion does matter – and not money. In the end his primal fear of anything silver – a bullet, a silver medal, all came true. The fear of second place, second best, was all true, 100 per cent true. He was a werewolf. A certifiable monster. Because how else can you explain his fear of silver?

If only you could have been here. How I wish you could have been here. Dearest Amber . . . I know you are the last person on earth to have vengeance in your heart, and in many ways I am like you. But after all we've been through, you would surely have felt something, to see the face of one who has never known fear, never feared another or respected anyone or any life, suddenly turn deathly pale when

279

confronted with the puking ghost of his own worst fears. And if that isn't retribution, then I don't know what is.

He was just six paces away. Perhaps even less. The last time that happened, my whole life flashed by before me as if it was the end. He was just six paces away to my right, and there couldn't have been two people less alike on the face of the earth. But even so, I was still just a boy, you know? An insect, an ant, insignificant, with my small sun-burned neck and arms set against a smoking war-torn field. My opponent on the other hand had the backing of the multi-decorated pagoda wherein sat his benevolent restaurant-owning uncles and aunts and University-educated brothers and sisters, all waiting, all expecting routine glory and an even more glorious feast to follow. All of that changed when my results were announced: twenty-five ounces to my older rival's nineteen.

The bag-eyed judge couldn't pronounce my name, and in the end, ironically, it was the Colonel who, the president of all things, walked up and said it all. 'Twenty-five ounces.' Looking down at me, he said what nobody else there could have dared to say. 'Well done, son! Well done! Excellent work!' Then he winked me a hawk's wink, telling me: 'You do realise you have just outdone somebody much older than you?' which to put it simply, blew it all to embers. 'Congratulations! Be proud of yourself!' and that, I mildly was. The silver hand on my shoulder was like the flat side of a heavy Arthurian blade. The Colonel was smiling at me as if he was rather enjoying the show, a side of him I have never seen.

But you should have seen 'Millions/Brilliant'. Or Raymond Loh, as he is known, The Big Bad Wolf. You should have, because I couldn't.

In a city where you absolutely have to be a winner to be 'visible', the concept of winning is an obsession, a daily preoccupation. And when suddenly you're no longer a winner, *the* winner, the tops, what else can you do? You 'disappear'. Become a nobody. Ashes.

I was looking at him. I glared. My dog-eyes focused, the aperture closing down to near F22 against the evening shimmer in what was the clearest vision I have ever experienced in my whole life. I saw a horizon of faces, with some still adamant against releasing the medal to me. They stared. They stood up, in the streaming, unblemished light of the unmistakable ... but still I couldn't see him. No matter how pristine my vision – I could recognise everything else, every tree, every herb's name, every bird, every lip-sucking fruit that's ever fallen out of the blue fish-eyed sky – *but I couldn't tell who this shadow was, standing a few yards from me now.* Who was this person with a bloodied nose, miserable because of a Big Voice blow? Who? A block of wood? Half pig/half donkey? Or was it The Big Bad Wolf?

I looked again. I shrugged. And then he had gone, vanished. The person who had stolen our tortoise, broken my thumb and murdered my dog had gone for ever. All that was left of him was a trail of dust. All that was left to see was high blood pressure, from his family – from his father in particular, who came down on him like a ton of bricks, as Mad Uncle had said he would. I thought of that cartoon moment when you are no longer 'Great Killer of Dogs' but a radioactive rooster running so fast you burn and become Kentucky Fried. Which is OK for a mortal like me, but not a Supernatural. Your face woefully distorted like a Kabuki mask and your father behind you, a cane in his hand, at the age you are, the name you are, 'Millions/Brilliant', cannot be OK. And neither is puking the way he made my dog puke. Totally not OK. Ultimate face loss. And maybe, just maybe, from here it will all be downhill for him, as if he'd failed to get into Cambridge or Oxford, failed all family Great Expectations.

But that wasn't the point here. The point was: *It's over*. I just want my silence back. My monkish ways. And yes, like the weevils we long ago without knowing, crippled, I can't help but feel some sorrow. The same dignified sorrow Bruce felt when he laid Chuck to rest at the fight's end. He was just another fellow human, after all. And now, that 'millions' look Loh once had was no longer, and in its place I saw a slow, hesitant, pale-nosed face turn towards me, so white and blank on this red-hot planetary Mars of a day, as if it was asking, 'Is this what you call losing?' Its look of shock was the one you wear when you don't want to look at something rotten and alive with maggots that will give you nightmares. Or the one you'd get if you'd been hit face on by a truck, or the big fat bulging belly of a giant Buddha. Perhaps a part of him still wanted to come after me, finish me off once and for all. But there was Big Voice and the Colonel next to me now. And it was over. The Day of the Locust mythology, over. The day's end.

I was finally left alone at 7.55 p.m. Another twenty

paces from the podium where funny-looking flower girls waited and a medal, but my memory is blank. Whether I walked those twenty unacknowledged paces or not, is a blank. I don't remember that Path of Glory. All I know is that the winner's medal was placed around my grimy neck, the first time it had ever been awarded to anyone from the outside. All this done and completed in a matter of twenty minutes. This was something you don't see every day. It was as if it was meant to be. My destiny. My time. My day. As if nothing is impossible.

If only Ar-Fun were here, then a picture or an impression could have been made. She could have drawn the scene of Big Voice being walked away by the Colonel (possibly the last time I'll ever see him), all bruised yet still smiling with his head held high, a nod in my direction as if to say: 'You did good!' It could have been a picture of remarkable triumph. A sky filled with angels. Just maybe. Just maybe his destiny was no Triad but something else. I like to think so. At least the crowd seemed to feel that way.

Come back to Hong Kong in twelve years' time, Amber. Or come back before, and you will find my name and *25 oz* inscribed onto the stones at the local Locust Hall of Fame. The only thing you won't find is me. I will have disappeared, just as the mysterious 1933 joint winner disappeared. Except in 1973 there was no joint win. Just one winner.

What I need is a set of wings. What I needed was a team to celebrate. A couple of Nestlé ice creams, some 7UP, Fanta, Green Spot orange, guava nectar, Vitasoy milk, sugar cane, a wag from Echo's flattering bushy tail. Items that would have made me think that you and the others were still with me. Walking with me as the icy spray of water from the three fire engines doused the field, melting away the heat and pressure. Melting away all signs and existence of Supernaturals. All pain, all disappearances, all the snakes and creatures left enamelled to the earth after the fire, all harshness of reality. I had survived. I was charred and wet. Face black, eyes closed, coming out of the white smoking field with all of you beside me, carrying the prize in the form of insects. Eyes opening. Emerging. Transforming. A winner.

Yes, what I needed was a day ending like that. And do you know, there was something not far from it.

Maybe you think I am writing this down just to please you? Or maybe I have been eating Grass Lizards, after all. But that's OK. It doesn't matter. Because I am moving on. I have to. The world is after me now. The crowds, the dogs, the silent faces unable to speak or cheer but whose desire is to become winners – they are all tailing me, trying to keep up and unable to express what they felt as I left the podium in deep thought. Was it for the same reason I chased angels? Believing that once you catch something, you can become it?

I have to plan out my next move. I've walked victorious through the mighty shadows of the Locust Hall of Fame so there's no way I can hang around. Every move I make from now on will be watched. There is no future here for me, as Mad Dog rightly said. Lord Baltimore and Echo died because we didn't live in reality. So now, reality it is.

After all this is over, I am going to buy five bottles of 7UP. I am going to open them and drink a toast to us all. To those of us who should be here, should be laughing and knowing this is a good time. I am also going to cry like a baby, the tears burning down my face. I won't care what anyone thinks. It's good to cry, right?

I walked like some cool hawk down the Hallway of Myth as if I'd just won a million dollars, and the people who were supposed to stone and hate me instead felt only awe. It was as if we had all come out of a drowning, were dazed. And not just by my fire-dancing triumph but by the atmosphere of the day – the air, the charged sky, the landscape swirling in sparks and stars with the two straw giants flaming and collapsing in the background like skyscrapers.

From now on, I am going to give the Clint Eastwood silence to anyone who tries to look down on me or Big Voice. I am going to bark and crawl into university and graduate no matter what. I am also, and I think this has to be the most encouraging item on the list, I am also going to do a '*jang hay*'. Literally translated as struggle/breathe. Meaning: stand up for yourself. Meaning: don't let anybody turn you into dog meat. Meaning: the ant lion has completed its metamorphosis and is now a lacewing and can ride on air. Also meaning: 'That's for my dog! For Lord B!'

But it is over. Meaning: tomorrow I am going to come through the door smiling like Gene Kelly and not have my head down ashamed I don't have this or that. All that is over. I have my goals now, my own dreams for the future. I know I could probably go on all day and never get it right, because there's no translating it. No easy way around it. But one thing is for sure: Big Voice did, and I believe him with all my beating heart, he *did* go skyward with almost supernatural grace and football away the *3+6* sign into a billion pieces the same way Bruce did to the *No Dogs or Chinese* sign at the park in *Fist of Fury*. Yes. No doubt about that. People actually gave Bruce standing ovations in cinemas across HK after that scene. It touched a nation's nerve. And you could say that in that kick, Bruce did a little '*jang hay*' for all of us. The message was: 'At last! You did it! After eons of *not* doing it, of eating humble pie and dirt, you finally gritted your teeth and did it! You are SOMEBODY.'

In the future, if anyone should ask, that's what I am going to tell them. *The beauty of the impossible was, and is, not for me.* I am also going to find that ace flyer and say: 'Father! I've done it! I've survived being a child so why don't you tell me the secret of life?' So yes. Spread the word. I am going to do all that and more. I am going to do it with style.

After today I am going straight, getting smart. I am going to be just like everybody else. Live in reality. Live in a flat. Live in a city, in an 8 by 12-foot square room with television and Calor gas, with angels singing on the veranda. With stairs and lifts and windows everywhere you go. Live for and through money. Because I want to be just like you, Amber. Plan ahead. See into things. Read thoughts. Invest. Get a regular job. Get into reality. Forget angels. Forget games. Forget escape and enter the harshness of the real world. Get into running Snakes and bribing police. I have to learn to do these things. This is my rite of passage. I am about to

286

become a changed person. No longer a locust junkie but an adult. A responsible person.

What do you think?

It's the only way to go. I no longer want to be someone still content with small-time victories. A locust for a Coke. A swing for a dress. I don't want to be still concerned with returning to the village and taking life lying down again, in that sleeping posture.

But the old truth is: I did.

I did . . .

I approached the village with a slow sadness. I had stopped crying and was tired, exceedingly tired, my face stiff with dried tears. I had approached the village knowing that somewhere within, under the last shadows, someone I loved more than anything else, laid motionless. I approached the white spot where I felt rain on my cheeks yet the sky was clear, without cloud.

But what happens is this:

Mad Uncle is standing there, instead of the blood, the dog, the death. He is standing – something I've never seen before. Relieved to see him, I instinctively move up to show him the medal. I watch him take it. See him grin at it, his lip bent like a sprung bow, seeming quite impressed. I want to ask him something yet am powerless to do so.

'I know what you desire to know,' he says, holding a broad stick, more for defence than for steadying his old body. 'You are thinking: is resurrection possible? But what I say is: *what if you never died in the first place . . .*'

As I said, I am still not sure where I stand in the world today. As I pause, about to end this letter, I look around, trying to work out where I am. I think it's 8.50 p.m. I think Mad Uncle is waiting for me, beckoning me with the offer of a chilled drink somewhere ahead on the road out of what used to be a village. But there is something unusual. The light. It seems to hang on, as if it doesn't want to go – like my feelings for you. I think I can see what I am after now. I'll have to leave. Go as far away as possible, I reckon.

Take care, Amber.

You will find me by the Sacred Swing, if you come on 21 June 1985, in twelve years' time. No matter what happens, I'll be here. I'll be waiting for you. I promise.

Love,

Sundance.

I fold the letter against the lukewarm surface of the road. Then slide it into an envelope.

I am still unable to find any traces of blood or gunshot shells. No matter how far down I lean into the ground, no matter how many times I brush my palm across the surface, I feel only the usual things – Longan blossoms, grit, seeds, dusk, a village hung in silence, a click beetle, the kind that can look dead yet has the clever trick of unclicking itself back into life. Just the regular everyday things.

As I stand up, about to leave, there is a sudden shift in the valley breeze. I watch it unsettle the avenue of trees in front of me, like a wave on a calm lake.

I find myself waving goodbye to Grandma using my half-singed straw hat. To Grandma, bless her! Who seems to only nod, in the distance, an OK nod as if she'll see me again tomorrow. She hurries the animals through the process of closing up, shutting down. I see the quivering pond with its distorted reflection of ghost-white buildings. I keep looking at them as if waiting for something to happen. That right moment. Right time. Right place.

I keep looking back because there is no avoiding it. Five people and a dog are moving up the hills. A bright figure. A girl. A smile, I think. She is waving at me. Then the boy with the straw hat next to her, turns and waves also. I think I know who they are. I am sure I do.

The robed figure of Mad Uncle is moving faster than a sledge somewhere ahead of me. As I hurry after him, I hear a strange unearthly tremble in the air, like the sound of some huge tidal wave coming steadily closer and closer. It is frightening and exhilarating all at once, as if it's about to smash in and swamp me, but yet when I look around there's not a thing to see. But maybe it's just me, because I am in the wavelength of growth and change. I am experiencing an important rite of passage.

As I catch up to Mad Uncle, almost reaching his pulsating life-giving radiance, I am thinking maybe I should add that to the letter, so I pull out the envelope and pause, to witness another swerve of light.

When I reach Mad Uncle I will hold onto his wrinkled yet reassuring hand. A healing hand. The resurrectionist hand that has kept me and will continue to keep thousands of others alive till the moment of his own beatification.

When I reach him I know I will have a new name, and also A Letter From America. By the time I reach him, thanks to him, my evening shadow will be as long as his, and by that time I know I will be a man.

PS. Dear Amber, As I left, the strange oceanic warbling finally reached its peak and thundered directly over me till I could see a squadron of three Royal Air Corps fighters drift over like a diamond – something that's never happened before. So calm and idle it seemed as if they were strolling right alongside me. And I know I could, if I wished it, also see familiar visual signs which would suggest we were walking among not just one, but several angels, by the Latin name of Garralax angelsis.

Po Wah Lam was born in Liverpool and lived the early part of his childhood in Hong Kong. After studying interior design at Brunel University, he was the first person to be awarded the David Wong Writing Fellowship at the University of East Anglia. He can regularly be found working at his little family restaurant. He is currently working on his next book.

OTHER BLACKAMBER TITLES

Alex Wheatle

Brixton Rock

Faraway rhythms of the Caribbean mix and merge with the beats of Brixton to create an inner city landscape which depicts 1980's London. Alex Wheatle both moves and entertains us with his deadly inside knowledge, making Brixton Rock *a wonderfully funny, gripping and riotous read.*

Brenton Brown is a 16-year-old mixed-race youth who has lived in a children's home all his life – until now. Released into the laid-back care of a Lambeth Council hostel for teen-agers, and armed with his fortnightly dole cheque, Brenton starts to learn what life is about. . . . He and his hostel-mate, Floyd, go to all-night raves, duck and dive around the locale and hang out with their brethren. Despite the fun on offer, however, the youth has his share of the blues. Brenton has never met his mother. He is haunted by her loss and hates her for abandoning him. Desperate to find his identity, he decides to search for her knowing that, until he does, he will remain restless and incomplete – a person with no prospects.

The best thing happens: Brenton is reunited with his mother, Cynthia. And then the worst: he falls helplessly in love with his beautiful half-sister, Juliet. This forbidden pas-sion causes both of them deep anguish. At the same time, Brenton meets his Nemesis in the shape of Terry Flynn, a killer who scars him for life. Brenton seeks revenge. All this leads to an explosive climax with the disturbed adolescent struggling to hold on to his sanity.

All BlackAmber Books are available from your local bookshop.

For a regular update on BlackAmber's latest release, with extracts, reviews and events, visit:

www.blackamber.com